Praise for Lau

'A gripping and dark psychologi
sitting' – **Harlan Coben,** ***The***

'Dark and spellbinding… All of Sims' deliciously wicked powers are on full display in this compulsive and unforgettable novel. A classic' – **Mona Awad, author of *Bunny***

'No one writes about obsession like Laura Sims' – **Samantha Downing, author of *A Twisted Love Story***

'A marvellously intense, read-in-one-sitting game of cat and mouse among the book stacks' – ***Guardian***

'Openly indebted to Shirley Jackson and Patricia Highsmith, this is a terrific two-hander' – ***Sunday Times***

'Fun and entertaining' – ***Glamour***

'Sims plumbs the depths of obsession and madness as she has each woman tell the story in alternating chapters, deftly building the tension until the explosive ending' – ***Washington Post***

'Bringing workplace politics to a fever pitch, *How Can I Help You* is a delicious mystery begging to be enjoyed beachside… Sure to satisfy just about any thriller craving' – ***Rolling Stone***

Also by Laura Sims

How Can I Help You
Looker

Poetry
Staying Alive
My God Is This a Man
Stranger
Practice, Restraint

Nonfiction
Fare Forward: Letters from David Markson

THE MAN

LAURA SIMS

VERVE BOOKS

First published in the UK in 2026
by VERVE Books Ltd., Harpenden, UK
vervebooks.co.uk

@VERVE_Books

A CIP catalogue record for this book is available from the British Library.

ISBN
978-0-85730-950-1 (Paperback)
978-0-85730-951-8 (eBook)

2 4 6 8 10 9 7 5 3 1

Typeset in 11 on 13.5pt Minion Pro
by Avocet Typeset, Bideford, Devon, EX39 2BP
Printed and bound in Great Britain by CPI Group (UK) Ltd, Croydon CR0 4YY

FSC www.fsc.org
MIX
Paper | Supporting responsible forestry
FSC® C013604

The manufacturer's authorised representative in the EU for product safety is Easy Access System Europe, Mustamäe tee 50, 10621 Tallinn, Estonia
gpsr.requests@easproject.com

For Corey and Caleb, my favorite men

‘The camera is my little friend’
– Vivian Maier

‘I think it does, a little, hurt to be photographed’
– Diane Arbus

This novel contains depictions of stalking and sexual violence.

I

The Wild Edges of Things

1

I SPOT HER THROUGH MY NIKON lens at the annual Columbus Day Parade. Beyond the majorettes' ecstatic rouged faces and kicking legs, a teenage girl stands apart from the cheering crowd, darkly clothed and oddly still amidst the revelry. Her eyes were averted but now she looks straight at me, her mouth tremulous, mascaraed tears tracking down her face, offering up her misery like a gift.

I take it. I take one shot after another until she turns quickly and disappears into the crowd.

I have to stop myself from running after her. She reminds me of the young girl I once was, raw and hurting. I feel a stab of pain in my side and press hard against the spot while closing my eyes. I haven't felt this for a long, long time.

A blare from the band's trumpet startles me back to the present. The pain has ebbed and the girl is gone, so I lift my camera and shoot a small boy with his eyes trained upward on the yellow balloon he holds in his hand. Next, I shoot a middle-aged woman lost in thought, her hands clapping but her face a blank mask. I keep moving, keep shooting, relishing each shutter click, all the while knowing that every picture will pale in comparison to the ones I've taken of the tortured girl.

I can't quite believe she was real.

As soon as I get home, I lock myself in the darkroom and work furiously until the negatives are hanging to dry. Later, staring at my contact sheet under the loupe in the bright light of my kitchen, I see proof of the girl's existence, and that her photographs are as good as I hoped they would be. Or feared: a new and terrible spasm goes through me. I sit down hard on a chair, waiting for it to pass. When it does, I stare at her some more. I'm not sure how long it's been when I hear someone clearing his throat and glance up to find Tom standing in the doorway. Looking tentative, as if he's caught me doing something obscene. I manage to give him my best smile.

'Dinner's lasagna. It'll be ready in thirty minutes or so,' I tell him. He frowns slightly and scans my face. Drops his eyes for a moment to the contact sheet.

'Get any good ones today?' he asks, and I nod but don't elaborate or share. Instead, I ask him to set the dining room table, then turn my attention back to my loupe, to the contact sheet, and to the girl I've caught on film. *Parade Girl*, I'll call her, since I'll never know her name.

2

PROFESSOR SORENSON LOOKS UP FROM the handful of prints I've given him and studies me like he's seeing me for the first time: the quiet woman in his Introduction to Photography class. The one who's lingered timidly until everyone else finished their first 'portfolio check' and left. Now we stand across from each other in the empty, semi-darkened lecture hall, and I'm pleased at his surprise; my pictures aren't what he expected: smiling children, flowers in bloom, or middle-aged women raising wineglasses in a birthday toast.

'Judith, right?' he says. When I nod, he drops his eyes again to the photographs. He's moving through the pack slowly, drawing closer to *Parade Girl*. It may be the best picture I've ever taken, but I nearly left it out. I feared he'd look into her face, into those tearing eyes, and see the younger me – like I did. *Ridiculous*, I tell myself. *Impossible.* But I hold my breath, waiting for his reaction. When he reaches her, I watch his eyes move slowly over every inch of her face and the people around her with flags waving, mouths shouting. He shakes his head but doesn't look up.

'This is terrific,' he says, quiet enough to be talking to himself. 'Just terrific.' I let out my breath, relieved, though my cheeks warm with his words of praise. I can suddenly hear the loud ticking of the classroom clock. 'Every single one of these is stunning, Judith. You have an uncanny eye.' I'm too flustered to respond at first, so I reach for my pictures. But when he hands them to me – reluctantly, it seems – I simply want to hand them back. To keep living in the moment of watching him love my photographs.

'Thank you, Professor,' I say at last.

'Call me Paul. Everyone else does.' He smiles. 'And you've got nothing to thank me for – the pleasure is all mine. Have you thought about submitting these to magazines? There's –'

'No,' I say. He's taken aback. But the thought of making my pictures public makes my skin crawl. As if he's asked me to stand naked on the town green – though that wasn't his intention, I know. 'Thank you,' I add, putting more emphasis on the words this time. Professor – Paul – nods and holds up his hands.

'I get it,' he says, though I know he doesn't; he can't. 'It's a private passion. But you should think about it.' I lie and say I will, then thank him again and turn to go. But before I can get to the top of the steps, he calls my name: *Judith*. I like hearing him say it, knowing that now he knows exactly who I am.

'Bring me your work anytime. I'd love to see more.'

I haven't thought beyond tonight, past satisfying a class requirement. I never dreamed Paul would react this way – or that I'd *want* to show him more. But the force behind his words and his pleading smile act on me like a stiff old-fashioned – my grandmother's drink – coursing through my veins.

What could it hurt, to show him more?

3

'WHAT DOES THAT EVEN MEAN?' Tom asks, forking up a bite of steak. He's puzzled by Paul's comment about my 'uncanny eye.' I don't know why I mentioned it; he doesn't like hearing about photography class. *Why go to school for something you're already good at?* he asked when I first brought up taking the year-long class at the local community college. Really, he didn't like the change it would mean – the change in our Tuesday nights, or the possible change in me. And now I've blurted out what Paul said last night, and Tom is resentful. Confused, and possibly suspicious, too – of my male professor taking an interest. He chews and looks at me.

'It means I see things… differently, I guess.' The back of my neck burns. I wish I'd kept it to myself. *Pride will out*, I suppose – like Grandmother used to say. 'Or maybe the professor didn't know what to say, but he knew he had to say something,' I offer with a half-hearted laugh, careful to say *the professor*, not *Paul*. It gives me too much of a thrill to say *Paul*, and Tom would see it in my face.

We go on cutting, chewing, and swallowing the steak, asparagus, and potatoes au gratin: our habitual Wednesday-night meal, one that hasn't changed since before Tom Junior left home. Nothing more is said about Paul, or photography class, or my 'uncanny eye.' I'm relieved he's let it go, but wistful, too. Tom tells me about his day, about the ongoing politics of the Harrington Public Works Department. Normally I get caught up in these reports: *Travis left the meeting abruptly? Sven and Jonathan said that only to you? Are you sure?* Tonight, though, I drift away, savoring Paul's words and the look on his face when he saw my pictures: open-eyed, surprised, more alert than I'd ever seen him, even in the midst of one of his energized lectures.

If he'd been a dog, his ears would have perked up. Like our little Rosie. Dead for three weeks now. Buried in the backyard, under the magnificent cherry tree. Tom wouldn't let me help. He was sad, too, I knew, and wanted time to himself with Rosie in her box and the growing pile of dirt by his worn leather work shoes. I watched from the back window, wiping my tears with a dish towel. Sweet Rosie, my Rosie. Tom Junior had called in disbelief, as if he'd thought she would go on whining for scraps by the dining room table forever, Tom ceaselessly shooing her away while we all laughed.

I'd believed it, too.

I blink back tears and take a bite of potatoes. It sticks in my throat. I have to gulp water to keep from choking. Tom stares at me bug-eyed.

'You OK, Judy?'

I drag the cloth napkin across my mouth, nod and smile. 'I'm fine,' I say, and reach to put my hand over his. He squeezes my fingers. I don't want Tom getting worked up. The doctor said he should be calm and steady, so I have to be calm and steady, too.

When I came home from wandering a nearby town with my camera last Sunday to find Tom slumped on the living room rug, I instantly thought of Rosie: how I'd found her stretched out, too still and silent to be sleeping. Her little chest should have been rising and falling; I should have heard her adorable snore. I knelt by Tom and shook him just the way I'd shaken Rosie. *Tom! Tom!* I said, until I heard the slightest groan. I waited until I heard one more, just the smallest sound and a puff of breath. Then I ran to the kitchen phone and called the ambulance, dismayed by the operator's nonchalance. *Where did your husband collapse, ma'am? Can you find his pulse? Does he seem to be breathing? Is the house number clearly displayed? If not, you may want to wait on your porch.*

I had no intention of waiting outside. I stayed by Tom, smoothing his thinned hair back from his forehead, talking to him the way I used to talk to Tom Junior when he was young and drowsy with sickness. *It's OK, honey, you'll be fine. Just hang on. You'll feel better soon. It's all right.* But the whole time I was vibrating with fear. I tried to bargain with the god I'd never fully believed in, even after all the forced churchgoing of my youth: *No more. Not now. Not ever, please. Please.*

Even fixed in that pleading state, though, I stared at Tom's slack face and wanted my camera. It was just behind me, just out of reach; I'd dropped it as I came in the door. In my head I left myself trembling on the carpet and saw him coldly, as if through the camera lens: the loose O of his mouth, the slight twitching of his eyelids over his large, straight nose. I noticed the blue carpet fiber that sprung up like a solid sea around his pale still form, and saw how I would frame it all. Except I wouldn't, of course; that would have been ghoulish and wrong.

I'd taken pictures of Rosie after she'd died, kneeling on the same blue carpet and lowering the lens to be level with her little face that had always been grinning and mischievous in life but had frozen now, solidified. I took a few shots to preserve this last memory of her, but once I developed the film, I stored the prints in the locked filing cabinet drawer that holds my private documents, the ones that even Tom hasn't seen. Rosie's death photos would rest in a file beside the brittle, yellowed article from my old hometown paper that reads, 'Local Girl Attacked by Afternoon Intruder.' I didn't like putting Rosie next to such ugliness, but I couldn't face her death any more than I could face the past, so I left her there.

My other reminders from that long-ago time can't be locked in a drawer. Moving my free hand under the table now, I find the scarring along my inner thighs: the bumps and ridges and bubbled skin that have been mine for years. Just after we made love for the first time, I told Tom the scarring was from a kitchen accident – a terrible spill. Even though I'm not sure he believed me, he acted as though he did, and has never brought it up since. It's remarkable, really – that in all these years he's never mentioned it. Not once. The most he does is run his hand over the spot now and then, saying nothing – but making me shiver and recoil.

He squeezes my hand again, bringing me back to the here and now. To the dining room table and to the life we've built in this small brick house on our quiet, tree-lined street. The past retreats – Rosie's death, Tom's sudden collapse, my ancient incident – but I sense it all hovering. Waiting for something: a window, an opening.

4

IN TOWN THE NEXT DAY, I shop for champagne and a gift for Samantha and Hal's twenty-fifth anniversary party. As I walk along Main Street, acquaintances ask after Tom's health or comment on Rosie's absence and I have to tell them, *He's doing just fine*, or, *Rosie died three weeks ago.* Most people respond lightly to Rosie's death, offering mild sympathy – she was only a dog, after all. A pet. But she was my constant companion, beside me for more hours of the day than Tom, even. I whispered to her when she curled on my lap; she always listened intently. She held all my secrets, never judging me or loving me less for them.

I can't say that in public, though. I simply say, 'Thank you,' and move along.

Toward the end of the street, I pause in front of Mr Katz's old toy store, whose oddly formal window display hasn't changed in years: dusty teddy bears, alphabet blocks, and empty-eyed dolls. But what's different today, what catches my eye is… myself. From the neck down, I'm a dark female shape reflected in the center of the window, with blue sky surrounding me and one wilted teddy bear caught in the bell of my skirt. Above it all, my face looms, bright and alive. I've seen myself reflected in windows before, of course, but something about this, about the composition, sets the back of my neck tingling. I fish my Nikon out of my purse, lift it chest-high, and click the button.

I think of Paul admiring the finished print, saying, *Incredible. The composition is striking. That uncanny eye of yours at work again, Judith.*

Pure nonsense, of course. I don't even know if it will come out well. Or if I'll show Paul more pictures after all. He said he wanted to see them, but what if he was simply being polite? I believed him at the time, but now, with a little distance, I realize I may have been starstruck, naïve. Paul has had a picture in *Harper's*, after all; what could he possibly see in mine?

I glance back at the window: there I am, floating in the world. Not quite embodied, not quite real. Like a phantom or an alternate self with no past, present, or future. *Who is this person*, I wonder. I know her face, but she isn't quite me. I feel dizzy and my vision blurs. When I step to the right, the spell breaks. The image alters, the composition dissolves; I return to my body, to myself, a bit shaken.

I turn and walk back toward the heart of town, trying to recapture my business state of mind. *To the liquor store*, I remind myself. *And then to Virginia's Boutique for a vase or a nice frame.*

Samantha and Hal, our longtime neighbors, have asked me to be their photographer. I know what they want: posed, artificial shots of pairs and groups of people with fixed smiles. All the same, I'm glad to have a purpose for the evening, and to have a chance to wear my dark blue satin cocktail dress with the deep V-neck, matching heels, and Grandmother's pearls. I walk briskly toward the liquor store, appreciating the sound of my low heels hitting the sidewalk and the tinkling bell of the door when I pull it open.

I'm here, I tell myself as I greet Lance, the owner. *I am Judith Stanley.*

5

THE FIRST HOUR OF THE party goes just as I expected it would, gathering guests in small groups and pairs and counting down to 'Say "Happy Anniversary"!' Faced with the camera lens, some fiddle with their hair or try to smooth away fat by smoothing their clothes, while others freeze in place with gleaming plastic smiles. In either case, the resulting shots will be lifeless, like the studio family portraits from years ago that hang on my own living room walls.

Samantha will be pleased.

As the hours pass, the party's taut atmosphere begins to loosen. Voices rise, raucous male laughter explodes now and then, and a low bank of cigarette smoke hangs just below the living room ceiling. Someone has cranked up the volume on the background jazz music – Hal's favorite – and a few guests sway languidly to the beat. I start to tense at every loud sound, as if wandering through a hostile landscape. I don't like noise, crowds, or parties; I try gulping champagne to fortify myself. As the wine warms and loosens me, I start to drift through the rooms more easily, hoping to catch a glimpse of Tom.

Patty, my neighbor from across the street, calls me over to her group of three. Her nails dig into my wrist as she leans close and practically shouts, 'Is Tom really OK? My god, when we saw the ambulance, we thought he was dead.'

I pull away from her. She probably wouldn't have put it that way if she weren't a little drunk, but it still rubs me wrong.

Diana and Mercy, the two neighbors standing with Patty, eye me expectantly.

'He's fine,' I say. 'Just look at him.' I point across the room to where Tom holds court in a circle of semi-balding men. He's telling a story, gesturing broadly, with the men all nodding along.

'He does look well,' Patty admits, taking a drag from her cigarette and blowing smoke beside my head. I squint as her eyes search my face. 'And how are *you*? First Rosie, then Tom.' She looks sorrowful, but also intrigued. It isn't *her* pain or grief, after all, and besides, I'm a curious case: a respectable mother and housewife who won't join the bridge club because she prefers taking pictures. Walks everywhere with that camera in hand, snapping pictures left and right. Is it a hobby or a bad habit? *Hard to tell*, Patty might say.

'Sorry, I see Samantha calling me over. She and Hal need their anniversary portrait taken. Lovely to see you ladies.' I slip from Patty's grasp and walk toward the far corner of the room. Samantha hasn't called me over, of course; she and Hal have already posed several times. Now she has her arms slung around Hal's neck and is planting a kiss on his cheek; he rears back with a quick, surprised grimace. I raise my camera quickly, capturing the moment before his features relax into a smile. They look at me when they see the flash, blinking and smiling, Samantha leaning into Hal. I take another shot for show and wave at them before walking away.

When I raise the first print later from its acid bath, I'll see a drunk, disgusted husband and a sweetly adoring wife. It isn't the whole truth about them, but it's part, and I've caught and recorded it with my uncanny eye. I feel slightly guilty but too lit up after taking a *real* photograph to feel truly bad.

I think Paul would encourage my behavior, my almost-lack of remorse. *Photography is an art, and art can be a razor blade, peeling back layers of civility to reveal stark truths*, he told us recently. I found myself nodding along, writing it down.

I move through the rooms now, hungry for more – more opportunities to reveal stark truths. I feel like I'm ruling the party in my blue satin heels, catching glimpses here and there of the gathering's dark underside. I notice the Millers from three doors down, huddled in a corner, clearly having a subdued but vicious fight. Their faces are taut with anger, though they're surrounded by blissful party noise. They stare at me with the flash, but I've quickly aimed the lens to the left of them, at a larger group of happy, laughing people. I move on, spotting and shooting: a smoking man – a stranger to me – leering openly at Rhoda Staunton; my neighbor Maura looking sick to her stomach before rushing from the room; and Tom himself, my Tom, mouth and eyes wide as he entertains his pals. I hardly notice it's him, my husband, when I focus and shoot; I only see a man acting like a clown. I won't show Tom the finished print, of course – and I tell myself I won't show Paul either.

Unless it's very good. Unless all of these party pictures are as good as I think they might be. Unless I feel a distinct need – or even a responsibility – to share my photographs with my professor who specifically requested them. *Almost an assignment*, I tell myself.

I jump when a hand touches the cool, bare flesh of my upper arm. I think, irrationally, that someone's come to punish me for my cruelly revealing pictures, but it's only Samantha. She's beaming.

'Did you get everyone?' She leans toward me, a little off-kilter, blowing hot booze breath in my face. I tell her I have. Her mouth drops open and she grabs me by both arms.

'You!' She sends another blast my way. 'You and Tom! We have to get your picture, too!'

I try to demur, but Samantha won't hear of it. She takes my hand and pulls me along behind her. We extract Tom from his group and Samantha plucks the Nikon from my hands.

'Oh,' I say, reaching out for it protectively. I give her tense instructions on how to focus, none of which she hears; she tells us to smile. I'm certain Tom is grinning; I can smell the booze and cigarette smoke on him, and he leans into me a little more than usual, his hand hot on the small of my back. It's too hot, really, so hot I want to shake it off. When Samantha finishes and hands the camera back, I loop the strap around my neck with a grateful sigh.

'I hope you're watching it a bit, Tom,' I say quietly, scanning his face. 'The doctor said – '

He waves me away. 'I'm fine, fine. He told me to relax, didn't he? I'm feeling pretty relaxed.' He laughs and gives me a wet kiss on the cheek, not unlike the one Samantha gave Hal. I probably look like Hal did, grimacing. I don't like wet kisses or drunk men. I don't like my husband when he isn't himself, and he isn't himself right now – too loose and hot and silly. The party is loose and hot and silly, too – and becoming more so by the minute. I tell Tom I want to go home, but he shakes his head slowly like a child. So I leave him to go to the bathroom.

I'm eager to sit in a locked, quiet room and close my eyes for a moment. But when I open the door to what I think is the bathroom, the slice of hall light reveals a darkened bedroom instead – the master bedroom. There on the king-size bed, a shirtless man is pinning a naked woman down, pressing the flesh of her V-ed arms as he grunts and moves against her. Her head is flopped back but she brings it up, sees me, and says, 'Oh,' with her mouth so perfectly circular that, even in my shock, I think about lifting my camera to my eye. But I'm frozen. The man never stops moving and grunting but the woman keeps her head up, staring at me, terrified. I don't know whether she's terrified at the sight of me or if it's the man who terrifies her, if it's what he's doing, how he's pinned her down.

'Stop!' she screams, finally – at me or the man, or both of us – and I slam the door, walk quickly down the hall. I try another door: locked. I try the next door. It swings open to reveal a small, empty bathroom. I lock the door behind me and lean heavily against it, closing my eyes. Pain goes searing through my middle. I wrap my arms around myself and stumble over to sit on the closed toilet lid. I hunch my body and tell myself, *It was just a couple having sex in the dark. Having fun.* But I don't believe it. I never saw his face, but I recognized the *kind* of man he was: the kind who'd held me down and branded my thighs.

I never saw *his* face, either. Or – I could never remember it, even though Grandmother and the police kept pressing me about it. *Think, Judith, what color were his eyes?* I couldn't tell them. When I tried to recall his features, they blurred into an awful mask. Grandmother would sigh in frustration, and tell me he'd never be caught if I couldn't remember. As if the burden were mine – as if I alone were responsible for what he'd done.

I feel responsible now, too. When the woman – a stranger – looked up at me, she reminded me of Parade Girl, though there were no tears marring her face. She was in trouble, though, and I left her there. Left her to suffer alone.

I unlock the door and go tearing past a confused guest who's been waiting for the bathroom. I fling open the door to the bedroom and see… nothing, no one. Only a bedside lamp casting a yellow glow over the newly tranquil scene. I step closer and study the bed, spotting a few telltale wrinkles in the otherwise smooth duvet fabric. They tried to tidy things before they fled. I leave and look down the hall toward the living room. Everything is the same: the nodding, talking, laughing heads, the skein of smoke hanging in the air. The smell of booze. As I draw closer, I smell more: light body odor mingled with heavy perfume; the tang of imported cheese on people's plates; and smoke, smoke everywhere. Veiling everything. I scan all the faces, looking for the couple. I go from room to crowded room, ignoring Tom as he waves me over to where he stands with two neighbors. I walk on through the dining room, my eyes furiously searching. But they're nowhere. They've disappeared. He took her somewhere – or they left together happily, willingly. Or the woman managed to run away.

'Judith,' Tom says. Right behind me. When I turn, I can tell he's sobered up a little. 'Everything all right?'

'I was just – looking for a couple I saw. Someone I thought I recognized.'

Tom furrows his brow and scans my face. 'One couple just left. I don't think we know them, but I saw them leave,' he says. My chest tightens at this, to hear they left together. *If* it was them. If it was, it means the woman didn't escape, that he led her out with his hand gripping the back of her neck, pushing her forward. She might have smiled at Samantha and Hal and wished them well in a tremulous voice before vanishing through the door, into the night, with the man close behind.

'Judith?' Tom asks. My eyes refocus on his face. He looks as weary as I feel.

'I'm tired, that's all. Can we go home now?' I lean my head against his chest, inhaling the familiar Tom smell of drugstore soap, sweat, and warm skin. A good man, a pure man. Nothing like the one I saw tonight.

I pull back from Tom with a tired smile. He takes my hand and leads me home.

6

I DREAM OF THE COUPLE – if that's what they were. The woman and the man.

In the dream the man has hot irons for hands. He's bringing them toward her face, which is turned to me, frozen not in terror but annoyed surprise. I tell her to move, to get up and run, but she just lies there, looking. He brings his iron hands up and scalds her, causing her mouth to form that same O, but without sound. The smell of burning flesh fills the room and when I scream, I'm muted, too.

I turn away from her smoldering cheeks and wake in the dark next to Tom, tears streaming down my face and onto the pillow.

Save your tears for your pillow, Grandmother told me when I was a child. And I did. I saved them all for my pillow and here I am, soaking it some forty years later.

Leave the past in the past, she also told me, with something like disgust. I've struggled my whole life to obey.

7

EARLY THE NEXT MORNING, WHILE Tom is still sleeping, I slip downstairs to the darkroom and pull the door closed behind me. I woke thinking I may have captured the couple on film, in one of my wider party shots, and was eager to see the pictures anyway – not the stiff, posed ones I took for Samantha, but the *real* ones.

My lingering anxiety – after the party, then the dream – fades quickly as I set to work. Fishing out the rolls from my camera bag, I begin with one, carefully threading the film onto the reel before dunking it in the first tank, then into the fixer. The work clears my head and grounds me with purpose; I move through the steps automatically, in a contented trance, washing the reel, then trimming and hanging the negatives to dry.

Later in the day, once I've prepared and eaten an early dinner with Tom, I head downstairs again. I love how the dark swallows me as I descend the steps. It's a good dark down here, a private, soothing dark. My heart beats quickly as I take down the negatives and begin to print. If I could hurry the process, I would – but it isn't until after ten o'clock, after I've fiddled with the cropping and exposure, that my pictures are ready to hang on the line. I'm tired, and Tom is confused by my working so late – I'm not usually in such a hurry – but I told him over dinner that Samantha wants her prints ready tomorrow. *It isn't like she's paying you*, he said, and then returned to his food with that slight grimace I've learned is just part of his aging face.

I wake at 3:00 am, a time when I usually read for a while to lull myself back to sleep. Tonight, though, I pull on a robe and rise without disturbing Tom. After collecting the dried prints from the darkroom, I spread them out on the dining room table and begin peering at each one. I search first for the couple – or the woman's face, rather, since I never saw *his*. I don't see the couple in any shot, and the more I don't see them, the more relieved I am. As if what happened in the master bedroom never happened at all, since the proof isn't in the prints. But the memory lingers. I saw it; it was real. I start over, searching for her face again. Nothing the second time; nothing the third time, either. My eyes begin to ache.

I tell myself to leave it alone, to step back from this wearying task and just review the pictures, starting with the portraits of Samantha and Hal. I think they'll be pleased with how vibrant and happy they look – Samantha with her shining black hair and Hal with his straight white teeth and crisp blue button-down shirt, their faces close together. Thriving after twenty-five years with each other, it seems.

No sign of that grimace I captured in the later hours.

I move on to the 'real' pictures and linger over one of our neighbor Janet, a loud and plain-faced divorcée who's buxom and wears enough bright lipstick to muster a dull suburban glamour. I've caught her with a wide-open mouth, roaring with laughter. She looks ready to eat the trio of men who lean in as if offering themselves up for consumption. Like Saturn, about to devour his child – though hers is a careless and sensual devouring. *Will Paul like it?* I wonder, which makes me realize: *I will show these to Paul.* The hesitation I've felt these past few days has vanished. I *will* show him. Will I share the one of Tom, too? It turned out so well, so brutally revealing. My stomach sinks to think of Paul seeing my husband this way, but if I don't tell him who Tom is, and if Tom himself never knows, the harm is practically nonexistent, isn't it?

I can't answer my own question so I leave the party pictures behind for the prints I took of myself in the toy store window. I study the first image with a hitch in my breath, remembering the odd sensation that passed through me. Will I see some phantom version of myself? But it's me. I see my solid, unsmiling face, the familiar shape of my body. The sky around me, and the sad teddy bear inside the dark outline of my reflected skirt. There's something odd in the background, though, reflected faintly behind me: a human-shaped smudge or shadow near the top right-hand corner of the print. I bring it closer to try to make it out. An imperfection, or a person? It's hard to tell. If someone was standing behind me, watching, I didn't notice at the time, but they would have been so far away – across the street, in a space between two houses – I could have easily missed them.

Missed *him*.

The more I look, the more certain I am that it's a man. I can't see any details of his heavily shadowed body or face, but I can tell he's looking toward my reflection in the window.

It's him. It must be him. Cold spreads through my body like liquid.

It can't be him, but the sudden spike of pain in my side says otherwise.

Before last night, I rarely thought of him, about the *fact* of my long-ago attacker. The long, placid surface of my adult life had made the past seem implausible – made *him* seem implausible. But now, this hellish jolt: a sign of his existence in every version of my toy store self-portrait. It doesn't appear in the party pictures taken with the same roll of film, so I'm fairly certain it isn't an impurity – though the party backgrounds are darker, less visible. Maybe it's there, and I've missed it? I feel a slight surge of hope that fades quickly.

I return to the pictures I took in town. It can't be him; it simply can't. They never caught him, but even if he were still alive, why and how would he find me *now*, halfway across the country, over thirty years later? The figure was more likely a random passerby, someone who paused to watch me taking photographs.

I tell myself this, but my body rejects it.

Staring at that ominous shape, I think of Grandmother reading aloud from the news article about the search for my attacker over dinner one night, as nonchalantly as if it had nothing to do with me. I sat there shaking violently until the fork in my hand clattered to my plate, which earned me a scolding.

Soon after, my father disappeared. Or – he took a job in Montana and never returned. Grandmother blamed me – for his leaving, for getting attacked. For not recalling the man's face, which led to the police department's long, futile search. For becoming strange and withdrawn, an object of both pity and curiosity in our town.

Around this time, I found my father's Kodak 35, bought on a whim and abandoned in a desk drawer with rolls of unused film. Nearly housebound, except for school – which was a torment after the attack – I started taking pictures: of gleaming doorknobs, sunlit windows, the gloomy staircase leading to the attic. I loved the heft of the camera in my hands, the sound it made when I advanced the film, and the neat click of the button. I loved how the camera rendered everything I saw precise and comprehensible. It made me feel safe, warming to my hand and showing me wonders in the world – even in my own tainted corner of it.

The more I used the camera, the more nuanced my photographs became. I felt intense anticipation and delight whenever I went to pick up my prints from the shop. I'd keep the pictures hidden away in old shoeboxes on the top shelf of my closet and sit cross-legged on the floor of my room to flip through them, seeing how I'd captured and remade the world in each small rectangle, how I'd controlled the wild edges of things. It flooded me with relief: proof of this small power I had.

Soon enough, I finished high school and was able to move far away. After Tom and I met at a cousin's wedding, we married and settled in Harrington, New Jersey, and for many years I used the camera the way a good wife and mother should: to capture birthdays, school plays, graduations, vacations. I felt proud of myself, living the way Grandmother would have liked, leaving the past in the past, moving forward, always forward. *People forget all kinds of things. People live by forgetting*, I once read in a book. It soothed and consoled me, told me I was doing well. I was fine. When I touched my scars, the past would bubble up, but I'd smother it quickly, move on.

Maybe that's why I hear Grandmother now, sense her disgust like hot breath on the back of my neck. *What are you doing, Judith? Awake in the night, worrying over this nothing, this smudge?* I quickly gather the prints into a neat pile, store them in a kitchen drawer, and pour myself a cup of cold water.

Drinking it clears my head but when I look down I expect to see Rosie, her little tail wagging. I choke back a sob, hold it in with a hand pressed to my mouth. Grandmother's voice tells me to *go back upstairs*, and I will, I will. If only I believed that sleep would change what I've seen.

8

When Paul ends class, the students around me pack up their belongings and leave – except for three young women I call 'the fangirls' who spend the lecture tossing their hair or smoothing it in place, crossing and uncrossing their long, stockinged legs. They turn their heads in unison to track Paul's movements as he walks and talks. I envy them their fresh young beauty, but none of it has earned them anything near the attention Paul has gladly given me.

When the fangirls leave, they hardly look at me, so focused are they on swaying their hips as they climb the steps, casting looks over their shoulders at a seemingly oblivious Paul. At the last moment, I see his eyes flick up, take in the sight of their retreating backsides. But then he spots me, seated and waiting.

'Judith,' he says, and it sounds perfunctory. 'Sorry, but did you have pictures to show me?' He's smiling but I can tell he's distracted and tired. Drained from teaching, and it's after nine o'clock. I've been foolish to wait. I thrust my envelope of photographs back into my bag and pack the rest of my things.

'I can show you another time,' I say, rising to go.

'No, I'd love to see them now.' He sounds suddenly brighter, a little revived. I hesitate before walking down with my envelope, but of course I do. It's what I've come here to do; it's what I thought about at the party and what I've thought about ever since: *sharing my pictures with Paul.* As I stand beside him, trying to see them through his eyes, I notice how I've emphasized the shadowy corners of Samantha's living room, the shadows beneath Janet's eyes, her wide-open, shadowy mouth – the shadows everywhere on this so-called joyous occasion.

Shadows in the bedroom, too. That ugly coupling. I fight to bring my focus back to Paul and the pictures in his hand. Not the pictures I didn't, couldn't, take that night. The ones I can't erase from my mind. If I'd managed to capture the man and woman on film, maybe I'd be able to move on and forget them. But they linger, indelible and grossly alive.

'Man, Judith, these are fantastic,' Paul says. He says it quietly, but it startles me from my dark reverie. His eyes are glued to the photograph of Janet with her head thrown back, mouth gaping. I'm so pleased by his comment that I start to babble.

'She looks like Saturn, doesn't she? The one who ate his children. Or child. His son. But obviously those are – men.'

Paul nods absent-mindedly. His eyes are roving over every last detail.

'The mundane made ominous and mythical, right?' he says without looking up. I love the way he's phrased it and long to write it down.

Paul runs his hand through his thick, nearly shoulder-length hair – something he does often during class – and keeps flipping through the pictures. He praises the one of Hal grimacing at Samantha's kiss, and pauses at the photograph of Tom, too. I stop breathing for a moment.

'This one – he looks like the guy who makes jokes at parties to please everyone.' I cringe inwardly at the delight in Paul's eyes but nod along, smiling, having earned my ounce of approval at Tom's expense.

Paul keeps flipping through the photographs, praising them. I stay where I am, soaking up his words. Tom's humiliation forgotten, or shoved aside. As Paul nears the self-portrait, the picture I most wanted to share, I start to panic. I wanted to see if he would notice the small figure in the background, but now

I'm overwhelmed by the opposite desire: to *not* know, to not share, to not submit the picture to Paul's searching gaze. I reach out and grab all the photographs from his hands. He looks up, startled and confused.

'I'm not –'

'I'm sorry. The last one isn't good. I can't share it yet,' I say, awkward and rushed. 'Thank you, Paul. I'm sorry to have taken up your time.'

'Not at all. It's a total pleasure to see these. And please remember what I said last week, about submitting to photography magazines. I really think you should consider it. It's a shame to – hide these away.'

The intensity in his warm brown eyes makes my pulse quicken. Like a scared little rabbit's. A *pleased* and scared little rabbit's.

'Thank you, Paul. You're very kind.'

'It isn't kindness,' he says. 'I've never offered to help a student with publication before. I never expected to. But believe me when I say these are extraordinary. I'd be honored to help you send them out. I think they'd find a great home. They *deserve* to find a great home.'

Extraordinary, he said. *Extraordinary.* Even better than *uncanny.* The dim, ordinary lecture hall brightens in the glow of Paul's words. Even so, they can't sway me. I never want strangers' eyes on me again, searching me, prying me open. I don't want strangers' eyes on my photographs, either; to me it's the same. And I can't explain any of that to Paul.

'Thank you very much, Paul. I will think about it.' He nods and bids me good night, polite but subdued. I'm sad to see the fire leave his eyes – because I've denied him the pleasure of helping me. I feel heavy as I walk away, retreating to that withdrawn and solitary place inside of me.

'Judith,' Paul calls before the door swings shut behind me. 'I hope you'll bring some new pictures next week.'

Everything shifts. I leave the room feeling buoyant and light.

9

PAUL'S DICTUM *THERE ARE WORTHY subjects everywhere* is foremost in my mind as I stroll through the small town of Suttonville the next morning, Nikon in hand. At first I see nothing but closed storefronts and half-empty parking lots in the shabby downtown, but finally I spot a 'worthy subject': an ancient-looking liquor store display. Incandescent with late-morning light, the bottles lined up on the mirror-backed shelves look like liquid candy; I have the urge to bring one to my lips and take a great, burning drink. One to burn away my grief over Rosie, my worry over Tom's health. Another to wash away the awful image of the couple from the party. A third to forget the strange man I caught in my photographs.

One photograph, I remind myself. Multiple shots of the same few minutes, the same location. A fluke.

I spot myself reflected in the mirror behind the rows and rows of bottles. I didn't intend to take another self-portrait, but the shot is too good not to take. I raise my camera to the top of my chest and try to relax my stern-looking face. From the neck down I'm made of bottles, shining and bright. I see a sudden flash of movement reflected behind me and turn, startled, to see a man passing by on the opposite side of the street. But he's just an ordinary man, not the least bit interested in me or what I'm doing.

When I look back, I check the mirror for any sign of someone reflected behind me; I'm certain there's no one, nothing. I take the shot. I try different expressions and postures, and before long I realize I've been here quite a while. The light has changed to a bright, flat white.

I move on from the liquor store, snapping shots here and there: of three underfed but regal stray cats on a doorstep, and of a middle-aged woman like me, cleanly dressed but harried, leaving the grocery store with paper bags bundled in her arms. She gives me a hard look that will only make the picture better. In last week's class, I jotted down a note that said, *The subject's response doesn't matter. All that matters is doing what's right for the photograph.* It's easy to apply because the camera makes me bolder than I am. So does Paul. It's safe to think of him, of his words and ideas and predilections, now that I'm in the flow. I'm moving and choosing easily; Paul's words just give me an extra lift.

I take pictures of eloquently empty doorways, a broken window gleaming with sunlight, a man leaning against a tree with his legs crossed, his hat pulled down over his eyes. I keep up a frantic pace until my stomach tells me it's well past lunchtime. It's hard to stop but I snap a few final shots and then turn back to the car, spent and deeply satisfied.

10

I'M STARING AT THE PRINTS of my liquor store self-portrait, spread out on the dining room table under bright chandelier light. I tell myself the smudge, the shadow, won't be there; it *can't* be there. I checked behind me and saw nothing, no one, before taking the shot. But here it is in every last version: a small, dark figure in the top right corner, by a cluster of trees. Somehow he found me. He followed me.

The side of my body throbs. I clutch my waist and look away, squeezing my eyes shut like a child. *It will be gone when I open my eyes.* But it's still there when I look at the prints again. Of course it is. It's as real and undeniable as everything else I see: the trees beside it, the rows of liquor bottles, the sidewalk, my own placid face. I choose one out of the batch and try keeping my eyes glued to the center of the portrait, not the margins, taking comfort in my gem-filled form and my strong, steady gaze. How could someone like this be afraid of a shadow? I stare for as long as I can, smiling and feeling no pain, no pain at all. But I can't resist the pull of the top right corner forever.

There it is, the dark shape of a man – and the pain shoots back. I gasp and put the print down, catching sight of my bare feet on the carpet. My lovely blue carpet, running through the house like a calming sea. If only Rosie were there, too, panting up at me. I'd hold her and feel her hot little breath in my face. She'd negate the shadow man somehow, my Rosie. But she isn't there – *she's* been negated. Another throb of hurt. I hunch over with it, my hands gripping the back of a chair.

When I can, I sweep the prints into a haphazard pile and carry them right to the kitchen trash can. I will not tell Tom and risk his health; I will not show Paul and risk his interference, his prodding questions. I stand by the trash can with the prints in hand, feeling the waste of what I'm about to do like a dull ache at the back of my head. Or maybe that dull ache was already there – maybe it came from straining my eyes, or from looking too long at a troubling thing.

The phone rings, loud and insistent.

I startle. The prints drop to the floor.

'Stanley residence,' I manage in a trembling voice.

'Judith! I can't thank you enough! You're so *good*. You should open a shop,' Samantha says in a rush. I exhale and lean against the kitchen wall, grateful to hear my neighbor's voice, even as I bristle at her suggestion of my opening 'a shop.' I can't stand the idea, though I know she thinks she's praising me by saying it. Spending my days posing children on stools; fixing stray hairs around strained faces; gently folding hands together on laps in front of fake scenes of autumn leaves, cherry blossoms, or blue sky – all of it stinks of boredom and death. But to most people, owning a studio represents the pinnacle of a photographer's achievement.

'I'm so glad you like them. It was a wonderful party. You and Hal seemed very happy,' I add, though I'm remembering Hal's grimace, and imagine for a moment how badly Samantha would react if she ever saw the photograph – which she never will. And how would she react to what I saw in her master bedroom? On her pristine blue duvet? I start to lose myself in what I witnessed, when Samantha's voice brings me back to the surface of our shared pleasantries.

'We were happy, and we are! We had a fabulous time, and we're so glad you and Tom could come. He seems to be doing well.' A note of sudden solemnity in her voice.

'Yes, Tom is perfectly fine,' I say, because Tom *is* fine. He had a ministroke, the doctors said – but no one needs to know those specifics or the lingering threat of recurrence, and no one will. Not Samantha, not anyone else in town. Our neighbors have pried for days now, but Tom and I won't crack. It's a private matter. A *Stanley* matter.

And it *won't* happen again. Not if I watch over him, keep him calm.

'Well, I'm glad to hear that,' she says, but I can hear the letdown in her voice. 'When the ambulance came and took him, I was terrified for you!' It's close to what Patty said at the party, but Samantha's comment pierces me deeply today. I go rigid, remembering the two vigorous young men who packed Tom onto a stretcher and carried him out the front door. There were flashing red lights that drew the neighbors to their porches, hands clasped to their chests or over their mouths. They were scared for us, yes, but beyond that, they were greatly relieved to *not be us*. To be spared the imminent threat of death.

'Thank you, Samantha, we're fine now,' I say a little crisply. 'I've got to get something in the oven before Tom gets home. I'm so glad you liked the pictures.'

'Oh – I've left something on your front porch. A token of thanks. And I'll be your best customer when you open that studio!'

Long after we've hung up, I lean against the wall with the phone pressed to my ear, listening to the dial tone. I can't stand everyone knowing our business. Digging for details. Gossiping behind our backs. I remember lying in my dark bedroom when I was sixteen, just after the attack, hearing a neighbor in our kitchen say to Grandmother, *The poor girl, to be ruined that way!* I lay there feeling ruin all over my body, when I had only felt pain and confusion before. Now shame was added in: I was *ruined*.

I couldn't hear my grandmother's response – it was low and rumbling, probably sharing key details: my torn dress, the gross smell of burnt flesh. She'd used my incident as coinage in town, gathering sympathy and praise for what she'd endured, how well she'd cared for me – despite the humiliation of it all and my ruined state.

I stop wallowing and kneel to gather up the scattered prints. There's still an ache, but when I pick up the first liquor store self-portrait – the best version, I think – sadness overrides my fear: I wanted so badly to share this one with Paul.

And then I realize: I can reprint the photo and *crop the man out.*

It won't mar the composition, and it won't take long. It won't eradicate the man, either – not in real life. But at least it will mean *I can show Paul my pictures.* I can satisfy my stupid little desire – and the thought of desire makes me blush, makes me tremble. I toss the tainted pictures in the trash, making sure they're face down.

Once the cropped prints are dry, I scan each one for the figure, but it's gone – of course. I'm triumphant, but drained, too, as if I've excised something crucial from myself: the tip of an inner organ, or part of a limb. I can't explain it any more than I can explain the man's presence in my pictures, but I feel puzzled and oddly bereft.

Tom will be home soon. I tuck the pictures away and remember, suddenly, the gift Samantha said she'd left. It's there on the front porch: a blue bottle of Bombay Sapphire gin with a silver bow around its neck. What a strange coincidence, given my liquor store self-portrait; I'm certain Bombay Sapphire was one of the bottles on the shelf. I think of Samantha being 'the man,' hanging back as I take my pictures, dressed in all black. The thought of her – cheerful and feminine and always impeccably dressed – skulking around after me through a dingy small town makes me laugh, standing there on my doorstep. I peer into the aqua blue side of the bottle and see my own distorted, smiling face.

11

THE MAN IS EVERYWHERE – marring every background of my latest self-portraits.

He appears in the rushed one I took in the hardware store window bristling with tools, with the shovel and rope fitting inside the outline of my reflected figure. He's there in the shot I took at the edge of the town's pond – a silhouette that turned out beautifully. My own shadow stretches over the green, brackish water, but *his* shadow is there, too, on the opposite side of the pond, just barely visible in a barren field. He's there in the ones I took in an old, abandoned dress shop window, fitting myself between two bald and naked but eerily smiling mannequins. He's in every one, watching me, though I saw no sign of him today.

Now I want to burn the whole roll and be done with it.

But I don't. I can't do it. At least I've been smart this time, catching him on my contact sheets so I can crop before I print, saving time and precious materials. It gives me a slight sense of control, and the printing process soothes me. When I hang up the newly shadow-free prints, I'm deeply relieved. I feel none of that odd sense of loss I felt the first time, but stare lovingly at what I've made – and remade – and congratulate myself for having put things right.

And for having made these images ready for Paul, I think with a pulse of pride. I get caught up in a vision of handing Paul the new photos, watching him shake his head in wonder as he flips through them. Especially when he sees the self-portraits. *What will he make of them*, I wonder.

The telephone rings, shrill in the quiet house. We don't get many midday calls. My hope is that it's Tom Junior checking in during a lunch break, as he sometimes does. I hurry to the kitchen, eager to hear his voice.

'Hello, Stanley residence,' I say, out of breath. I repeat my greeting when there's silence on the other end, but no one responds. As I press the phone closer to my ear, I start to hear something: the sound of shallow breathing. I follow the rhythm of it, staring at the small pineapples lining our dark green wallpaper. The sound is soothing. Mesmerizing, even.

'Hello? Who is this?' I ask in a whisper. No answer; only the breathing goes on. My eyes have nearly closed. I'm leaning my head against the wall and drifting off when an image invades my mind: my ravaged inner thighs, just as they were right after the attack, raw and blistered and bleeding. I'm back there again, in that other kitchen with Grandmother's high-pitched scream. The moment she found me. I gasp and open my eyes to the sight of row after row of cheerful yellow pineapples, and the words fly out of me:

'Leave me alone!' I slam the phone into its cradle and sit down hard on the nearest kitchen chair. The pain has come searing back, but I know it will pass if I sit quietly and wait for ten or twenty minutes until the call recedes from my mind. Then I can rise and take Rosie for a walk. A walk will clear my head. I look around wildly for Rosie – and then I remember.

When Tom touches my shoulder gently, so gently, I'm curled on the floor beneath the kitchen phone. Hours have passed – I see the muted light of dusk through the small curtained window and feel stiff and foolish and scared. When he helps me up and holds me against him, I whisper, 'Rosie,' through my tears. And nothing else.

12

TOM WANTED ME TO STAY home and rest today, but I promised him I'd be fine. It was just a passing moment of grief, I told him, though I knew what he'd seen: his wife in the fetal position on the kitchen floor. I told him I needed fresh air, that I'd stay local and rest when I came home. I wouldn't rush to the darkroom. That pacified him – and it freed me, though I don't know how free I am today, walking listlessly through our local park, snapping pictures here and there without *looking deeply*, as Paul urges us to do. I see things but don't feel them. It's too painful to feel them. I keep revisiting the memory of my freshly burnt flesh, and the sound of the caller's breath in my ear. Was it him? No, it wasn't *him* – but it was someone. The someone who follows me.

I come to the reflecting pool by the playground in this sad, distracted state of mind. The photographer in me stirs, at last, at the sight of my shadow stretching over the dark blue water. If I could only raise my camera, it would make a better silhouette photo than yesterday's. But I know what I'll see when I develop the film: the man somewhere, across the water. I can't see him even as I stare in that direction, but I'm certain he's watching me.

Maybe I should try to find him.

I'm terrified by the idea but my legs move anyway, walking me around the reflecting pool and into the trees beyond it. A narrow path leads deeper into the small woods; I walk along it for a while, looking left and right, jumping at the slightest sound. No one is here, and even the birds and squirrels have gone quiet. I feel as foolish as I did on the telephone yesterday, talking to no one, listening to almost nothing, but I call out anyway.

'Hello?'

No answer. But why would he answer?

'Are you there?' I shout, feeling foolish but bold, too. 'Why are you following me?'

I look all around until I'm turning in slow circles, crunching leaves beneath my feet. I'm certain he's here somewhere, but he hides himself well. Maybe he curls himself into the shape of a rock, or climbs a tree. It sounds ludicrous, but otherwise I can't explain his damned invisibility. And then his damned *visibility.*

Like a dark god of some kind.

Walking out of the woods, I feel as haunted as I would have if I'd seen him. I look over my shoulder again and again. He doesn't appear. He won't, I know. I should go home, but I can't stand having wasted the day. I turn into the playground, distracted and bitter but resolute. I bring the camera up to my eye and begin snapping haphazardly. Children playing in the fountain, on the jungle gym, and flying down the slide. Children laughing, a baby screaming miserably, two siblings fighting over a cup full of dry cereal until it spills. I'm engrossed, even though I'm still not really *feeling*, when someone taps me on the shoulder. I whirl around.

'Why are you taking pictures of our children?' A stout woman with a thick but unplaceable accent glares at me. Behind her a small group has gathered, staring disdainfully. I forgot that I no longer belong in this world – the world of women with young children. I'm a suspicious intruder, especially with my camera in hand. I'm jealous for a moment – of these children, so fiercely protected from harm. I mumble an embarrassed response and leave quickly through the playground gate. The first woman swings it shut and locks it behind me.

13

I've made Tom's favorite for dinner: chicken piccata over pasta with a fresh spinach salad on the side. Tom tells me it's delicious, but his compliments can't disperse the fog that's descended since I came home today. I take small bites of the meal I've prepared and think: *This is the best thing I made today – to be consumed and processed and eliminated quickly. A literal waste.*

When I look up, Tom is watching me closely.

'Where'd you go today?' he asks, trying to sound casual and unconcerned. He takes a long swallow of milk and waits for a satisfying report from his wife. I wipe my mouth, clear my throat, and deliver it.

'Nowhere – just downtown. Nothing much came of it,' I say lightly, holding back a dark slew of words: *I tried to find the man who's been following me but couldn't – even though I know he was somewhere nearby. He's the man who called yesterday and the man in my pictures who might have branded me years ago. Those scars on my thighs are not from an accident. You've known that, though, haven't you? You just haven't wanted to know and I've never wanted to upset you.*

'I don't believe that,' he says, and for a tense moment I think I've said it all aloud – or that Tom has read my mind somehow. 'I'm sure you got some good shots, hon. Can I see them?' he asks, instantly calming my fears. He didn't read my mind, of course, and his request is a simple one. He rarely asks to see my pictures – but when he does, I try to filter out the 'weird' ones. No need for that today, though, so I get up from the table and bring him the contact sheets; the prints are still hanging to dry. I'm not even sure why I bothered to process them, but I'd taken a full roll, had an empty afternoon, and somewhere in the back of my mind was the thought, *What if there's a good one?*

'These are wonderful, Judith. You're too hard on yourself. I can see these in a magazine. They're just as good as the ones in *Life*.'

I thank him, but Tom's approval only confirms what I know: there *aren't* any good ones. Not any truly good ones. As I clear the plates, I imagine showing this batch to Paul. He would take them, expectant and smiling through his well-trimmed beard, saying, *Judith, what gems do you have for me today?* And I would smile tremulously back, knowing I was giving him not gems but duds. I would watch his smile falter as he searched through the pack for just one that stood out, one that proved he hadn't been wrong about this unlikely talent, this quiet housewife. He wouldn't meet my eyes when he was done. He would take the bunch and tap the edges against the desk, as I've seen him do with other students' work, then hold them out as if they might taint him. *Very nice*, he'd say, as he's done with the others. *Very nice pictures.*

I look up in the darkened kitchen window over the sink as I fill one tub with hot, soapy water. I look startled in the reflection. Startled and sad. I could grab my Nikon now and capture it, this image of a pathetic, pained woman, but wouldn't he be standing just behind me?

The man, I mean. Not Tom.

14

PAUL SPEAKS ABOUT SYMMETRY AND the 'rule of thirds,' gesturing animatedly, and I'm as rapt as a fangirl. It may partly be my delight at being out of the house, away from lingering memories of the past few days, but Paul's magnetism accounts for the rest. I encountered good teachers in high school, teachers I liked and admired, but Paul is something else: a showman, a magician. But it isn't just show; he's brilliant and knowledgeable. He says he's had only modest success in the photography world – an exhibit here and there, his picture in *Harper's* magazine once – but to me he sounds terrifically accomplished, and I suspect he's downplaying it all out of modesty.

When I glance at the clock and see how close we are to the end of class, I start to envision the moment I'll hand him my prints. *Not* the forgettable ones from yesterday, but the earlier ones – including, this time, my cropped self-portraits. My pulse races at the thought of Paul seeing those pictures – too soon, and not soon enough. I want him to hurry and end this, I want the fangirls to leave quickly, with everyone else, and I want to share the silent room with Paul.

'So, when you're out hunting for pictures – which is your only homework, by the way,' Paul concludes to light laughter, 'look for patterns. Identify symmetry. Try not to make your pictures *too* perfect, but do strive for balance. Interesting, striking balance. That's all for tonight. Have a great evening, everyone.' He holds up his hand in a wave, and the noise of students packing bags and leaving fills the room.

I see the fangirls step into the aisle and think they're leaving, too – but they walk toward Paul instead of up and out. They've never done this before, approached him so directly; I grow agitated watching them cluster around him, monopolizing him and his time. The dark-eyed, dark-haired one who's the boldest of the three speaks while the other two nod and clasp their binders to their chests. I can't hear what she's asking – the girl's voice is low – but I see Paul smile as he answers. It's a different smile from the ones he gives in class – more intimate and even suggestive, maybe? I begin to wonder if I'm a fool, a burden to Paul, waiting here, rushing him through this enticing flirtation with a gorgeous girl. Here I am, tiresome old Judith, interfering with what he probably really wants. He's a relatively young man himself, after all. Not that age matters: he's a *man*.

I stand abruptly, making more noise than I'd hoped to, and start to walk out.

'Judith, I'll be with you in just a moment,' Paul calls out. 'Charlie, does that cover it? Did I answer your question?' he asks kindly, but with a hint of impatience. All three girls nod as if they were all named Charlie. On their way out, they eye me with curiosity – especially the one I'm nearly certain *is* Charlie – but all I care about is the sound of their retreating boot heels and the door shutting firmly behind them.

Paul and I are alone now. I'm relieved and scared and ready as I walk down the steps – quietly, in my sensible flat shoes.

'Judith, what have you got for me tonight?' Paul asks, leaning back against the table where his papers and prints are piled in tidy stacks. He has an eager look on his face as I pass him the envelope with a trembling hand. I'm unreasonably nervous as Paul begins to flip through, drawing closer to my self-portraits in the back of the pack. He keeps his eyes glued to the pictures, scanning every inch of them.

'I've said you have an uncanny eye, haven't I?' Paul murmurs without looking up. 'It's really true. These are... incredible. You didn't need my lecture on patterns and symmetry today, that's for damn sure. I could have used these as examples.'

I murmur my thanks, but I don't think he hears. Finally, he reaches the first self-portrait, the one taken in the liquor store window. He stares. Then bursts out laughing. He's laughed in class before, but never like this – with unleashed glee. I'm petrified, thinking he must be laughing at me, at the silliness of making myself the subject.

'Holy shit, Judith.' I find the curse word jarring, but I'm beginning to see that he *likes* what I've done – he's staring down at it with that same look of love in his eyes I saw when he studied Parade Girl. Relief floods through me.

'This is gorgeous! Just look at this composition,' he says as if it weren't my own picture. He runs a hand through his hair and pulls at his short beard, moving on, flipping through the next ones. My eyes dart to the corners, checking the spots where the figure once stood. Nothing there, every time. Of course not. When he finally looks up, he holds my gaze and speaks softly, urgently.

'I've never seen such inventive and formally just... *wow* self-portraits, Judith. I really haven't. No one's doing work like this – *no one*.' He drags his hand through his hair yet again. I see the bulge of his arm muscle beneath his shirt and feel as giddy as one of the fangirls.

'You know what I'm going to say now, don't you?' he asks, his eyebrows raised. I nod and shift my eyes away from his face. 'So I won't say it. But you know, if you ever want to pursue that route, I'm here to help, in any way I can.' He looks at the wall clock behind me as he hands me the pictures. He's already thinking of something else, a plan he has with friends or a girlfriend. As much as he seems to love my pictures, they're not a real part of his life – even though this time with Paul is a real part of mine.

I don't want it to end. It wouldn't have to if I simply said, *Yes, please help me publish these.* We would stay longer, discussing and strategizing; he would put off his plans or ignore them. But I can't do it. I take the pictures back, thanking him. It seems as if the lights have dimmed – but they're always dim in this lecture hall.

'Can I walk you to your car?' he asks, and a new flutter goes through me.

I'm conscious of my body as I walk down the hall beside him, matching my stride to his, feeling his physical closeness. He's talking fast, telling me about how he lucked into his cheap apartment in the East Village, and this leads him to urge me to visit the city.

'You really should, Judith. We're going there later with the class, but you need to get there sooner. I can't imagine the pictures you'll take there. On the subway alone! You'll be snapping shots left and right.' I'm swept up in Paul's enthusiasm, already envisioning myself there, catching the train tomorrow morning and coming back by late afternoon. Tom won't love the idea of me roaming around Manhattan alone. In fact, he'll loathe it. But Paul is right; there isn't a place more filled with unusual, wondrous, disturbing sights: a photographer's heaven.

That settles it. I'll go.

Will the man find me there?

'Paul,' I say abruptly. We're almost to the parking lot, almost out of time. 'Is there ever an impurity that could cause a – a mark to appear on your photographs? But only on certain photographs?'

'Yes and no,' he says, thinking for a moment. 'If it's a film impurity, you'd see it in every photograph, not select ones. But I didn't notice anything like that in the ones you showed me.'

I know this, of course, but my heart sinks anyway. I nod and say, 'I was just wondering. It's happened before – not with these latest ones, though.'

'You must have had a bad roll.' I lie and say yes, that must be it. It's the closest I've come to telling anyone about the man in my pictures; now I feel as if I've stepped back from a cliff's edge onto firm ground. Relieved but melancholy – alone with my secret again.

When we reach my car – our old family Buick – he hovers behind me as I unlock the door. As soon as I'm safely in, he bids me good night. I watch him walk toward his own car, noting his long, loping stride, and think what an excellent photo this would make – Paul striding across the heavily shadowed parking lot, moving through pools of light cast by the streetlamps. *Moody and striking*, he'd say, when I showed it to him. *I love the deep contrast here – the man striding in and out of darkness and light.*

15

THAT NIGHT, LYING NEXT TO a deeply sleeping Tom, I find it hard to wind down. Usually I read before bed, but I've had my copy of *The French Lieutenant's Woman* propped open on my chest for almost an hour before I quietly close it and set it on my nightstand. I shut my eyes and replay everything that happened after class: the rapt look on Paul's face as he reviewed my pictures, then his outburst of joyful profanity at the sight of my liquor store self-portrait. Lying here in the dark, with Tom's quiet presence nearly an absence, my head fills with Paul's words, facial expressions, and the stark wonder and desire in his eyes.

Not desire for *me*, of course; I understand that.

But his desire for my *photographs* is a real, nearly palpable presence, one that sets a burning engine going in my chest. I turn on my side as if to keep Tom from sensing my excitement, and review my plan for tomorrow. I'll start from Penn Station in Midtown and head north, then loop back to catch the three o'clock train to make it home before Tom. I'll tell him about my day trip when it's over, when I've come back. No need to worry him, or risk having him tell me to stay home. Though part of me – a small part – longs to be told exactly that, to let the trip go, to not put myself at risk of encountering the man.

But I don't 'encounter' him, do I? He hangs in the background, behind me somewhere, appearing only in my pictures. Or he calls and breathes into the telephone. *He's cowardly*, I tell myself.

And he'll be lost in the commotion of the city. I'll be safer there than I've been in small towns.

Tom shifts beside me, and I freeze. I stay rigid until I hear a light snore, then try to let my body relax. It doesn't work. Pushing the covers aside, I rise creakily and walk to the bathroom for one of the sleeping pills the doctor prescribed after Tom's incident. I need a full night's rest.

16

I'M AS NERVOUS AND EXCITED as a child boarding the crowded nine o'clock train. I've been to the city many times, of course, but never as a *photographer*. Though I'm hesitant to call myself that, it gives me confidence as I stare at commuters in fresh suits, dresses, and shoes waxed to a shine, many of them with bright faces to match, rattling their newspapers purposefully. I desperately want to lift my camera and capture every last person, but I feel shy, even with Paul's words from a recent lecture ringing in my ear: *Photographers should have a one-track mind when they're out in the field. Shoot! Shoot! Shoot!* He punched the air as he said the last part, and everyone laughed. But they listened, too; I listened deeply. I want to obey but I tell myself I'm not quite 'in the field' yet; I'm in a small, contained train car. I'll shed my reserve when my heels hit the city sidewalk.

And I do. With my first breath of Penn Station's humid, tar-heavy air, all hesitation drops away. I shoot: the somber conductor as he stands, regal or simply very tired, by the long silver line of his train; a small homeless family huddled in the hallway with a cardboard sign that reads *PLEASE*; and the blurring bodies and faces of commuters set within the endless river of human momentum. The river splits around me as if I were a rock – a rock with a camera, shooting everything, everyone. I'm sweating before long, but the moment I ride the escalator up to the street, the cool air revives me. I stand staring at the autumn-blue sky caught between tall buildings, amazed by it all and relieved to be here, as if I've traveled many hours, many miles, to an unknown place.

At first, I simply walk. It's a joy to navigate the city streets, to drink in the many and varied faces passing by. I watch them hungrily and no one flinches when I lift my camera, snapping photographs, even inches from a face. I feel giddy, snapping left and right. I don't have a set destination in mind, only a direction: north. Toward Central Park, I suppose. On my way I can flow left or turn right, finding pockets of color and life here and there.

When I pass a string of enticing store windows somewhere along Forty-Eighth Street, I interrupt my heady obsession with the odd contours of people's faces to zoom in on my own. But my finger falters on the shutter button; I know the man could be nearby despite how safe I feel. I turn and look behind me for a long while, checking every male figure and face for *him* – and finding nothing – but I can't quite take the picture, either, with all that terrible space behind my back. A moment later, I stride over to a shiny new Cadillac parked at the curb. I lean into the side mirror and see my face reflected with only a sliver of the street, buildings, and sky behind me. This will do. I set up the shot carefully, feeling clever; he can't possibly squeeze into this one, even if he's here somewhere. I've outmaneuvered him, and it gives me a great lift.

I go on finding shots that limit background space: my face reflected in a silver plate on display in a store window; my face reflected in the side of a toaster left on someone's stoop. It's still possible the man might appear in minuscule form behind me, but I push forward with growing confidence. *If he's there, I'll crop him out*, I tell myself – as if that were the main concern.

Turning onto Fifth Avenue, I'm distracted again by the restless flow of people. I feel bolder than ever before, so bold that even the stone-faced New Yorkers find me intrusive. I take an extreme close-up of a surprised workingman, whose tanned and deeply lined face reminds me of the earth scored by valleys and rivers. I shoot two middle-aged lovers kissing passionately on a park bench, then shoot a grinning child with dirty tear marks on her face: a younger, less desolate version of Parade Girl. After I've taken several shots, her grandmother heaves herself up from a nearby bench to threaten me.

'Get away, get out of here,' she says, like I'm a stray dog. Her reaction angers me, even though she's justified in shooing me away. It may be that she reminds me a little of my own grandmother – who was also large and formidable – but this is a grandmother who cares enough to protect her grandchild. When I stand my ground and snap a picture of the woman herself, she explodes into profanity and moves toward me quickly. I turn and run, knowing she can't run far; she'd leave the child behind. Soon enough, the sound of her voice fades, and I'm leaning on a low wall to catch my breath. I'm exhilarated by what I've done, even if it's somewhat wrong. I've followed Paul's dictum: *Shoot! Shoot! Shoot!*

I'll have several rolls of good pictures to show for it. To show *him*.

I move on and stand on a crowded curb before a crosswalk, feeling smug about my hasty escape and my photographic bravado. When the light turns, there's a rush to cross. I'm almost to the other side when someone grips my arm and leans in close to my ear – so close I can feel a moist spray of breath. I think it's the grandmother at first, and try to pull away, but the hand – a man's hand, I realize – holds me fast.

'Judith, you're a selfish fucking bitch,' he hisses, dropping my arm and striding off before I can see his face, or anything but his hand and the tan sleeve of his jacket. I follow the disappearing back of his head with my eyes, too frozen to do more than notice his average height and short brown hair. And then he's gone. I walk in a daze to the sidewalk, letting my old pain rip through me.

I'm doubled over, gripping the railing in front of a department store, when a man's voice asks, 'Are you all right?' My pulse rockets but it's a different man – a different voice. Even so I look up, terrified, into his kind, concerned face.

'Do you need help?' he asks.

I shake my head. 'I'm fine. Fine.' I straighten up and begin to hobble away despite the pain. I don't thank him, because I can't push out the words. It's not until I'm halfway down a residential block that I pause to sit on the steps of a row house, still clutching my side. I stare back in the direction of the crosswalk. Is my harasser nearby? Has he followed me?

I try to remember his voice, even though I flinch from the memory of his words. *Selfish fucking bitch.* Most terrifying of all was that he used *my name.* Said it in a voice that was masculine, ageless, smooth – have I heard it before? Years and years ago, maybe, in a shabby, close kitchen?

Behind me, I only see empty sidewalk and one long, black car moving slowly down the street. He hasn't followed me. No one has. I'm oddly alone here – as if I were back in one of the semi-deserted towns I frequent, as I probably should be. Bile and bitterness fill my mouth. I think of Tom, how he doesn't even know I'm here and how furious he would be if he knew what just happened. Furious at the man, yes, but also furious at *me.* I've been reckless and it makes me regret the recent past.

When the pain finally passes, I rise slowly from the steps and make my way toward the train station, thinking only of getting back. I planned on having lunch here, but now I just want to be home. I want freshly vacuumed carpet beneath my feet; I want to see our family photographs on the wall and my small, shining crystal figurines on the shelves. I want curtains to pull across windows, a front door to slam shut and lock. For one sweet moment I think of Rosie, waiting at home for me, but then the moment passes and Rosie disintegrates – back to the pile of bones and moldy flesh she surely is by now. Another spasm runs through me but I manage to turn right on Seventh, hand clutching my side, and run toward the station. My eyes flit to the side every now and then – is that him, walking beside me? An average, brown-haired man in a crisp white shirt. And another, and another – they're everywhere. I push myself to walk as fast as I can, trying to leave him, leave all of them behind.

The city seems different now. Clouds hang low in the sky, casting gray light everywhere. People's eyes dart toward mine as if I'm tainted, strange. I feel tainted and strange, but I keep pushing forward until I'm inside the station, in the NJ Transit waiting room, and finally on the westbound train. I collapse into a seat, breathing heavily, dabbing sweat from my face with my handkerchief. It isn't crowded at this hour, but I'm glad to have people around me. Normal-looking people, not people who grab women in crosswalks and call them vicious names.

My breath slowly steadies and the pain ebbs as the train starts to move; we leave the city farther and farther behind. I lean my forehead against the smudged window, staring out at the wetlands caught between the frantic crush of the city and the orderly green lawns of home, and if I could, I'd raise my camera to capture the sight. But I'm limp and fatigued. All I can do is stare, and think one thing: *He knows my name. He came and taunted me. Touched me. Said my name.*

I close my eyes for the rest of the journey and shove all thoughts of him from my mind. I think of dinner, an upcoming dentist appointment, and the three shirts of Tom's that need ironing tonight. I won't run to the darkroom when I'm home, though there's plenty of time. I'm not ready to see those vivid images, those stark reminders of the day and what happened inside it.

When I reach our quiet little station and walk through the empty, tree-lined streets, relief overwhelms me. It isn't long before I'm steps away from our tidy brick home. Thinking of how the neighbors might react if they saw me is the only thing that keeps me from running pell-mell for the dark blue door.

17

'I WENT TO THE CITY TODAY,' I tell Tom as he chews his salad. I've been moving my fork through my bowl, stabbing a lettuce leaf here and there, but I haven't been able to bring any food to my mouth. Blurting out my confession – one sliver of the story, the only sliver I plan to give him – frees me enough to take my first real bite. I chew and swallow it in a mouth gone dry.

'What for?' he asks. I see a flash of something in his eyes, hear the tremor in his voice. 'You didn't take the subway, did you?' We've seen evening news programs about escalating violence on the subway: robberies at gunpoint, stabbings on the platforms or in the flickering, failing light of a train car. I shake my head, imagining what might happen if I said, *I didn't take the subway but a man assaulted me on the street in broad daylight.* His eyes might roll back in his head; he might slide from his chair to the floor. I know what it would look like: Tom on the ground, limp and barely breathing. I close my eyes to try to wipe the image from my mind.

When I open them again, Tom is there, giving me that look he gave Tom Junior whenever he misbehaved at dinner – when he spit food from his mouth as a toddler or sat sullen at the table in his teenage years. Once he left home, Tom told me he could finally fully digest, but I found the endless calm oppressive. I hated our too-easy small talk and the sounds of our eating. Even Rosie's presence couldn't distract me from the desperate scrambling I felt or the voice in my head asking, *What now?*

What and who are you, Judith Stanley? I was no longer a mother and I felt suddenly old, my new life an ill-fitting skin.

It was then – three years ago now – that I started wandering the neighborhood, the town, the neighboring towns, like something of a ghost. I drifted through places that were mostly familiar to me, feeling oddly disconnected from myself. I had no purpose – only to drift. But I began noticing things: the wine-colored birthmark staining the side of a beautiful storekeeper's face, or the dark interior of an abandoned house seen through the gaping front door. I saw the wounded, scarred underside of the world I knew well, and I wanted my camera. I'd used it mostly for family pictures since Tom Junior's birth, but now I started carrying it everywhere – much to my husband's confusion. I moved through emptiness and filled it with image after image; then I made my darkroom and taught myself how to process film. Before long, I was living in the middle of a rich new phase of life.

And then: Tom's episode. Rosie's death.

And now: the shadow, the caller, the man in the crosswalk. Sullying everything. Forcing me to hide more from Tom.

'I wanted to get better pictures. More pictures. There are simply more people there, Tom,' I say, sounding defensive and slightly condescending. 'I'm tired of my usual circuit. I'm running out of subjects. Paul says –'

'I don't care what *Paul* says,' Tom says with sudden heat, banging his glass down so hard that milk sloshes and spills onto the table. There'll be a ring now. I wait a moment, staring into Tom's red face, knowing it mirrors my own. I've forgotten to say *Professor Sorenson*. But I press on, too worked up to stop.

'I used to go to the city all the time, remember? And I can take care of myself,' I add, though I can hear the echo of the man's words in my ear even before I finish talking: *selfish fucking bitch*. And here I am, making the insult ring true: telling my husband a half-truth so I can continue to *do what I want*. Tom exhales loudly and something shakes loose in me.

'I'm sorry,' I say. 'I just – needed to go.'

'I don't like the idea of you roaming around the city like that, taking pictures,' Tom says, softer now. 'I know some people get angry. Did you run into any trouble?' I take a breath and tell Tom about the grandmother who scolded me for taking pictures of her girl. I turn it into a funny story, telling him how she reared up to challenge me and then I took her picture, too, knowing she couldn't chase after me. Tom laughs, his whole body shaking as it always does. I love his laugh. The sound of it wipes away the tension between us and clears my mind of the dark moments from the day. We spend a contented evening together, reading side by side on the couch, then curled together in bed, with Tom's arm firmly around me.

18

THERE HE IS. A FRANTIC pulse beats through me as I scrutinize fresh prints the next day. I spot him first in the picture I took in the Cadillac's side mirror, the one I thought was too cleverly composed to leave room for him. I can see why I missed it on the contact sheet: the dark figure behind and to the side of me is so small that I have to squint through my loupe to see it in the full-sized print. But even without the visual proof, I would recognize him by the sick feeling in my gut, the agonizing twist in my side. I struggle to stay upright as I pore over the other self-portraits for some time, seeing him in every last frame.

Suddenly the urge to leave, to get out, overtakes me.

I burst out of the house into the crisp morning air and walk briskly around the block. I long to have Rosie beside me, moving her short legs in triple time to match my stride. The pain fades as I circle the block once, then twice, checking now and then over my shoulder. I see no one, not even Patty on her front porch, waving me over for a chat; I'd welcome that today. I'd even welcome her prying questions. On my third time around, I've calmed enough to go home, to the self-portraits marred by that unmistakable small figure whose placement makes it impossible to crop. I take a breath and tell myself it doesn't matter, that the figure is so minuscule, it's hardly even there. It's as if I've cropped it already, cleansed the image of the man's presence. Paul – or anyone – would need a magnifier to see it, which renders the man as inconsequential as a regular passerby.

He isn't, of course – not in real life. The thought of him: the knowledge of his presence in the world, the words he spoke to me yesterday, and the memory of his grip on my arm make me feverish with fear. *When I go out tomorrow,* I decide, *I'll stay closer to home – and I'll bring Tom Junior's knife.*

I remembered it last night: the folding knife he kept in a box with compasses, twine, and other Boy Scouts paraphernalia. I take it out now and open the sharp, serrated blade, turning it this way and that; it's a little rusty at the edges, but no matter. Just as I thrust it into my imagined attacker, the telephone rings. I fold the knife but keep it in my hand and rush to the kitchen.

'Hello, Stanley residence.'

No answer.

'Hello?' I repeat, impatient but apprehensive. There's nothing but silence – and then the slow, shallow breathing I heard the other day. I can almost feel the small wind of it in my ear.

'What do you want?' I ask, clutching the telephone cord. I lean against the door frame and stare at the pineapple wallpaper just as I did before. I know it's the man; I hear his breath. It feels intimate in a way that makes me recoil but also press my ear closer to the phone. If I could just make sense of his breath. If I could remember it – or know it. I'm beginning to lose myself in the rhythm of it – my eyelids drifting down, down – when the caller slams his phone into its cradle. I flinch but go on staring at the wall, still twining my fingers through the cord, listening to the dial tone as if it would answer the question I asked and the others I didn't. *Who are you? What do you want? Why are you doing this to me?*

The dial tone goes on and on as if the phone never rang, as if I only heard this flat, persistent, meaningless sound from the moment I picked up the receiver.

I remember the knife and slowly open my hand to stare at its silvery sides. The pain hasn't come. Because of the knife? Because it protects me? *I'll give him this,* I think grimly. If he comes at me again, if he nears me or touches me, I'll give him this blade in the chest, neck, arm, face – whatever's closest. It's what I wanted to do all those years ago but couldn't. I lay there and received his harm, and then he vanished.

Only to reappear now? To lurk in the background of my pictures, to breathe into my ear on the telephone? I shake the illogical thought from my head and slip the knife into my purse. I'll go everywhere with it now – even to class tonight.

19

THE LECTURE HALL IS DIM but for the glowing black-and-white images projected on the screen: sunlight pouring through a row of windows, then the interplay of light and dark among trees. Paul stands with his back to us, waving his hands over the pictures as he speaks.

'Light is the essence of what we photographers do,' he says. 'We're never looking at people, places, or things, but at light, always light.' His words give me a thrilling lift. I stay sharply tuned in as he goes on speaking about how light draws the viewer's eye – the excess of it, the slant of it, the way shadows enhance or diminish it. How brutal hard light can be, and how melancholy soft light. It's poetry, all of it, even when he turns to the practical side of things, telling us how to 'dodge' and 'burn' in the darkroom to deepen or lessen shadows. The fangirls in front of me scribble notes, chew the ends of their pens, and exchange glances when Paul combs his fingers through his hair or tugs his trim beard. I can't say I blame them, but I don't envy their youthful, wriggling lust. I've tamed mine, directed it, turned it toward the end of class, when I'll be alone with Paul, showing him my city pictures.

I'm especially proud of the self-portrait I took in the Cadillac's side mirror. But I'm nervous to show him, scared he'll somehow spot the impossibly small man. I know he won't – but still I imagine confessing: *That man has been following me everywhere. He grabbed me in the city, in a crosswalk. He calls me, too. I've started carrying a knife.*

How would he react? He might look at me like I was crazy or damaged, the way my friends did years ago, when the news article came out: 'Local Girl Attacked by Afternoon Intruder.' Girls who'd been my bosom friends helped spread the rumors that I'd made it all up. They whispered in the halls, said I was *neglected at home*, that I *wanted attention*. Things their parents probably said – things that weren't entirely untrue. Instead of fighting the tide of gossip, I gave up, withdrew from everyone, and counted the days until I could leave town.

Suddenly I hear my name spoken aloud. It takes me a moment to remember where I am, and to recognize Paul's voice.

'Judith, have you brought any photographs that might illustrate what I've been saying about light?' Paul looks at me expectantly, a smile twitching the corners of his mouth. I sit unmoving, filled with dread, as every classmate turns to stare with expressions that range from curious and kind to envious, openly skeptical.

'Oh,' I say aloud. I fumble with the envelope of pictures I've brought to share with *Paul*, only with Paul, trying to hide my surprised anger. Holding the pictures, I look him squarely in the eye and say, 'I don't think so.' I hope he'll understand this as a refusal – and I'm certain he does, but even so, he climbs the stairs two at a time with a determined look on his face. Unless I want to make a bigger spectacle of myself, I have to hand the pictures over. When he reaches me, I do. Then I watch as he shuffles quickly through the city prints, in front of everyone. I envisioned this moment so differently – it's ruined now. All I can do is sit, paralyzed by fear, feeling the stillness of the room like a crushing weight until Paul speaks, quietly, only to me.

'Judith, these are marvelous. Just marvelous.'

Charlie, the dark-haired leader of the fangirls, is sitting closest to me; she overhears Paul's comment and turns to whisper it. I'm returned to the awful days of high school as I watch them play a game of Telephone, passing the news down their little line. I have to remind myself they aren't saying I'm a liar or a ruined whore; they're saying that Paul, our professor, thinks my pictures are 'marvelous.' Despite everything, I can't help being pleased.

Paul chooses one without asking for my input or permission and walks to the front of the class. *My pictures belong to Paul now*, I think, suddenly panicked. They don't, of course, though he's acting like they do. He gives the chosen photograph to a student in the front row, a sloppy-looking young man who may or may not have clean hands. My shoulders tighten as I watch him take it.

The students pass my pictures around while Paul leans casually against the table up front, lost in thought, oblivious to what he must know is my great discomfort as pairs of eyes that aren't his, aren't mine, aren't Tom's, scour an image I've created. I'm sick to my stomach. I want to scream. If Paul thinks this will convince me to send work to a magazine, he's wrong. He thinks he merely has to push me, like he's pushing me now, but that only shows how little he knows me – and I thought he knew me better. Silly, perhaps, but I thought his communion with my photographs would have taught him more about *me*. I sit straight-backed and stiff with fury until the student two chairs down from me hands me my photograph with a shy smile.

'Far out,' he says, and seems to mean it. I take it from him and finally see the image Paul chose. It's the young lovers standing on a street corner. Late-afternoon shadows drape them while the sun bathes their faces in white light. They stand close together, their hands clasped, but look separate: two bright ovals drifting through the darkness of space and time. I knew it would be brutal when I took it, that it would throw their young romance into the harshest light. But Paul has told us to be ruthless – something I never needed to be told.

I pass it to the next student with my own shy smile.

Once the picture has made its way around the room, Paul takes it gently from the last person's hand and returns to the podium. He sets it down and stares at it for a moment. The class is quiet, attentive. I wonder if anyone – or everyone – can hear the loud thudding of my heart. Finally, he clears his throat.

'As you've all seen, Judith has done a phenomenal job of using the time of day and the slant of light to separate these two lovebirds who are physically quite close.' He looks up and finds my eyes. I tell myself to be still, to sit here and endure this, or enjoy it – or both at once.

'We can see how alone they are, how distant they are from each other – even if they can't see it themselves. It's beautiful – beautiful and cruel,' he ends, glancing around the silent classroom. '*This* is what I mean by harnessing light, everyone. Exactly this.' Some students nod, others stare forward in what could be indifference, denial, or simply deep attention. I glance at the clock on the wall and will time to move faster.

When Charlie's hand shoots up, I cringe. I'm sitting in a high school class again, waiting for the insult to arrive. But when Paul calls on her, she turns to me with a friendly and frankly admiring look on her face.

'Judith, how did you get this shot? Can you walk us through it?' Though I can tell she isn't trying to stump me, I feel stumped. And panicky. How *did* I get the shot? I think back through the noise in my head to that day in the city, to that quiet moment when I came upon the couple.

'I-I was on Fifth Avenue, close to the park. I happened to turn down a side street and saw them from a distance. As I walked closer, I noticed how the light was hitting them, hitting their faces. I got as close as I could, framed the shot, and took it. Took several. This turned out to be the best version,' I say. Charlie nods and smiles, then asks if the couple noticed me. I shake my head, growing more comfortable in the glow of her friendly attention.

'No, not at all. Though it wouldn't have mattered if they had.' Soft laughter ripples through the class. Paul gives me an approving look.

'Exactly the right attitude. This kind of masterful result is what you get when you're unafraid.' Pride sears through me; I blink back unexpected tears. He goes on talking to the class, but I'm stuck on the word: *masterful.*

20

I TRY TO KEEP MY EYES glued to the words I've jotted down as students pass by on their way out of class: *Light is everything. Hard = brutal / soft = melancholy. Dodge / burn.* I glance up quickly once, only to have a young woman with permed blonde hair and red glasses catch my eye. She looks like she wants to say something but is too timid. I give her a friendly smile even though I'm still so angry at Paul – even if he did use the word *masterful*. Once the room empties out, I wait for Paul to acknowledge me, to acknowledge what he's done, but he goes on placidly collecting his books and papers. I walk slowly down the stairs. He doesn't look up until I'm standing right in front of him.

'I know you must be pissed off,' he says, raising his eyes at last. He looks only partly regretful, mostly pleased. 'I know I should have asked for your permission first, but I didn't because I knew what you'd say. Look. Those were just kids seeing your picture – and it wasn't so bad, was it?' I hear the question, know the answer he expects, and refuse to give it.

'Maybe not tonight or even any time soon, but someday I think you'll want to share your work with people who matter – art editors, gallerists, and… everyone else. As you know, I can help you. I'd *love* to help you. You could have more of a successful run than I ever did – you could have a *career*.' He leans on this last word with an intensity that borders on fury. For a moment, I can't do anything but smile at him like a little fool, like one of those girls with bare legs to cross and curled eyelashes to bat.

But the moment passes; I'm *not* one of those girls, after all. I want Paul to know that he's crossed a line.

'You shouldn't have done it. You had no right to pass my picture around without asking my permission. The rest of it is – nothing I'm interested in, as you know.' Though I mean to sound cold and unshakable, I can't keep my voice from trembling. I sound more like the vexed mother of Tom Junior at the maddening height of his adolescence, when I would snap at him and watch him shrug. Still, Paul looks abashed.

'I apologize, Judith. I really do. I got carried away – your work makes me do crazy things.' He gives an embarrassed smile at this, and I inch toward forgiving him. Too quickly, I know, but I'm relieved, too, when the tension between us breaks.

'Look, I fully acknowledge my guilt. But tell me the truth. Did you enjoy it? Just a little?' His playful question sends me toppling back to my grandmother's kitchen floor. *You enjoyed that, didn't you? You little slut.* I'd forgotten – or smothered – the words; they sound fresh now, as if the man just poured them in my ear. Or as if Paul himself meant to echo those vicious original words. But he couldn't have, could he? I stand frozen before Paul, staring, unsure, but he just shakes his head and laughs a little. He's lighthearted and markedly different from my kitchen assailant. He's Paul. Simply Paul.

When he holds out his hand, I obediently place my envelope of pictures in it.

'I didn't get a chance to take these in during class. I was just looking for the light, you know?' I nod, still a bit dazed, and watch him flip through. When he gets to the side mirror self-portrait, my stomach clenches. Will he see it there? Minuscule, just outside the curve of the mirror. *Hey, what's this?* he'll say, his finger hovering over the spot. But it doesn't happen. It's too small, and even if he saw a man standing in the background, what would he care? I exhale, feeling at once relieved and let down.

Paul moves on, oblivious. He shakes his head in wonder at every picture. I hear him mumble about techniques I've used to great effect. I never think about techniques when I'm out 'in the field.' I don't think about anything; I see, I feel, I focus and shoot.

When he's done, he looks a bit dazed himself. 'You've reached a whole new level with these, Judith. I knew shooting in the city would give you a boost. I mean, you have a solid thing in these small towns. But these new ones, they're something else.' He flips through the prints once more, like he can't get enough of them. I tell him I'm glad I went, and I appreciate his praise, all the while hearing the crosswalk man saying *selfish fucking bitch* and knowing I won't go back. Paul will have to settle for my less exalted small-town photographs. As will I.

Paul is unusually quiet as we walk from the classroom to my car. When I start up the engine, he leans down into my open window.

'Judith, you should keep going to the city. And you know what else I want to say. I won't beg, though. I know it's not something you want.' I can only just see his face in the darkness, but his hand, resting on the windowsill, is lit by the overhead lamps. I can see every line, every freckle and hair. And it's close to where my left hand rests on the steering wheel, so close I can imagine him grabbing my hand the way he grabs my pictures – urgently, hungrily. I clear my throat.

'Thank you, Paul,' I say as lightly as I can. 'I'll try to go back. It's tricky, though, with my… family schedule.' I feel a sinking as I say this. There is no 'family schedule,' of course, and when my mind flashes back to those crowded city streets, to the roar of its trains, to its wildly diverse faces, I long to go back. Right away. But I can't. Or – I shouldn't. Not after what happened. In the small towns I visit, the man might trail me, he might watch me, but he's never *touched* me. The city's energy sets him loose, I think – in the same way it sets me free.

The way it *set* me free: past tense. I clench my teeth as Paul walks to his car, and then I drive off with my window down, letting the cold wind tear at my hair, sting my face, and bring tears to my eyes. I wipe the tears away angrily, telling myself it does no good, no good at all, to cry. But it eases something in me. By the time I pull up to the house, I'm fairly calm. It's only when I step outside that I feel unsettled again. Exposed. The front door seems miles away. I stand still, eyes darting around in the darkness, seeing slight movement in the neighbor's bushes, hearing the wind pick up and rattle the fallen leaves. Suddenly, our porch light comes on; I slam the car door and run toward it just as Tom opens the door.

'Judy?' he says, then, 'Oh.' I brush by him, panting, on my way inside.

'I got spooked!' I say, trying to sound carefree. There's nothing more wonderful to me now than the sound of the front door closing, the lock sliding into place.

21

THESE ARE BAD, I TELL myself, with each click of the shutter button. *Nothing like what I'd take in the city.* And it's true – I'm just repeating myself here in Mason, another small New Jersey town where I'm taking the same photographs I've taken in other small New Jersey towns. If I showed Paul the results, he would give me a pitying smile, then turn away. So I turn away myself; I let the camera dangle around my neck as I walk up and down the small grid of streets without touching it again. I've wasted enough film this morning as it is. It feels rotten but slightly better than forcing the effort on a hopeless day.

I'm relieved when I finally turn off the main street to find my car. A row of nearly identical houses, painted shades of white, blue, and gray, line the street. Most are tidy, with wooden porches and small, clean lawns. I think of how I'll set my camera on the side table at home, not bothering to process any film. Then I'll soothe myself with a cup of tea and my four o'clock cooking show. I try to tell myself I've done enough today, that I've earned these small rewards, but it isn't true, of course – what I've done amounts to nothing. I walk along, simmering with disquiet.

A car is suddenly idling beside me. A long blue Buick with white leather seats. The windows are down but I can't see the driver – only his hands, lean but muscular-looking and tan, gripping the white steering wheel. *Mean hands*, I think, and then I envision Paul's very different hand, aglow in the parking lot light. The driver loosens one of his from the wheel and lays it flat on the seat beside him. My throat tightens.

'Get in, Judith,' he says. Low and gravelly. Commanding. I should run, but my feet go padding along toward my car – slowly, so slowly – as if I were out for a leisurely stroll, or caught in a dream. And then the pain tears through me. I want to stop and lean against a nearby tree, but I know I have to push through it, keep moving.

The car matches my pace, its engine idling softly.

'Get in,' he says again, higher-pitched now, impatient. I try to focus on his voice, to remember it; is it familiar? From the telephone, or the crosswalk, or from long, long ago? Trying to fix it in my mind worsens the pain, so I stop. I scan the houses beside me for help, but they're locked and silent; it's the middle of a workday. I creep closer and closer to my car with one hand on my hip, my clawed fingers digging in to try to ease the stabbing sensation. *Stabbing.* The knife. With my shaking free hand, I reach into my purse, draw the knife out, unfold the blade, and point it toward the driver. It feels cold and good in my hand; it makes the pain subside a little.

'You can't reach me with that, Judith,' he laughs, and though it's true, I still grip the weapon. I can't reach him *now*, no, but maybe soon? If he comes closer.

When I get to my car, the man pulls up and brakes, blocking the driver's-side door. Even so, I want the familiar shelter of my car's interior; I reach for my keys, fling open the passenger door, and slam it once I've crawled inside. I hold the knife out, training it on him as steadily as I can, and close my eyes to the pressure of his presence. If I were to open them, turn my head, I'd see him – either in profile or staring me full in the face. But I can't bear the thought of it. I tell myself I *need* to look so I can identify him at last, but some unidentifiable force comes pouring off the man like scent and keeps my eyes sealed.

Then I realize: I could photograph him, even without looking at him. All I have to do is lift my camera in his direction and shoot. He may be out of focus, but it would be better than nothing. And it might even startle him, send him away.

I set the knife down beside me to free my hands. I sense him looking at me, quietly laughing, as if he knows what I'm about to do. The futility of it. I do it anyway; I lift the camera, turn the lens toward him and shoot, advance the film and shoot again, all with my eyes closed. I can feel him facing the camera head-on and smiling. Posing, even – like all the partygoers at Samantha and Hal's. I haven't thought of the party, of that couple in the bedroom, in some time. How the man on top of her was smiling – wasn't he? Taking pleasure in all of it, even in my watching.

I drop the camera like it's hot to the touch.

'What now, Judith?' I hear him shout. His windows are down, mine rolled up, and I wish my closed eyes could prevent me from hearing him, too. I sit like this, boxed in by his car and his unending menace, waiting for him to reach through the glass and metal somehow to touch me irrevocably. Minutes pass, or maybe an hour, or more. There's nothing in the world but the sound of his engine, idling. Then a car honks loudly, piercing the quiet; my eyes fly open.

I see the tail end of the blue Buick gliding past, followed closely by another car. The man is going, then he's gone, and I won't wait for him to circle back and find me. I veer out of the spot and drive wildly for home, obsessively checking my rearview mirror the whole way – on the small roads, the highway, then the small roads again – and even when I pull into the driveway and park with a lurch, I look behind me, expecting to see the blue Buick ease into view. But it doesn't.

I walk quickly to the house, lock the front door behind me, and stand there against it, breathing heavily.

I expect the telephone to ring. I expect him to be there, breathing, on the other end of the line. Saying, *Judith, you got away but I can still reach you. My mean hands can always reach you.* I stand in place against the door for a very long time, afraid to move because I'm certain if I move, if I set down my things and give up my vigilance, the telephone will ring. I go on standing until the silence has lasted so long that it melts me a little. My first steps are tentative – I inch away from the door, and then I go wincing through the house.

The burst of cheerful noise when I turn on the television is welcome. I turn it up loud enough to cover all sound – even the ringing of a telephone.

22

I'VE MADE A TERRIBLE MEAL – overcooked chicken, wilted green beans, bland instant mashed potatoes – but Tom eats it all valiantly, complimenting the 'delicious food' as he takes one forkful after another. I've been fighting back the tears that have come and gone all afternoon, but Tom's habitual kindness unlocks them; they slide down my face. They come faster and faster, until I'm gasping with sobs. I put my face in my hands to try to hide, but there's no hiding now.

'Judith! What is it?' Tom's fork clatters to his plate as he reaches for my wrist. He grabs it too hard and I cry out, as though he were the man in the crosswalk. Or the man in the long blue car. Or the caller. The dark figure in my pictures. All the men or the one man who torments me. Tom lets go, and through my hands I can see the stricken look on his face.

'Judy. What is it? What happened?' I can only shake my head back and forth. When Rosie died, I cried like this, and again at Tom's hospital bedside. I cried like this when Tom Junior was born, when the nurse held the tiny bundle out to me. I held him and wept out all the pain, all the hardship and horror of my childhood. The kind nurse gave me tissues but she should have brought a bucket and mop instead. Tom, beside me, made soft shushing sounds, as if I were a baby myself. I kept saying through my tears, *I'm all right, I'm all right. Just overwhelmed.* But since Tom didn't know the whole story of my youth, I couldn't articulate the immense and complicated joy I felt, knowing my child would grow up with two loving parents in a stable home.

When I was done sobbing, it felt like I'd gone through a monumental cleansing. As if the flood of my tears had washed out the past like it was a rotten bridge. The feeling ebbed, but I always remembered it and the soft peace that descended after my wild sobs. I floated in that space for as long as I could.

When I've quieted a little, and regained my composure, I let my hands fall and look Tom squarely in the eye.

'There's a man who's been – calling me,' I say quietly. I can't tell him the worst of it, the whole truth of it. The words won't come out – just as they haven't whenever I've tried to tell him about my early attacker.

'He says terrible things. I don't know why he's calling me, or why it upset me just now, but he does and it did.' Tom, whose face has reddened, asks me what the man says, and the lie comes quickly:

'He says he wants to… do things to me. He calls me names.' That part, at least, is true. Tom pushes back his chair and stands, pacing in our small dining room.

'When does he call?'

'In the middle of the day, or the late afternoon.'

'We should call the police.' He looks furious and certain, but my blood freezes. Tom doesn't know my history with the police: how they accused me of letting my attacker in, of being complicit in my own torment. How, later, they suggested I'd made it all up – and my grandmother believed them. The whole town believed them, eventually, when the man never materialized, and no witnesses came forward. I can't bear to have the police here, digging and prodding, doubting me, uncovering my past. I shake my head slowly.

'No police,' I say in a hoarse whisper. Tom sits down in his chair again, and holds my cold, trembling hands in his.

'We should call them, just to get it on record,' he says softly.

'It won't help. And besides, it's just some… idiot. A troubled teenager,' I say, lying again and scrambling to seem composed.

Tom gives my hands a squeeze and nods once. 'OK. We won't call. Not yet. But from now on, when you're home alone, don't answer the telephone. Just let it ring.'

'I can't do that, Tom. What if something happened to you? Or Tom Junior.'

'Well, if you pick up and it's him, hang up *immediately.* Don't listen to a word. And tell me when I get home – or call me at work.' I nod, relieved that he's moved past calling the police – though I shouldn't be relieved at all. Nothing's changed or improved; I'm still alone with my pursuer and I've told my husband a slim half-truth. I tell myself I'm shielding Tom to save his health, but really, would it hurt or kill him to know? Why hold so tightly to my secrets?

Because I love them, just a little? Cherish them as wholly mine?

Do I love the man, the shadow, too? I wonder, and a shiver runs through me. Tom sees and rubs my forearms with his warm hands. I give him a watery smile. He's the man here with me now in our cozy home; the main presence in my life. But there are others, and the others find me everywhere I am, everywhere I go. They circle the two of us, surrounding us, drawing close. But Tom doesn't know.

There is no hope for you, I think, looking at my Tom like he's some kind of doomed suitor. He just gives me a loving smile.

23

WHILE WASHING THE NEXT MORNING'S breakfast dishes, I think of the man's terrifying, tan hand spread against the white leather car seat and remember taking pictures of his face.

A plate slips and shatters in the sink.

'Judith?' Tom calls from the other room.

'I'm fine, it's fine,' I sing back, trying to sound carefree, like the woman who's opened her heart and now feels as light as a bird. The pointed shards say otherwise. I stare at one in particular – a perfect triangle with a sharp tip – for a long while before dropping it into the trash with the rest, then washing the tiny fragments down the drain.

'What happened?' Tom asks, standing in the doorway.

'Just an accident. A soapy dish slipped. It happens.' I smile.

Once I've sent Tom off to work with a kiss, I walk slowly down the cellar stairs to the darkroom, gripping the thin railing as I go. I tremble at the door and make a promise to myself: *If I have a clear picture of him, I will tell Tom everything. We will go to the police.* I move through the steps mindlessly: mix the chemicals, load and soak the film, rinse it, hang the negatives to dry. After lunch I print the negatives, then wait impatiently for them to dry. Once enough time has passed, I rip them down from the line and take them upstairs. First I see the hard proof of my mediocre shooting day – then I hold my breath and squint at the shots taken inside the car.

There's nothing in any of them. Only a blue and white blur, something that might – or might not – be the dashboard of his car. Alongside my frustration, I feel a sliver of relief as sharp as the plate shard: *Now I won't tell Tom anything. I won't have to visit the police.*

24

I WAKE STARING AT THE CEILING, knowing I'll stay home again today. The man can call me here, of course, but he can't *reach* me. Touch me. I'll be safe behind our bolted doors, and I can hang up the telephone – just as Tom directed. If I have to call Tom at work, he'll rush home. I hate feeling this trapped and controlled, but I tell myself I'll strike out to take pictures very soon. Maybe even tomorrow. I hang my hope on *tomorrow*, and the idea of it shines in my mind. I cling to it: *I'll go out tomorrow.* Today I'll be cautious, and being cautious will somehow earn me the right to be less cautious, to be reckless, even, *tomorrow.*

'I could stay home today,' Tom offers, shrugging as he lingers by the door. 'Call in sick.'

'I'm fine, Tom, really. I'll be fine. Just a little tired is all.'

'What if the guy calls?'

'He didn't call yesterday.'

'Judy.'

'If he calls, I'll hang up, and then I'll call you at work right away. Now go, you'll be late.' I give him a quick kiss goodbye and send him out the door – not before scanning the street for the man's blue car. No sign of it anywhere.

The door pops back open before I can lock it.

'And lock the door,' he adds, forgetting for a moment that the threat – as he perceives it – comes from *inside* the house. I lock the door and sigh when I hear his car pull out of the drive, as if Tom himself were the danger.

I look around the silent, empty house. Wondering what to do first. Dust and vacuum the living room? I've dressed in my cleaning clothes to do just that, but standing here now, the cleaning spirit leaves me. The row of crystal figurines I've slowly collected catches my eye, shining in the morning light: the sparrow, the owl, the squirrel, the field mouse, and the little dog like Rosie. They throw spots of light around the walls, and that seals it: I fetch my camera, telling myself I'll start cleaning the moment I'm done.

I'm surprised by how much I like the challenge of turning our everyday objects and rooms into pictures – *good* pictures. After the crystal figurines, I move on to Tom's and my coats hanging like emptied skins in the hall closet. Then I head deeper into the house. As the sunlight shifts from morning to afternoon, our rooms become shadowed, strange terrain. I capture the inner dark of the bedroom closet, its door cracked; the solemnity of our queen-sized bed, which offers the slight imprints of our separate bodies; and the steps leading up to the attic, seemingly dissolving as they rise into darkness.

I pause in the bathroom, glancing in the mirror. I've avoided every other mirror: the one over our living room mantel, another in our dining room. But this one is unavoidable; I start to back out, but I'm held by my own image, my camera poised in midair.

I can stand in such a way that my cosmetic mirror, attached beside the main mirror and angled toward it, reflects me back to myself ad infinitum. The hairs along my arms stand up the way they do whenever I find an exciting composition, and I can almost hear Paul call it *electric and original.*

But I can't take it. I stand forever with the camera in hand, looking in the mirror and longing to preserve the image, but terrified at what might be behind me when I print the film: the man reflected ad infinitum too.

I set the camera down on the back of the toilet and wash my face in cool water at the sink. When I look up, there is only one of me. No figure looms behind me. I feel great relief and a vast disappointment – relieved to be safe, bereft to give up on such a striking picture. I move to pick up my camera but stop myself before touching it. I tell myself I'll get it later, when I'm done with my cleaning. I glance at the camera once more, sitting in such an odd place, before I turn away.

25

THE PHONE SHRILLS DURING DINNER, making me jump. It's only then that I realize what silence I've lived with all day. Not a sound, except for the white noise of vacuuming the carpet, or the watery sound of mopping the kitchen floor. The phone never rang; no one knocked; not one person disturbed my solitude – though it felt more like abject loneliness by the end of the day. When Tom returned home, I surprised him with a fierce embrace. But Tom's entrance was a welcome interruption; the telephone's ring is not. It sullies my house – my spotless rooms and straightened pillows. I feel sullied myself, though I'm showered and dressed for dinner.

Tom gives me a steady look and pushes his chair back from the table. I sit unmoving, my fork frozen in air, as I listen to Tom in the kitchen.

'Hello, Stanley residence.'

'Hello? Who is this?' I swallow. Will the man just breathe and laugh, or will he say vile things? Will he tell Tom the full truth of how my thighs were scarred? Will he tell him I'm…

Tom returns. He gives me a wobbly smile.

'Wrong number. They wanted someone named Gunderson.' Relief floods through me, but it's temporary. There will be another call sometime, probably soon. Or the man will come to our door instead. He'll ask for Tom and I'll stand behind him, absorbing all the terrible words. Digesting them. Becoming them – right in the presence of my husband.

I try to eat my food, but when I've chewed and chewed, I find I can't swallow. *If I swallow it, I'll become those things, won't I?* I push the chewed meat into my napkin when Tom turns his worried eyes away from me for a moment, and then I set my fork down carefully.

26

PAUL IS QUIETER THAN USUAL tonight, thumbing through my pictures. Probably disappointed by my light and dark interiors, my mundane objects and lifeless scenes. I watch him pause at certain ones and wonder what they are. I stand there, fidgeting like a schoolgirl – like one of his fangirls.

Finally, he looks up.

'These are wonderful, Judith. And unexpected.' He hands them back to me, which sinks my rising spirits, but then he looks the way he always does after seeing my photographs: bright-eyed and alive.

'I expected to see more self-portraits – in mirrors, in a toaster oven, that sort of thing?' I think of the stunning photograph I failed to take in the bathroom mirror and freeze. How can I explain why I spent the day inside, surrounded by reflective surfaces, without taking a single self-portrait? But Paul was commenting more than questioning. I'm relieved when he goes on.

'But I didn't actually miss them. I mean, I *did* miss them, I love your self-portraits, but… it's astonishing to me how much emotion you convey in *all* of your photographs, even these, of objects and interiors. I can still *feel* them, you know? Feel the weight of the house and the life of these things, and your life inside all of it. It's really something.' He's staring off into the dim classroom as he speaks. Even though he's speaking about *my life*, he doesn't need me here, I realize; he's communing so deeply with my pictures that I could be… a desk, or the fine point of his sharpened pencil, or nothing at all.

'Thank you, Paul,' I say, louder than usual, trying to remind him that I'm here, that I exist. 'I-I purposely avoided taking self-portraits. I think I might rely on them too much.'

'No, no way. You've got much more to explore there. And you will – there's plenty of time for more of those. But these interiors turned out beautifully. More for the portfolio. They show your range,' he says significantly. But he doesn't say the rest, which both relieves and frustrates me. I want him to say it now – maybe I would say yes. Just for the hell of it, just to prove that I can, and to see the pleasure it would bring him.

'I do think you should go back to the city, though,' he continues, a bit brusquely. 'I really noticed a leap in your skills when you went, and I think it would push you further, in a way staying home and staying local simply cannot.' I let the silence stretch and distend between us, with Paul waiting for me to promise I'll go there right away, go tomorrow – like I did the last time he suggested this.

'I've been so busy,' I lie, speaking at last. 'I've had to stay close to home.'

'I see,' is all he says, and I can sense him studying me, studying my face and the way my hands clench together at my waist, smothering the truth between them.

27

'I'M SURE I DON'T NEED to point out that most of these phenomenal photographs were taken in New York City,' Paul says toward the end of our next class. 'If you've been there – I'm sure you've made the trek all the way from New Jersey at some point – then you know how the city stirs the imagination and provides endless chances for amazing shots.'

Paul's lecture on the great street photographers of recent years is like a taunt; I've spent a week doing nothing, stifling my imagination, denying any chance at all for taking 'amazing shots.' Could Paul know, somehow, that I haven't touched my camera in days? Instead, I've focused on large-scale domestic chores: sorting through boxes in the bedroom closet, clearing the attic of old toys and board games, dropping several loads at the donation center. I've felt useful and noble, standing dirt-streaked and sweaty in the shower after these long, physical days. Simple days. Empty ones, too.

When I set the camera down in the bathroom more than a week ago now, I picked it up once, later, to retrieve the film roll, then I set it down again. I left it sitting there, day after day. It wasn't a decision I made, but simply something that happened. I couldn't *stop* it from happening. I finally asked Tom to carry my camera to the darkroom for me – mainly so I wouldn't have to see it every time I used the toilet or sink – and he gave me a questioning look but complied. I know I've done right, because I haven't seen the man or heard his hateful voice in over a week.

What's new is the gnawing emptiness. It lands with full force when I wake in the morning, giving me the foggy sense that I've misplaced something; then the sense of loss grows until I name it, acknowledge what's happened, and along with that, who or what I've become: *Mrs Judith Stanley, mother and housewife* – that's all.

But what's caused this? The camera's sudden absence, or the man's?

I thought about quitting the class. What was the point, if I was no longer taking photographs? And what would I say when Paul asked for my photos? But I told myself my sudden quitting would worry Tom – even if he didn't love me going to the class – so here I am, staring at the vibrant images up on the overhead, most of them taken by Garry Winogrand, Lee Friedlander, Diane Arbus, and Robert Frank. I feel a faint stirring at the sight of them, like a sleeping foot tingling – painfully – back to life. I'm so caught up that I'm only half-aware of Paul, standing center stage with his hands on his hips, looking pleased with himself.

'I'm sure you've all long since lost your syllabus,' he says to laughter. 'And have probably forgotten about our field trip to the city next Friday.' I sit, stunned for a moment. I'm not a twenty-year-old and yet I forgot all about it, in the blur of the last weeks. Now I remember Paul mentioning it to me directly, and seeing it on the syllabus long ago. I look up to find Paul staring at me.

'We'll leave from Harrison station at nine o'clock and spend the day there. If you can't go, you'd better have a really great excuse. Dead grandma or a sudden, debilitating illness.' The students laugh again, and Paul glances around the room while I avoid his gaze. *I won't go. I'll make up an excuse, it doesn't matter. It's not as if I care about my class grade.* But I know Paul will be disappointed, and I hate the thought of disappointing him, even as I sit here, empty-handed, having set my camera aside.

'So, show up at the station next Friday with your cameras and as many rolls of film as you can comfortably carry. We'll visit a gallery first to see the Samantha Laertes exhibit. Remember the slides I showed you last week? Powerful stuff, and the show is getting great reviews. Then we'll hit the streets. Any questions?'

After a brief cascade of questions, class winds to a close. I want to slip out quickly, but students block the aisle in small groups, chatting about the trip as I try to push past them up the stairs. I've almost made it to the door when Paul calls my name.

I could ignore him and just keep walking. But I can't. I could never ignore Paul – or be rude enough to ignore any professor's summons. I turn and walk down, facing the curious looks of my fellow students; one of them is Charlie. But her look is softer, more companionable somehow. Like she's telling me it's all right, she's on my side. I catch her smile and feel buoyed by it.

Paul eyes me when I step to the lectern empty-handed.

'No pictures today?'

'No. It's been a busy week.' He nods but looks let down. His disappointment feels like a steady pressure against my temples. A headache forming.

'You'll be there next Friday?'

'Yes, I'm – looking forward to it.' I meant to say the opposite, of course, but the words failed me.

'Good,' Paul says. He's clearly relieved. 'I may have planned this for the whole class, but I'm mainly happy we're going for *you.*'

'Oh.' I can't hide my uncomfortable pleasure or my swiftly reddening face. 'That's… so nice of you to say, Paul.'

He gives a soft laugh. 'It isn't nice, Judith. I've told you before – I'm not encouraging you out of *niceness.* I want you to take more pictures in the city, and I think Samantha's work might inspire you, too. So… I'll see you on the platform next Friday at 9 am sharp, yeah?' He holds my gaze. What can I do but nod my throbbing head and say goodbye?

28

'WHAT KIND OF COLLEGE CLASS goes on a field trip?' Tom asks, brow scrunched over the hunk of bread he's torn from the warm loaf on the restaurant table between us. As he slathers it with butter, I remember Paul's words: *I'm mainly happy we're going for* you. How he leaned on the *you*. If Tom knew, he'd be furious. I drain the last of my wine and ask the waiter for another.

'I don't understand why you'd go when you aren't even interested in taking pictures anymore,' Tom continues, eyeing the fresh glass of red – my third tonight. I always drink more than usual during our Saturday dinners out, but a third glass must strike him as wild. I *feel* wild. I've felt this way ever since Tuesday night's class – a reversal of the deadness I felt in the days before. A reversal that briefly transforms my terror into reckless joy at the thought of using my camera in the city again, of risking yet another encounter with the man. I've convinced myself I'll be safe, tucked inside the large class group, ushered through the streets by Paul. The man wouldn't dare approach me then, would he? The wine says he would not. The wine says I'll be fine. Better than fine. It gives me a kind of giddy power as I try to reason with Tom.

'I haven't been taking pictures lately, but that doesn't mean I've given it up. I just – needed a break. And needed to take care of some housework. The field trip isn't negotiable, Tom. It's a class requirement. It's not up to me.'

Tom keeps his eyes on his buttery bread; I wait for him to say it isn't a real class or that I should quit the class anyway, or that he doesn't trust Paul, but instead, he simply nods.

'Just be careful, Judy,' Tom says once he's swallowed his bread and chased it with wine. He, too, is drinking more than usual; maybe that's why it's been easy to sway him. 'Callers can be stalkers, too, you know. I haven't wanted to say this before, but this guy could be following you. When you're out taking pictures, or even just running errands in town. It drives me crazy, thinking of it. Who's to stop him from following you into the city, too?'

Tom has come so close to the truth that I stare at him, speechless. Now would be the time to tell him everything, tell him he's right, but instead I reassure him with my standard set of lies: *That isn't happening, they're only phone calls, I haven't noticed anyone strange when I'm out and about.*

'I'll be fine,' I say, smiling with all the warmth the wine has given me. 'Perfectly fine.'

29

On the train ride in, I close my eyes and listen to my classmates' bright chatter, Paul's low, distinctive voice cutting in now and then. I don't join in the conversation, but the sound of it soothes my nerves. After defending the field trip to Tom and nursing dreams all week of how exciting my time in the city would be, I woke this morning cold with fear. I could have balked and stayed home, but the thought of Paul's puzzled disappointment – and all the pictures I might take – lured me to the station, with my camera and several film rolls packed carefully in my purse. Paul's eyes lit up when he saw me – as if he wasn't sure I'd show, until I did.

When I fetched my camera from my darkroom this morning, I stood holding it, relishing its cool, dense weight. A sense of rightness washed through me that's persisted since leaving my house. Now there's a light touch on my shoulder and I look up, expecting Paul. But it's Charlie – the fangirl who asked how I'd taken the picture of that dramatically lighted couple. I try to hide my surprise.

'Hi, Judith. How are you?' She drops into the seat next to mine, speaking as if we were old friends; it puts me right at ease and reminds me that I've missed having young people around since Tom Junior left home.

'Excited for the trip?' I ask.

She nods. 'It's funny, but I feel like a kindergartener, you know? Going on a field trip. I come to the city plenty, but this feels different. More fun, more momentous.' I see the glint of humor and eagerness in her eyes and wonder what her photographs are like. Snapshots of friends and lovers grouped around candlelit tables, heavy with food and wine? Light-filled outdoor scenes – eternal picnics, joyous hikes? I can see it all now, on color film, possibly not exacting or artful but messy, youthful, and alive. She reminds me of a daughter I might have had – or a young version of myself, if I'd had a different life. A different *start* to life.

'I agree. It does feel momentous. I thought Paul might hand out permission slips.' We laugh together at this.

'I know I've only seen the one picture Paul shared, but it was *so* good. I haven't stopped thinking about it. Do you always take street photographs? Portraits, mostly?'

'Yes… and self-portraits, too. In windows, ponds, any reflective surfaces, really.' I haven't told this to anyone but Paul; should I have kept it to myself? I feel a tremor of regret. As if mentioning my self-portraits to a near-stranger might conjure the man, make him appear across the aisle from us or at our station stop, waiting for me, ready to taunt me. It's a ludicrous notion, but it grips me all the same – until Charlie's eager response deflects my worries.

'Self-portraits, really? How do you set them up? What other kinds of surfaces have you used?' She's leaning toward me, her smooth skin and bright eyes filling my vision, so eager to know what I've photographed and how I've done it. I answer her as best as I can, then turn the conversation to her own interests, asking her about her favorite photographic subjects and locations, her preferred camera, and so on – because I really want to know. She shyly asks if we might 'exchange work' sometime, and I tell her I'd love to – though I'm a little relieved when specifics are cut short by the train pulling into the station.

When Charlie returns to her friends, I reach into my bag for my camera, just to feel it for a moment, but instead, my fingers find the knife. I forgot about the knife; I wrap my hand around it and imagine pulling it out, unfolding it, and pointing it right at him, right at the man. I know I've done that before, unsuccessfully, but I tell myself that in the right situation – on a city street, for instance, though the thought makes me wince – I could hurt him. I know I could.

I *think* I could.

For now, I let it go, take out my Nikon and loop the strap around my neck. I love how snugly it fits against my chest. It feels like reuniting with an old friend.

Once Paul has shepherded us out of the station and into bright morning sunlight, I start shooting immediately, manically, hungry to capture everything I see: a young couple stepping out of a store with unlit cigarettes tucked between their lips; the same couple standing, heads bent together over a lighter flame. A babushka selling pretzels from a cart, and then her opposite: an elegant, painfully thin older woman dressed in black, her dark red lipstick like a bruise against her pale skin.

The whole spectrum of human life is suddenly laid out before me, mine for the taking. Just as Paul promised, just as he always said. He was right, of course, and though I knew it, I'd denied myself the truth of it since last time, the bad time. Now I revel in the city's great variety – but still, I'm troubled by glancing thoughts of the man. If a man shifts his eyes toward me, looks suspicious or interested, I stare at him and slip my hand into my purse. I keep an eye on our group, too, staying close enough to be safe – I hope.

When we reach Washington Square Park, teeming with young students, panhandlers, street musicians, and tourists, all jumbled together, Paul gathers us by the fountain and tells everyone to wander around and 'take shots.' I've already been consumed with doing exactly that, but I'm uneasy when my classmates scatter in different directions. I stand by the fountain, paralyzed, tracking them – even Paul, who wanders off, too –

until my eyes land on a perfect scene: a young couple on a bench with their mouths locked together. They're oblivious, at first, but as I draw nearer for a better angle, the boy looks up, his mouth still moving over the girl's. I capture the odd separateness of his staring eyes. In the print, he'll look like he's carelessly consuming her. I move through the park methodically after that, my mind turned off, my eye catching everything. I burn through two rolls in the park alone.

When our group moves farther downtown and stands at a stoplight, I spot a round cosmetic mirror that's been dropped in the gutter. When the light turns, even with people spilling around me, giving me looks, I lean over, center my image in the mirror's reflection, and snap. My first self-portrait of the day, and I'm certain it's a safe one: there can only be my face and the tops of buildings looming over me. No room for the man, unless he can fly. At the thought of him, and the memory of that other city crosswalk, I straighten, look nervously around, and notice the others far ahead, by the door to what must be the gallery. My camera bangs against my chest as I run to catch up.

30

I MOVE SLOWLY THROUGH THE ROOMS of the Samantha Laertes exhibit, absorbing each unsettling image of Chicago's outcasts: The poor, the mentally ill, the prostitutes, drug dealers, and addicts. Neglected elders and young runaways. In one face, one stance, I see defiance; in another, fleeting joy. A young homeless mother and her children, huddled together on a street corner, ooze despair amidst the well-shod pedestrians passing by. Each picture resembles a richly detailed oil painting that I could study forever. At the same time, each one compels me toward the door, toward the vibrant city streets. As transfixed as I am by Laertes's photographs, I'm also itching to go.

'She committed suicide,' Paul says, his voice suddenly by my ear. I turn to him, startled. It's the first time we've had a moment together today, and it may be the closest we've ever stood. It's awkward having his bearded face so close to mine, and I'm unsettled by what he's said. I knew she'd died young, but her brief biography on the wall doesn't mention suicide.

'They don't say it there,' he says, pointing, 'but she overdosed, and everyone who knew her knows she did it on purpose. Including me. She was severely depressed.'

'I-I'm sorry,' I say. 'I didn't know you were friends.' We both turn back to the picture before us, titled *Runaway*, of a gaunt, hunched teenager holding a black kitten.

'Not friends, exactly, but – acquaintances,' Paul says, shrugging. 'We, uh, both had photographs in an exhibit together once. After my *Harper's* publication. But that was a long time ago. A while ago. Anyway, it's a damn shame there won't be any more of her work.'

'It's powerful. I find it hard to look away. Her pictures have this… dark magnetism to them.'

'I knew you'd like them,' he says, sounding pleased. I keep staring at the photograph, but I'm distracted by Paul's closeness. I should thank him, I know – for bringing me here, for prodding me out of my stagnant confinement – but the words don't come, and there's only so much I can tell him. I suppose I'll thank him by taking good pictures today, though it's a selfish expression of gratitude.

'Your pictures could be hanging in a place like this, you know,' Paul says, without taking his eyes from *Runaway*. 'You have a great talent, like Samantha did. It shouldn't be wasted.' *Wasted.* What a word. Is that the sum total of what Paul thinks of me and my photographs? It burns like the man saying *selfish fucking bitch*, his rough hand gripping my arm. Or like my ear pressed up against the telephone. But haven't I felt *wasted*, too, these last few weeks? Not the way Paul means, but by giving up and putting my camera down, by hiding inside. A moment ago, I was going to thank him for putting an end to my *wasting*, but now I'm repulsed by his proximity. I notice new faults as I study his profile: the large pores of his nose and the shine on his forehead. The faint coffee tang of his breath as he continues to speak.

'I've had a hell of a time lately getting my own work out there. I'm not like you, Judith. I've taken some lucky shots, but most of my pictures come out too studied, too composed. I'm trying hard, you know, but earnestness doesn't win over the gallerists – or anyone. Your work has the effortless quality they want – that everyone wants. I may not be able to do it myself,' he says, sweeping his arm to take in the whole room. 'But I know it when I see it. That's a talent, too, I suppose – or a skill, at least.'

I compose myself for a moment before speaking. When I turn to Paul, I see how hopeful he is, his dark eyes holding mine expectantly. Like he thinks he's won me over already; like he thinks he's *won*. I take care with my words, and deliver them firmly.

'I'm sorry you've had such trouble, Paul, but you know how I feel. My pictures are private. I have no desire or need to share them more widely. And I don't think of it as a "waste," simply because my photographs won't be up on public walls,' I add with heat. Paul's gaze intensifies, hardens. I step back from him a little, though I'm vibrating with anger.

'It *is* a waste. It's irresponsible. Selfish, even. I don't believe this whole worry over privacy – I think you're just afraid. You want to curl up in your safe little life and reject anything that might challenge the way you've lived, that might set you free.' He shakes his head. 'Your work is trying to free you, Judith. Listen to it. And *share* it. Otherwise, yeah, it's a *fucking waste*.' He spits the last words. I stare at him, stunned. 'Judith –'

'I have to go,' I say. Paul grabs my arm and I nearly scream.

'Let me go,' I manage to whisper. He does, then lifts both hands in the air. I walk toward the door with him calling after me. The other students turn their heads, soaking up the drama between us, assuming things that aren't true. I push through the gallery's front door and stand on the sidewalk, shocked and blinking in the sunlight. There's a squeezing pressure in my head. I can't believe what Paul said, the language he used – foul and hateful, like the man's. Every inch of me says *flee*. So I do: I spot the nearest subway stairs and run for them.

31

I stumble down the stairs and into the tunnel that leads deep inside the station, looking over my shoulder now and then, but Paul hasn't followed me. He can't, of course; he can't leave the others behind. *And why would he bother following a* fucking waste? I think bitterly.

Standing on the platform, a sudden wind blows back my hair. The uptown train is coming. *Here I am, Paul, being free*, I think, stepping into the car. It's overheated and half-full, but I easily find a seat. I sink down onto the hard plastic, feeling as though I've escaped danger, but I've only escaped a humiliating public episode. I try to let it go as the train plows forward, but I can't help reliving the moment – my anger, Paul's fervid energy, the terrible embarrassment of those words.

The muggy heat and the swaying of the car through the dark make me drowsy, but even as my head nods, I stare around at my neighbors. I'm too tired and defeated to lift my camera from my purse, so I just take in their faces, knees, chests, hands, shoes, and eyes with faint hunger. My eyes flutter closed, then open. Closed, then open. Closed…

When I open my eyes again, I panic. I can tell time has passed; the subway car has emptied but for the man sitting next to me. Right next to me. I lean away from him a little and watch the stations blur by. I can't read the signs to get my bearings; the train speeds past every stop. The only person to ask for advice is the tall, slim man beside me, but he seems to be dozing.

I consider him carefully from the corner of my eye. He looks like a well-off businessman in his navy-blue suit and shining, tasseled brown loafers. I'm relieved to see that his hands, long and folded in his lap, are nothing like the Buick driver's hands. They're pale and almost feminine. His face, tipped forward and hidden under his wide hat brim, only reveals a somewhat pointy chin. As I look, I become more aware of the side of his body touching mine. I could get up and move, but if he woke, I'd be embarrassed. Embarrassed to have overreacted, embarrassed to be alone with him in an empty car. When I shift, the man stays still; he's asleep, as I suspected. A harmless rider, asleep on the train – nothing more.

Still, I think of the knife nestled deep in my purse. There if I need it.

I only have to make it to the next stop – if the train ever stops. I'll get out then and head downtown to Penn Station. A simple fix. For now, I watch the two of us reflected in the darkened train window: the top of his hat; his neatly folded hands; my pale, pinched face. My fingers itch to take a picture; I'm not too tired anymore. Mentally preparing the shot gives me energy. I reach into my purse and close my hand around the camera, preparing to lift it out.

His hand is instantly on my wrist. His cold fingers wrapping it, pressing it down. I try to wrench free and stand, but the pressure of his hand keeps me pinned in place, and then the old pain sears through me. I sink back against the seat and whisper, 'Let go.'

He tightens his grip until my wrist bones grind together.

'You're hurting me,' I manage through the sharp pain of my wrist and the deep burning in my middle. As the train slows, finally nearing a stop, the man releases my wrist but quickly brings his arm up to circle and clinch my neck, pinning me to his chest, his head over mine, his hot breath in my hair like a lover's. The way the first man's breath was in my hair, slow at first, then quickening, quickening, then slowing at last while I turned my head and retched.

When the train begins screeching to a stop, I reach up and back to scratch at his face; I think of what it looks like, my red nail marks along the skin of his face. I wait for his cries, but there's nothing – yet suddenly I'm free. His arms release me. The doors open. I throw myself onto the platform, stumbling to the ground, staring wildly at the doors as they close, expecting to see him come through behind me. He doesn't. He's let me go easily – so easily that it puzzles me. Wasn't he pinning me against his chest a moment ago? So desperate to have me that he nearly choked me? When the car passes by, I see nothing but strangers in the windows. No tall, pale, hatted man, but many more people than I remember. This must be a different car; I must have missed mine passing. Somewhere in the dark of the tunnel that man sits alone, flexing his hands and gently prodding the cuts to his face. Feeling bested and furious, vengeful. *Next time*, he thinks, *next time I'll put an end to this.*

I feel heavy, so heavy, as I start the long walk downtown, the camera like a small anvil around my neck. I've lost my quick, light city stride and stop to check behind me frequently. I don't see him; he hasn't found me yet. *But he will*, I think. *He will.* It isn't until I pass a butcher shop window and glimpse myself, caught between bloody sides of beef and dangling sausage links, that I'm moved to use my camera. There I am – wide-eyed, disheveled, and forlorn. But slightly defiant, too.

I raise the camera and shoot, knowing he'll be there, behind me somewhere. I look around fearfully, trying to spot him. When I shift my eyes back to the window, I'm startled to see: the woman split in two. The photographer thrilling to her hurt subject's face, and the hurt subject resentful of the woman with the camera.

32

I STAND UNDER THE SPRAY OF the hot shower for thirty minutes or more, trying to wash it all off. The whole day. The sensation of his iron grip on my wrist, my neck. My tumble through the subway car doors. I will never ride the subway again. Never go to the city again. Never go anywhere. I'll take my pictures here or nowhere; possibly nowhere. I was right to give it up before. And I'll give up the class, too – along with Paul's praise and censure. Why shouldn't I, anyway? *A fucking waste.*

Once I've toweled off and wrapped myself in a robe, I feel calmer, steadier. I try to tell myself a new story, a more logical one: The man on the train was just a pervert. What happened was a fluke. The train car I saw was a different car, the one after mine. I wipe fog from the bathroom mirror and study my wrist and neck, looking for bruises. I turn my wrist back and forth, turn my head back and forth, pulling at the skin of my neck, but there's nothing. No dark smudges where he touched me. No evidence of what occurred.

This heightens my sense of distance from what happened – as though I've drifted over it like a bird. It happened, but now I'm far away and safe at home. It doesn't matter now. Tom will be back from work in two hours, and we'll have a quiet evening made of dinner and light conversation, dishes and bed. I look at my camera bag bursting with film rolls on the hall table and feel distant from it, too. I'm not eager to process the film the way I usually am. Instead, I'm content to sit quietly in the living room, staring at my animal figurines.

Into this quiet the telephone explodes with its sudden, shrill ring.

Even though I shouldn't, I glide into the kitchen to answer it. *If it's him, I can call Tom at work. Or just handle it myself. I'm safe; he didn't get me. He got me, but I got away. I'm out of reach now.* Calm spreads through me as I reach for the phone.

'You have such deep regrets about going today, don't you, Judith? The way I handled you. Marked you, even if you can't see it. I can see it from here. You're covered in cuts and bruises, from here,' he says in a soft, confiding voice.

'Shut up,' I gasp, as the day comes hurtling back into focus: the cool, dry skin of the man's hands, his breath on my hair, the pressure on my neck and wrist. I clench the phone instead of hanging it up. I drift down into a crouch to try to ease the pain in my side.

'I mean I see your bruises from *here*, Judith. I see them *right now*.' I stand abruptly and look through the kitchen window, scanning the backyard for any sign of him.

'Shut up,' I repeat, though I'm breathless with hurt. I don't see him anywhere, but his seeming absence doesn't comfort me. I focus on familiar things to steady myself and gain control: the twisted branch of the cherry tree, the shape of the dirt mound that covers Rosie's bones, slightly flattened now from time and weather. The man doesn't speak again for a while, as if he's obeyed my command to *shut up*. The weight of his presence begins to lift and I step back from the window toward the phone's cradle, determined to hang up, but then he speaks in a low, gentle voice.

'When I walked through your grandmother's door that day and found you, you were willing. You wanted all of it – the burning, too. Because who would you be today if I hadn't marked you? Not Judith Stanley, right? Who?'

I scream into the receiver then and slam it down – again and again and again. Then I drop it so it hangs, swinging back and forth, sending its dial tone and then its urgent beeping into the air.

33

TOM FINDS ME SLUMPED AT the kitchen table, staring into space. I managed to sit myself down in a chair, but that was all. Then I watched the clock hands advancing and knew he was coming, that he would find me like this, that it would scare him, endanger his health, even, but I never moved – because I'm a *selfish fucking bitch*. A *fucking waste*.

As I went on sitting there, another Judith – the better one, the *unmarked* one – split off from me. She stood and put the phone back on its hook. She went to the kitchen sink and washed her face in cold water, dried it with the freshly laundered kitchen towel, tied the apron around her waist, and busied herself with chopping onions, carrots, and celery for the stew. She hummed a little tune. The call dropped from her mind or it had never happened and when Tom came home, she smiled and offered him her cheek. *How was work*, she asked, as always. And the evening unrolled like a smooth satin ribbon.

But the other Judith, the only one I know and am, looks into Tom's panicked eyes, hearing his frantic questions as if through water. I let the tears fall and say, 'Oh, Tom.' And I tell him almost everything.

34

THE POLICE OFFICERS WHO COME by have resigned expressions and tired eyes. They won't help; it's clear they consider this a waste of time. But Tom can't see it – he's too worked up, and wants to wring something from them: an answer, a resolution. I'm ashamed of having told him and ashamed to have them here, but what can I do but sit beside him on our sofa, observing the scene as if it has little to do with me?

Officer Denby, the one in charge, is short and stout, stuffed into his uniform; he has small, penetrating eyes. The other, Christenson, is his opposite: fair-haired and skittish; tall and long in the limbs, face, and hands. My eyes rove over the pair of them sitting in our armchairs and I desperately want my camera. It would be odd for me to fetch it, odder still for me to use it, so instead I watch, helpless, as Denby holds forth and Christenson picks at his hangnails. Denby has a habit of swiping a finger under his nose as if he were combing a ghost mustache. I see shot after shot pass by, evaporating as the men gesture and speak. I could have had a whole series of photographs by now, but I'm relegated to sitting here with my hands clasped together.

Tom does most of the talking, as if he, not I, were the victim. I don't mind. I've brought out coffee and a plate of store-bought cookies, but all of it goes untouched; the men talk while the coffee grows cold. Tom narrates my experience like I'm not here at all, like I'm a picture on the wall or a child at a grown-up party, invisible. I know this feeling – I remember it from back then. When my father sat beside me on the sofa and we faced one officer, not two. Just as I was back then, I'm surprised by the sound of my story, the one I've lived, coming from a man's lips. Like my father, Tom gets things wrong: he says the man in the crosswalk *pushed* me, and he says the man in the car was armed – when I was the only one with a weapon. I don't correct him on either point. Why should I? None of it matters. I take a quiet sip of coffee, but my cup clinks loudly against the porcelain plate. The detectives turn as if I've just appeared.

'Mrs Stanley, how long has this been going on? The, uh...' Denby, the lead man, looks down at his notes. 'The phone calls, the general harassment?' He sounds bored. I glance at Tom. The real answer is *thirty-four years*, but Tom doesn't know that. And he won't. To tell him now would be cruel, after keeping it from him so long.

'Six or seven weeks,' I say. 'It started after my husband came home from the hospital and our Rosie died.'

'Rosie?' Denby's head snaps up.

'Our dog,' Tom says, reddening. The men exchange a look. I feel like the foolish woman they think I am, for mentioning our dead dog. There's silence while Denby takes notes.

'Can you describe the man for us?' Denby's pen is poised in air, ready for definitive details. But I have nothing definitive to give him. I could never say, *He looks different each time, but somehow he's the same man.*

I look down and mutter, 'Tall. White. Brown-haired. Maybe... fifties? He's often wearing a hat.' Denby nods, recording my vague descriptors.

'Eye color? Or clothing he wore? Nose shape? Any more specifics you can give us will help.' Christenson isn't taking notes. His long hands are folded in his lap while he studies me. His gaze makes me feel guilty as I stammer a response.

'He's worn a suit before. He wore it on the subway. Navy blue. Nice shoes – brown loafers. And I saw a – pointy chin.' I can't bring myself to talk about his hands. I could say, *with long hands like yours*, indicating Christenson, but I think I'd vomit.

'Nothing else?' Denby asks. I shake my head and listen to the officer's pen scratch across the paper. The sound goes on for longer than it should, becoming so strident I want to cover my ears.

'Your husband tells us you have some photographs with the man in the background, is that right?' Denby asks when he's finally done writing.

'I do, though I've cropped him out. But I can reprint the negatives and – and leave him in.' The thought of *putting the man back in*, of tainting my cleansed pictures, makes me sick. It would be wrong – horribly wrong. But when Denby asks me to do just that and drop them by the station, I say I will. I sound firm and sure – and truthful – when I say it, but I doubt myself even as I utter the words. I can't picture myself doing it; I even wonder if I *can*.

Denby stands abruptly, and Christenson, taken off guard, rises as well.

'You should start taking notes whenever he calls, too. Record what he says. In the meantime, all we can really do is advise you to be cautious. We can't take action unless he physically harms you –'

'He *did* harm her. Did you hear a word I said?' Tom stands abruptly, towering over both men. I'm proud of his height and strength in the moment – even as I'm mortified. Denby holds his palms out as if to say, *Step back*.

'Tom,' I say softly.

'I just mean that without any physical evidence of –'

'You want physical evidence? You want her to come in bleeding, is that it? Then you'll "take action"?' I rise to stand beside Tom and put my hand on his arm. He flicks me off like I'm an insect. I know he's angry at me, too, for not telling him sooner. For putting him in this defensive position, for making him look foolish with my fuzzy details, my non-descriptions. Denby looks at him with weary impatience.

'Sir, we simply can't step in until we have something concrete to go on. The good news is that we have the report now. So when something else happens – *if* something happens, and if there's evidence, we can act quickly.'

Tom scoffs and the men argue more. I focus on the phrase *act quickly*, thinking not of police officers rushing to my side, sirens blaring, but of reaching into my purse for the knife and holding the blade to that face I haven't fully seen. The image fills me with a burning satisfaction – a hunger, even – to do it. I wasn't able to do it in the Buick or the subway car, but I feel ready now. Ready to stab him under the jaw, in that soft, tender spot, ready to see him clutch at the wound, helpless, as blood pours out.

'Ma'am,' Officer Denby says, pulling me back to the room. 'The best thing you can do is be cautious. Don't go out alone, whether it's day or night. Stay home. It's the best way to stay safe.'

I don't say a word. I just hold his gaze and hope he sees that he's offered us no help, that he's told me to imprison myself so the man can roam free. I look at Tom for support but he and Denby are finally in agreement; Tom nods at me, furrowing his brow. He wants me to stay home. He wants me to be like one of my crystal figurines, secure on the living room shelf. If I fell, I would land on soft carpet. Tom would pick me up, polish me, and put me back; it would be as if I'd never fallen, never left the house, never journeyed around taking unnecessary pictures.

'Bring us those photographs when you can, all right?' Denby says before leaving. I nod but feel stricken, again, at the thought. I won't do it, but I won't tell Tom. Christenson, who hasn't spoken, follows Denby out the door, and then the two men are gone.

35

THE NEXT DAY, LONG AFTER Tom has left – reluctantly – for work, long after I've run through small household chores and prepared a vegetable stew that's now simmering on the stove, I stare at our pineapple wallpaper and will it to stand in for fresh air and sunlight on my face. Back when Tom Junior was young, I never noticed my relative confinement. I would go about our housebound mornings feeling productive, fulfilled – unless I've forgotten how those days really were. Were they truly so simple, so engaging? I only used my camera as a perfunctory accessory back then, like every other busy mother; now my needed appendage hangs limply from a peg on the darkroom wall, and I slump at the kitchen table one floor above it, staring around, sensing the thinness of the wall between the present and my grandmother's house in those terrible days. They locked me up then, too, because the man was somewhere outside – even though he'd walked *inside* to harm me and could, I knew, return at any time.

Don't go out alone whether it's day or night. Stay home, Denby said. It's close to what the police officers from my past said, and just as meaningless. The man can reach me anywhere. Everywhere. Inside and outside don't matter. Both equally unsafe.

Still, I've promised Tom.

I glimpse autumn's high blue sky through the kitchen window. Branches twitching in a stiff breeze. Red and yellow leaves spinning to the ground. I long to put on my coat and walk briskly through them, my Nikon in hand, so instead I shift to the living room to flip through the latest *National Geographic* for the second or third time, hoping the color-saturated images will sate me. They did the first time, for a while. Now I stare hungrily at things I've never even *thought* of shooting before: castle ruins, dense jungles, isolated tribes. I stare at the photographers' bylines, too, reading what they've written to introduce their portfolios, and feel a flicker of want. Have I been wrong to cling so tightly to privacy? What has privacy won me, anyway? The man still found me, ferreted me out, invaded my life – and here I sit, locked at home.

An idea flickers in my mind – of giving Paul what he wants. Would it be so bad? Would Tom care so very much?

He would. I know he would.

I hear the barking of a dog outside, far off but recognizable. When it barks a second time, I'm certain: *It's Rosie.* Even though she's dead and gone. I *know* she's dead and gone, I took pictures of her, lifeless on the living room carpet, and watched Tom bury her, but: there it is again. Rosie. I know her bark like the sound of Tom Junior's voice: immediately, instinctively, like something carved from my own cells.

I rise, put on my coat – just as I imagined, though without this thrumming anxiety – and step outside. I stand still and listen on the front porch. Nothing, no sound. I remember my knife then and step back inside, rummage through my purse, and slide the folded blade into my coat pocket. That's when I hear it again – Rosie's distant bark.

I take deep breaths of the fresh, cold air as I walk the quiet streets, telling myself it's good that I'm out, telling myself I'm just strolling through the neighborhood, what could be the harm? But the sound of leaves rustling roughly in the wind and the sight of my neighbors' dark, hooded windows combine to rattle me. I look back over my shoulder again and again – seeing nothing – but I keep hurtling forward toward the sound. Even as I wrap my hand around the knife in my pocket, it comes again. Closer now. I move faster, passing identical, tidy homes and heedlessly following Rosie's bark until I reach an abandoned-looking house several blocks away. It's like my own house and every other but with peeling paint, an overgrown lawn, and a rusting car parked in the driveway. I don't remember ever seeing it, even on my longer walks with Rosie, but maybe we never turned down this street before.

But didn't we turn down every street in the neighborhood? There are only so many.

'Rosie?' I call, embarrassed at first, then letting my voice ring out. 'Rosie?'

She barks in response; she's inside. I step closer, crossing the weedy lawn to the nearest window until my face is just inches from the glass. Shading my eyes to peer inside, I find a room that looks like a ruin of my own living room: with a long couch and two armchairs, blue carpeting, oval coffee table, antique lamps. Everything layered in dust and unbearably shabby, as if the owners died or abandoned the place years ago.

But Rosie is in there somehow; I hear her again. A moment later, she trots into the terrible room.

Her ears are perked and her small pink tongue hangs out. She spots me at the window and yaps repeatedly. Urgently. I'm pawing at the window frame now, trying to lift it, when a wrinkled, wrecked face with milky blind eyes rears up before me.

'Get out! Get off my property!'

'Rosie!' I call. 'Rosie!'

I'm banging on the window, adding to the noise, and Rosie is jumping now as she barks, then turning in panicked circles. I never saw her behave like that – but was she ever so distressed, when she was mine? I beat harder on the window; in an instant, the glass shatters. All over the wrinkled face and my Rosie. I start to scramble over the windowsill, knocking out more glass as the person tries to push me back. The awful face bleeding now.

'Rosie!' I shout, expecting her to come. But when I look at her again, with half of me in the window, hanging over the sill, I freeze. It isn't her. It's a little dog that resembles her, yes – but this dog's ears are less upright, its coat a darker color. It's growling now, and yipping. Ugly. Nothing like my cheerful Rosie – gone, dead, buried in the backyard at home. Of course. It can't be her. I knew it couldn't be her.

I drop back to the ground, muttering apologies, and stumble away with the old woman's curses ringing in my ears and the dog still yipping, yipping.

It's only when I reach my lawn that I notice my hands – slick with blood. I've dripped blood on my lovely winter coat. My palms burn badly as I pick out the slivers of glass, then wipe my hands on the soft grass to clean them.

'Judith?' I hear behind me. A woman's voice – Patty's. The last person I would hope to see, the person who ogled us from her porch as Tom was carried out. The person who will spread the news from house to house: *I saw Judith Stanley disheveled and running, then wiping her bloody hands on the lawn.*

'Patty, hello,' I say, hiding my hands behind me.

'Everything all right?' she calls from her porch. Her hair is up in a rag and she's wearing an apron over her housecoat.

'I'm fine! Just getting some fresh air. You cleaning the house?' She nods but I can see her scanning me, looking for signs of disarray, noting that my hands are out of sight. Can she see the bloodstains on my coat from there? I turn and start walking toward my house, moving my hands to the front as I go.

'It's a good day for cleaning. Hope you have a nice day,' I call out. My voice wobbles, but I make it inside the house and lock the door behind me before crumbling apart.

36

I SIT BESIDE TOM ON THE couch, my hands wrapped in bandages. He rushed home from work after my nearly incoherent call, and after tending to me, he went to check on the furious old woman. She was fine, save for a few facial cuts and her unending outrage. He told her we would pay for the broken window and arranged for a repairman to visit her first thing tomorrow. Then he helped her cover the window with a tarp. He's telling me now how filthy it was inside her house, and then he looks at me significantly.

'The dog's name is Henry.'

I nod, ashamed. 'But it was Rosie's bark,' I say. 'I can't tell you –'

'You shouldn't have been out. Period. You promised to stay home! You even left a pot on the stove!' I hadn't forgotten about the pot on the stove – I was only leaving for a short time and knew it would be safe, simmering on low. I often leave the house with a pot on the stove. But I don't say that, Tom wouldn't understand.

'I'd planned to stay home. I meant to. But then I heard her.'

'How could you even think it was Rosie?'

'Tom, believe me. It *was* her. The bark was hers. You would have thought it was Rosie, too, if you'd heard what I heard.' I want to appear firm and strong and clear-headed, but I'm holding back tears. I don't want Tom to take my bandaged hand gently in his, to speak softly to me, to be kind, because the tears will spill over. They do, and I swipe at them impatiently.

'Whether you did or didn't hear Rosie is beside the point. You shouldn't have been out, wandering around.' *Like a dog off its leash, you mean*, I want to say. *Like a child toddling into the street.* I look in Tom's concerned face and see a trace of smug confirmation: that he's been right all along, that his errant wife needs to be scolded and confined.

'I took Tom Junior's hunting knife with me,' I blurt. 'I had it in my pocket. I've been carrying it – in my purse.' I want to impress him, but his eyes widen. He wipes a hand down his face and shakes his head.

'You think you'll be able to reach for it and unfold it in time, with this guy coming after you?' His flushed cheeks are worrying; I need to calm him down. I've been so lost in my own drama lately that I haven't considered Tom's health enough. Tom, who should be resting when he isn't at work, tinkering in the backyard or reading a magazine. Not patching up the neighbor's window his wife crashed through in search of their impossibly reanimated dog.

I *did* hear it, though. I did.

'I'm sorry, Tom. I convinced myself it was her – somehow. I think *he* did it, to lure me farther than I wanted to go. Maybe he has a dog… I mean a dog with a bark like Rosie's, and he…' I trail off as Tom stares at me.

'How would he do that, Judith? How would that even be possible?'

'I don't know. He often does impossible things. But I'm certain I heard her voice. Her bark. I wasn't mistaken. You don't have to believe me, but I wish you would.'

Tom doesn't answer but nods his head in a wobbly, broken way and eventually looks at me with brimming eyes.

'I can't lose you, Judy. You have to take care of yourself.' I said the same words – or almost the same words – to Tom when he finally came to after his episode. We were in his hospital room.

He was attached to monitors and an IV, and he looked so forlorn, so frail, not my usual sturdy Tom. I don't know if he's using the same phrasing on purpose or not, but I know I can't deny him. I don't want to.

'I will, Tom. I promise,' I tell him, because I can't add, *as long as the man lets me*. 'And I'm sorry about today. I don't – know what happened.' I hear the sound of breaking glass all over again and can't quite attach it to my own actions. Did I really *break a window*? I have to look down at my hands to convince myself I did. *Concrete evidence*, like Denby and Christenson demand. I give a little laugh, and Tom looks at me.

'Maybe we should go to the station now and show them my hands. Tell them *he* did this to me. Do you think they'd finally do something then?' I watch Tom closely – his cheek twitches first, and then he laughs. For a moment, my whole body relaxes. I reach my wounded hands to his face and bring it to mine.

37

DINNER IS A CALM AND soothing affair. It hurts to hold my spoon, but the stew I've made warms me, Tom's quiet presence warms me, the glow of our dining room table in the yellow light warms me. I'm safe now, and the memory of that ravaged face looming in the window seems remote, insubstantial, unreal. I can understand that it happened, but I can no longer feel it. The intense sting of it. The hell of the unkempt house and running home with that fake Rosie barking after me. The humiliation of hiding my torn hands behind my back as Patty stared. All past now, all gone. It happened to the old Judith, because I am the new one, the one basking and serene here, spooning up wholesome food with my bandaged hands. I take a deep breath over my steaming soup, and savor the food and the peacefulness of being with Tom. My love. My steady one. His eyes crinkle at me over his bowl.

'Delicious, Judy.'

'Thank you.'

38

IT FEELS LIKE SEVERAL MONTHS, not two weeks, have passed since I last entered the lecture hall. Paul isn't here yet, and I'm relieved. But I'm anxious – and terrified – to see him. What will he do when he sees me? Nothing? Or a noticeable *something* – a dismissal, or a distant, friendly acknowledgment? Walking to my seat, I note my classmates' interested glances – and then Charlie's friendly smile and wave. It helps, to see Charlie. I exhale and sit down, farther back than I usually do. I wait tensely for Paul.

It was hard convincing Tom that I needed to resume this sliver of my routine, that the days at home since the false Rosie incident had begun to make me hopelessly claustrophobic. When he agreed – on the condition that he would drive me here and pick me up – I felt triumphant. Euphoric. *Back to Paul's class.* A burst of activity to light the current gloom. But I hadn't dwelled on what it would actually be like. How I would hear my classmates whispering and feel the weight of their gazes returning me to that tense gallery scene, when Paul and I argued, when I fled.

I keep my eyes trained forward, reaching for the envelope of prints I've brought. So foolish, to bring them at all. To think Paul will want to see anything of mine anymore – and to have gone back into the darkroom in the first place. But they tugged at me, those undeveloped film rolls from the city. I kept seeing flashes of the images I'd captured; I knew they would print well. They *deserved* to be processed and printed. *It would be a crime*, I told myself, channeling Paul, *to neglect them*. So I blocked out the bad, the very bad, from the day in the city and spent a mostly blissful time in the darkroom. Later, when I saw the familiar figure marring the background of every self-portrait, it made me hurt, but I cropped it out and told myself the result would be well worth the biting discomfort.

The result of having finished pictures in hand, of course, but the result of having Paul see them and extol their virtues, too. If I could bring myself to show him.

Sitting here in class with the envelope shivering in my hand, I doubt I can do it. I can make an excuse, tell him I haven't had time.

But why should I even expect his interest, after all that's passed between us?

Paul finally walks through the door, an uncharacteristic five minutes late. He seems frazzled, unprepared. As if he didn't mean to walk into the room, didn't mean to stand under these stark lights, blinking up at us. Despite everything that's happened, the sight of him thrills me. I forgive him at once for saying *a fucking waste*, for making me feel small. He said it in the heat of the moment; I shouldn't have run away like a frightened child. I clutch my envelope now and think I really might do it: go down after class and try to show him. But what if he shrugs and turns away?

When Paul finally spots me, I can see he's both regretful and relieved. He's noticed my absence and hates that he might have caused it. I see it all in his eyes. *Paul forgives me and I forgive Paul*, I think. *I* will *show him my pictures.*

39

PAUL ANNOUNCES THAT HE ISN'T feeling well. After lecturing half-heartedly for thirty minutes, he ends class an hour early. Students around me glance at their wristwatches, shrug, start to close their notebooks and rise. I can see signs of sickness in Paul's pale, drawn face but I'm still deeply disappointed; I needed the full ninety minutes. After a few students wish him well, they swarm up the stairs and through the doors, eager for their extra fifty-plus minutes of freedom. I've turned to follow them, my heart sinking, when Paul calls me down.

'Judith, can I speak to you?' I freeze in place. There would have been a comfort in my careful slinking out the door, avoiding the moment of confrontation since the gallery. But I can't just ignore him; I obediently turn and make my way against the flow of exiting students. When Charlie passes me, she smiles.

'See you later, Judith.'

I try to force a matching smile, but it falters. 'Enjoy the extra free time,' I say awkwardly. Charlie's lanky blonde friend stares at me while chewing gum with her mouth half-open and with such energy that I hear my grandmother say, *Don't chew your cud like a cow.* I wish I could say it aloud.

'You too!' Charlie says. 'Hey, we have to exchange pictures sometime. After next class?' I give her a flustered nod and tell her I'd love to, but I wouldn't love to. I won't do it. I'll have to conveniently 'forget' and make up an excuse. Then I can review her work and praise it to the skies. I'd gladly do that.

'Pick your favorite ten and I'll pick mine,' Charlie says, squeezing my hand quickly before she leaves me in the aisle. I watch her go a little wistfully, trailed by her two dubious friends.

Once they pass, there's nothing but a few stragglers between Paul and me – and then they're gone. The class is suddenly empty and quiet. Very quiet. I swallow hard and stand before Paul, his stinging words ringing in my ear. His words, and then what followed: the flight down into the subway, the struggle with the long, pale man who crushed me against him. Even so, I'm here with an envelope of pictures he hasn't seen and I need him to see them. It's as simple as that.

'Judith,' he says softly. He gives me a melancholy smile. I can see he's struggling for the right words, but his mind is fogged with sickness, or he's too ashamed, or both at once. His discomfort makes my own discomfort flare, so I give him an easy out.

'You should go right home and get to bed,' I say. Maternal wisdom. Paul smiles and shakes his head, extending an open hand toward me.

'These are from that day in the city, aren't they?' he asks, his energy visibly lifting as he begins to look through. I say yes and wait, watching his eyes rove over the pictures. Despite the tension between us, there's nothing like the tactile pleasure of having my pictures in Paul's hands again.

He clears his throat. Never lifts his eyes.

'I'm very sorry about what happened, Judith.' I think for a strange, dislocated moment that he means what happened to me in the subway, then what happened to me in my neighborhood, with Rosie's double – but he can't mean either one.

'I really – I took out some personal frustrations on you.' He looks up with a rueful smile that doesn't quite reach his eyes. 'I think I mentioned I've had a hard time showing my work, that it isn't – ' He sighs and scrapes a hand down his face. 'It isn't going well. To say the least. Anyway, seeing your work, and your… reluctance to publish it has felt like salt in the wound sometimes.

But I never should have snapped that way. It was completely out of line. Forgive me?' he asks, like a lover, or a child.

'Of course. It's forgiven and forgotten,' I say quickly, though it isn't forgotten. The hurt lingers – like all my hurts. I have a reckless urge to tell him: *I'm ready, I want you to send these out to magazines and see what happens.* It isn't true, I'm not ready, I will *never* be ready – but wouldn't it smooth things over beautifully? It would seal our connection, too, keep us tethered beyond the class. And it would give Paul a project. I'd be doing it for both of us, but the whisper of pain that starts in my side keeps my lips sealed shut.

'See?' he says when he's looked through the packet twice. 'I was right to get you back to the city. These are just... vibrant and sublime, Judith.' He gives a prolonged sigh. I wait to hear his usual entreaties, preparing myself to say the word *yes* this time: *Please let me send these to magazines, Judith. Please let me help you publish.* But the entreaties don't come; his silence hangs in the air between us.

When he hands the envelope back to me, I shrink into my cowardly self.

'Keep up the great work,' Paul says in an easy, jovial tone that doesn't sound real. It shatters me to hear the wooden note in his voice.

Take my pictures, try to sell them, I nearly say. *Go on, take them!*

But the pain throbs, telling me, *If you let Paul sell your pictures, the man will come.* I'm crushed but I obey. Trembling, I tuck the envelope into my coat pocket and turn to go.

'I have to finish up a few things here, so I won't walk out with you tonight,' Paul says. I hear the strain in his voice despite his polite smile – he doesn't *want* to walk me out tonight. He's tired of me, tired of my refusals – even the unspoken ones. And he assumes I have my car. I could tell him I don't and ask for a ride; if we left right now, he'd get me home before Tom leaves the house. But Paul has things to 'finish up,' and I can't risk Tom missing me – he'd panic. I'll simply wait out front, under the lighted awning. If Paul leaves before I do, I'll say, *Tom is on his way.* Because he is – he could even be out there already, sitting in the car with the engine idling. I'm both stifled and cheered by the thought.

'Good night, Judith,' Paul says, barely looking up at me. 'Get home safe.'

I force it out: 'Good night.'

40

TEARS BURN MY EYES AS I walk outside. I fumble for a handkerchief in my purse, see the knife there, glinting in the bottom like a bright coin, and wipe my face with too much roughness. Angry at myself – but why? Angry for not having spoken up, for not having offered Paul something I can't give. I see Paul's car and wish it were mine. If I could drive home fast with the windows down, the cold air would clear my head. Instead, I have to stand here waiting. Hopefully not for long. I glance around at the circles of brightness cast by the overhead lights and see one light that's gone out in the back of the lot, beyond Paul's car. I stare into its darkness, not quite knowing why. I stare until a shape emerges slowly from the spot. A scream forms, and freezes, at the back of my throat.

I tell myself it's Tom, that he's here early, that for some reason the car is nowhere in sight, and for some reason Tom is shrouded in shadow and doesn't say a word, doesn't call my name as he draws near.

When the man steps into a pool of light, I see that it isn't Tom, of course; it's

the first man
the man in the blue Buick
the man in the crosswalk
the man on the telephone
the man in the subway car
the man lurking in the back corners of all my self-portraits. I

know him instantly, though his face remains shadowed. I think of my knife, nestled among my things: wallet, hairbrush, hand cream, and the old cherry cough drops I should have thrown out months ago. *The knife is right there*, I think. Almost calmly, through the thick sludge of terror. All I have to do is rummage in my purse and unfold it. But my hands stay where they are, hanging limp at my sides.

The man comes closer – or have I moved closer to him? I look over my shoulder and see that I've somehow passed Paul's car, that the school's entrance is just a dim beacon behind me. I can see the man more clearly now: the gleaming whites of his eyes. I've never seen his eyes before, or the vaguely oval shape of his face. I expect the sharp pang of my old pain to come as we draw closer, closer – but: nothing. Instead, the sight of him washes over me like a soothing wave. I feel myself drifting asleep, then I snap awake when his voice comes.

'You shouldn't be here, Judith. You should have stayed home like you were meant to. You should have stayed inside the building. You should have pulled out the knife before you stepped outside. I'll wait for you to do it now, if you like.'

His voice surrounds me on all sides, soft and malevolent. I close my eyes and open them after ages have gone by. He's still there, standing just a handful of feet away. I reach my hand into my purse – because he's told me to do it – and find the knife. I pull it out. Unfold it. He laughs as if the sight of it amuses him. The sound takes me back through the years, to my grandmother's house, to the first attack.

The day I was born, I think, and there is truth to it.

'It was you, wasn't it? All those years ago.' My voice rusty in the cold night.

His laugh rings out louder this time; I can't stand to hear it. I grip the knife tightly and hold it out toward him, watching the blade catch the light. I'm transfixed by it. It seems to float before me, detached from my hand. But it isn't detached; I step forward and slash at him. He gasps and his awful laughing stops. I can't see his mouth but I know his lips have drawn into a tight, serious line. He's afraid now, I can taste his fear like blood in my mouth. I want to spit but instead I stab him, lightly at first, then deeper. I hear his animal moans with each thrust of my knife, until I've stabbed him so much my hand is tired – all of me is tired – and I loosen my fingers to let the knife go.

The sound of it hitting the pavement is a hard, bright clatter.

My eyes drift open. I find myself on the ground, looking up at the night sky. The parking lot lights mostly obscure the stars, but I can still see them, faint and twinkling.

I feel tired, so terribly tired. And sore. My middle aches. I turn my head – with great effort – to look for the man, who must have fallen nearby. I only see the knife, though, covered in blood. No man. I turn my head the other way, toward the school: no man. He can't have escaped – I destroyed him. He's here somewhere, lost in the darkness. He must have stumbled or dragged himself out of sight.

While my eyes search for him, the school's front door opens and a man comes out. Paul. I open my mouth to yell, but I can only whisper. 'Paul,' I whisper. 'Paul.' But he doesn't hear or see me, far from him at the back of the lot. He walks decidedly to his car, oblivious, and starts it up.

'Paul!' I scream, my voice finally free. But the noise of his engine swallows it. He drives away, his red taillights blurred by my tears.

I'm left alone, waiting for Tom now. Willing him to come. But will he see me when he comes? If I can turn over, pull myself toward the school, I might make it before he arrives. But turning over hurts, and I'm so tired. I must be wounded, though I never felt the man's weapon, never even saw that he held one. My stomach aches. I lift my hands from my stomach so I can see them: slick, shiny, and smelling the iron smell of blood.

Is it his blood, or mine?

Or both of ours, mixed together?

The lights in the parking lot flicker all at once, then dim.

They grow dimmer. I'm frightened of the dark. I want Tom to come. *But there is still so much time before he comes*, I think hazily. The lights grow fainter. I stare at them, trying to hold them, but soon enough they're gone. I feel a shiver of fear before the darkness surrounds me, cool and soothing. It spills over my face and body. Fills my mouth.

It eases the pain of my stomach and the old pain beneath it and blots out every last painful inch of the world.

II

Like a Fucking King

1

WHEN THE TIME COMES, HE finds it remarkably easy to lie.

Paul sits across from Tom in the Stanleys' muted blue living room, surrounded by stiffly posed family portraits that Judith can't have liked, and lets the false words flow.

'That last night – the last time I saw her – Judith asked me to help her publish her photographs. And I said I would. Happily.'

He's relieved he didn't stammer or stumble, that he delivered the lie in his smoothest professorial voice, as if telling a student that the Leica was far superior to the Nikon, if you could afford it, or that black-and-white film, with its contrasts and shadows, could heighten the drama of any picture. He takes a quiet breath to calm his jittering heart, thankful that Tom can't know how sweaty his palms are against the fabric of his pants.

Tom looks weary and gray-faced but wary, too. Paul has never met him in person before now but can tell grief has flattened him; it hasn't been that long, after all. Eight weeks, give or take, since Judith died. Paul waited as long as he could before showing up, unannounced, on Tom's porch; he thinks now that eight weeks may have been too soon. But hell, eight *months* might have been too soon – there was no good time, so he may as well be here.

'She said that?' Tom squints, as if Paul's words pain him. He squinted like that when Paul introduced himself, too, because he knew who Paul was: the last person to see Judith alive, her professor, and a prime suspect – until the Harrington Police cleared him. The dregs of suspicion still cling to Paul, of course, but Tom was a suspect, too. He was cleared as well, and whoever killed Judith walked free. As far as Paul could tell, the case had drifted into limbo.

'She did. She might have told you I'd been encouraging her to publish? Ever since she first shared her photographs with me. They were like nothing I'd seen before. She was incredibly talented. But I'm sure you know that.' Paul hopes he doesn't come across as too eager or desperate to please.

'Yeah, she said you liked her pictures,' Tom says. He makes it sound dirty, as if Paul had complimented his wife's tits. Paul doesn't remember Judith's tits; they were always primly covered, never outlined by the tight shirts and sweaters many of his young coeds wore, and besides, Paul wasn't interested in her that way. But when he saw her first self-portrait, he felt semi-aroused. *God*, it was good! His response was only heightened by Judith's cluelessness about what she had, what she could do. Tom wouldn't like hearing any of that, but Paul wishes he could convey how momentous it was, discovering Judith.

He remembers how she lingered after class for the first portfolio check. He always tried to be kind about student work, unless it was one of the eager young men, younger versions of Paul himself, who came thrusting their imitative pictures in front of him like sacred gifts. Judith's name escaped him at first. *Jennifer? Janice?* He finally found the right one, and thought it perfectly fit the timid, middle-aged housewife before him, her hand visibly trembling as she gave him the envelope.

He expected nothing from her photographs, just as he expected nothing from any of his students' photographs. He had a store of polite phrases ready for what he was certain he'd see inside: *Lovely family you have. Attractive scenery. Is that your cat? I like the green you've captured here.* But Judith's pictures struck the smugness right out of him. He couldn't find words at first; they were just so good. So genuinely, purely, goddamn *good*. The high drama of her light work, her sly use of angles…

but most of all, the range and nuance of emotion that shone through every scene. Paul lost himself in looking, nearly forgot Judith was there.

He remembers thinking, *I want these.* Like her pictures were something he could steal – the way he stole groceries, books, booze, and clothes when he felt the urge. He wasn't proud of his stealing, but sometimes he couldn't help himself. Besides, he was good at it, and he'd never been caught. It also helped his budget and gave him a buzz, made him feel like he was floating over the squalor of life in the city – just the way it had helped him escape the dreary reality of his suburban home when he was younger. The buzz he got from stealing was intense – until it wore off, leaving him sprawled in a chair at what passed for his desk, fingering a green and yellow striped necktie he'd probably never wear again or drinking straight from a bottle of top-shelf whiskey and staring out his grimy window into his neighbor's grimy window across the narrow courtyard, wondering how this was his life. How he was a small-time crook and a community college instructor all of a sudden instead of the towering photography talent he'd meant to be – the towering talent he'd *been* for a few brief moments in time.

When Marty Janowski at *Harper's* had chosen one of his photographs – his lucky shot of two ragged but fierce young men slapping and shoving each other in front of a burning apartment in lower Manhattan – six years ago for a portfolio called 'Urban Struggle 1960–65,' he'd thought for certain he'd be lifted to the upper echelons of lasting artistic fame. There'd been a *burst* of near-fame – including glowing mentions of his piece in major newspapers and even a local TV interview, once – but the fanfare had died down quickly. He'd had solicitations from other editors and gallerists after that, but whenever they considered his body of work, they could see how sadly anomalous the great fight photograph was, and one after another, they passed.

But there were no anomalies in Judith's work; every print she'd brought him evidenced greatness. It was painfully clear that she could tap right into the marrow of the world just by lifting the camera to her eye. She made it look easy. He knew then that she could be what Paul never could: a *towering talent*. It wasn't fair and it wasn't right, but once he'd endured a spasm of envy, he eased into his mentor role and was able to give Judith what she deserved: heartfelt, enthusiastic praise. Judith flushed and stammered, thanking him, and then Paul told her, truthfully, that she really should try to publish her work in a magazine.

He fully expected another round of blushing gratitude, but her face changed and lengthened. Her features set. She said no, and meant it. Paul resented her once more for her firm, fixed denial of all the things she could easily have and he couldn't. He had never stopped submitting his work, never stopped gathering up his rejections and soldiering on – to no avail, thus far. And here was his unassuming student, gifted with immense talent but unwilling to reach for the artistic notoriety she could pluck like ripe fruit from the branch of a bare tree.

Paul could have changed course then; he could have avoided her after class, denying her the chance to share her work. Instead, he welcomed her whenever she lingered. He knew what would be best for her and her work, after all, and he felt driven to convince her to submit, send out, and publish. But aside from that, he was desperate for her pictures – they were gorgeous and surprising. Addictive, even. Judith seemed equally desperate for his attention; he was fast becoming her sole mentor, cheerleader, and photography friend. He believed he was helping her grow by feeding her technical knowledge, photography history, and the language of the field. And by encouraging her, of course. He encouraged her more forcefully than he'd ever encouraged himself – and he sincerely felt and believed every last encouraging word. He began to see himself as a crucial element in her artistic composition. Paul knows that if Judith had lived, she'd agree.

But that's now beside the point; Judith is gone, and Paul needs to convince her husband of something she never explicitly said to him. Otherwise, her pictures will sit in storage in this very house, and the world will never see them. Paul will never have the chance to *make* the world see them.

Paul refocuses on Tom, who sits across from him with his arms folded over his chest. There's been a lull, but now Tom speaks again.

'Judith told me you wanted her to publish her pictures, but she always refused. She wasn't interested in all that. I'm not interested, either.'

'It's true that she refused. Every time. Until that night,' Paul says, holding Tom's gaze the way an honest man would do. And he's *nearly* honest, saying this to Tom; maybe Judith couldn't admit to herself that she would have wanted this, but he believed he was carrying out her unspoken wishes, or the wishes she would have expressed if she'd gone on living, gone on hearing Paul's urgings. She was receptive to them, he knew she was; she would have come around, eventually.

'I have no proof she said it, of course. She didn't put it in writing. But, Tom, that was her last request. She was adamant. Impassioned, even. Almost as if she knew...' He lets the sentence trail off, worrying he's gone too far. When Tom grimaces and turns away, Paul wishes he hadn't mentioned *that night*.

For his own sake, too. He's been troubled, since then, by all the things he did and didn't do that night, like ending class early and heading to his office instead of walking Judith out. He was feeling sick at the time, and too weary even to press his case about publication. He just wanted to tie up a few loose ends and go home. He could tell Judith was troubled by his lack of attention and interest, but he was simply too exhausted to care.

When he learned of her death, he was truly shocked. Depressed, even. But he was grieving more than Judith's death – he was grieving the loss of his mentor role, too, as well as his access to her photographs. He thought it would pass, that he'd stop thinking about her work, just the way he'd eventually stopped thinking of Judith and expecting to see her in class. Instead, he grew fixated on her work, especially in the quiet evenings when he sat by a cracked-open window in his living room, wearing his winter coat, smoking cigarettes, and sipping rye. The pictures were there, weren't they, in her house? Just sitting there, in the care of someone who didn't know good photographs from bad, who had no idea that his wife was a *towering talent* – and what someone could do with that.

Someone like him.

Paul started to believe it was his duty – his calling, even – to bring Judith's work to light. He also thought it would help divert attention from the brutal ugliness of her death – which had landed on local and even national news – and refocus the public's gaze on her brilliant pictures instead. He would do that gladly, he thought, feeling noble and good as he exhaled a white cloud of smoke. He would put aside his own ambitions – such as they were – and give himself over to championing Judith's work.

And that exalted notion eventually brought him here, to Tom's living room, face-to-face with a man still chest-deep in grief.

2

'HAVE THERE BEEN ANY NEW leads… in the case?' Paul asks Tom cautiously. Tom shakes his head.

Tom was the one who found her – his wife of twenty-nine years, lying on the ground at the back of the lot, her mouth gaping open, blood pooling around her. The knife next to her, carelessly discarded by her killer. Paul learned later it was *her* knife, something she'd carried to protect herself from the stalker he'd only heard about after she died. But Tom had known about both – and the police posited he could have murdered her himself and made it look like the stalker's doing. The news grabbed hold of this story for a while, making Tom's living hell even more hellish, Paul assumed.

'Nope. They're pretty useless, the police. They haven't done a damn thing.'

'But they did a search, and interviewed people –'

'Like you,' Tom says sharply, looking up.

'And you,' Paul returns, though it feels like twisting a knife in a hollow man's back.

'Yes,' Tom concedes, sounding weary.

'Well, they were wrong in both cases,' Paul hastens to add. 'Should have been looking elsewhere from the start.' He expects some sign of agreement or appreciation from Tom, but it doesn't come. Instead, Tom asks:

'Why'd you end class early that night? I've been wondering. Why then? And why weren't you with her? Didn't you two…

talk after class? Isn't that when she told you she wanted your help with her pictures?' Tom's eyes, newly bright, fix on Paul.

'I-I told the police all this,' Paul says lamely.

'I know you did, but I'm asking you to tell me, too.'

'Of course. I understand. I ended class early because I wasn't feeling well – I told the class that, and the police know. Judith showed me the pictures she'd taken on our field trip – extraordinary, as always – and that's when she told me she wanted to see them published. Or hoped to have them published, and wanted my help. I was thrilled, Tom. I really was,' Paul says, smiling as he elaborates on the lie. 'I told her we'd talk about details the following week. I wanted her to bring me ten of her best prints, and she said she would. After that, I let her know I had to finish a few things in my office before leaving, so we said our goodbyes. I can't tell you how badly I wish I'd walked her out like I sometimes did. I would have seen she had no car, and...'

Would it have ended differently, though? Would she have accepted a ride from Paul when she knew Tom was coming? Wouldn't Paul have left her then, in front of the school, waving as he drove away, essentially offering her up to her killer? Paul wonders if Tom, too, is thinking all this through. He doesn't show any sign of doing so – or any sign at all. His face has loosened into sorrow and longing. When Paul speaks again, it's in a low, soft register.

'Look, all I want is to honor Judith's last wish, and bring her work to light. I could involve you as much or as little as you want.' When Tom gives a slight nod, Paul thinks he's won. He's gently nudged the man, in his delicate state, toward accepting his reasonable request. But then Tom comes abruptly back to life.

'So what's in it for you? Why are you so interested in publishing Judith's pictures?'

Paul stifles a nervous laugh. He feels exposed, and like he's underestimated Tom – or overestimated the stupor of his grief. *What's in it for Paul?* Well, all the things he's imagined in the weeks since recovering from the shock of Judith's death, some of which may be purely fantastical, none of which he'd say aloud, and all of which make him slightly queasy to acknowledge – even to himself: a warm and hitherto unimaginable welcome from the art world; the padding of his wallet with crisp new bills; and the jolt it might give his own photography career, such as it is, to be the spokesman for Judith's work.

Paul leans forward himself now. 'My main – my only interest is in bringing Judith's work to a wider audience. To the public. That's where her photographs belong.'

'No,' Tom says with a wave of his hand. 'They belong with us – with her family. Not with strangers, not the public,' he says dismissively. Paul tries to fight the feeling he has of sinking, of losing. He was so close, just a moment ago.

'Tom, remember. Judith came to me –'

'There's no proof of that,' Tom says flatly.

'How could there be?' Paul asks, his voice pitched higher than he'd like. Tom goes quiet. Paul lets the silence stretch between them before trying a different angle. A risky but convincing one, he hopes.

'Publishing Judith's photographs would be a powerful way to counteract the image people have of her now, from the late-night news. The housewife… slain in a parking lot. It's stark, but sadly true.'

'Don't talk about that. Don't say a word about it,' Tom's voice is low and menacing.

'Forgive me.' Paul scrambles to think of something else. He knows he's running out of time, that Tom's patience will soon vanish and he'll find himself back on the front porch, empty-handed. 'I also think you might – well, if things progress, it might provide some extra income for you and your son. I know that isn't –'

'Ah,' Tom says, lifting his eyebrows. 'There it is. You want money. That's what's in it for you. Got it. You can go now.' He stands and stalks to the door. Paul stands, too, but stays by the sofa holding his hands up, palms out. He's done begging; impatience and anger overtake him.

'No. That's not why I'm doing this. I've told you why I'm doing this, though you haven't heard. Maybe you don't understand. We're talking about a *magazine submission*, Tom. Magazines don't pay much. Believe me – a pittance like that isn't my motivation.' He knows he has little chance now of convincing Tom he isn't a rank opportunist, out to profit from a dead woman's work. Or worse – someone who may even have killed his wife for profit. Maybe Tom will call the police now to report what he's said – though Paul doubts Tom would bother calling the 'useless' cops.

Tom stands, opens the door, and motions for Paul to leave. What can he do but comply? He makes one last attempt before he goes.

'Judith wanted this,' he says, pressing forward with pure conviction. 'You're letting her down if you just plan to box up her photographs and store them away. It isn't what she wanted – not at the end. She wanted my help. She wanted an audience, too. She *told* me, Tom.' Tom looks at him with such violence that Paul waits for a punch; it doesn't come. A vein in Tom's forehead jumps out, but that's all.

Paul walks down the steps, and hears the door slam and lock behind him. Sitting behind the wheel, an ugly idea blossoms in his mind: of breaking into the house one day to find those damn pictures himself. He'd use a crowbar to pry open the back door, search the small house, and load every last print, roll, and negative into the trunk of his car. He'd have them all to himself then. He wouldn't be able to publish them, of course, but at least he would *own* them.

Until Tom sent the police after him – or came after Paul himself.

Paul won't do it, of course. He isn't *that* kind of thief – never has been. And the whole point is sharing the pictures, not hoarding them like some ghoul in a cave, like Tom, hunched over treasures he can't comprehend. Paul's outrage over this, as he drives home, fans the flames of his desire to have Judith's pictures, to *get* them.

And then to give them back, of course. To everyone. To the whole wide world.

3

On his way to the highway, Paul swerves into a grocery store parking lot. It's one of those large, pristine supermarkets you never see in the city, and even though he tells himself he's stopping because he needs to buy a few things, the itch under his skin tells him he won't be buying anything at all.

He's defiant about it, like the store *owes* him its goods. Owes him whatever he wants. Just like Tom Stanley owes him Judith's photographs but would rather let them sit and molder in their boxes. He takes a few brown paper bags from the stack he keeps in his trunk, tucks them under his arm, and heads for the entrance. He's seething as he grabs a cart and pushes it down one plentiful, brightly lighted aisle after another, dropping cans and boxes and produce in as he goes: diced tomatoes, linguine, fresh basil, mushrooms, nectarines, yellow potatoes. He doesn't usually go for toiletries, but then toiletries aren't available in the city markets where he usually shops, so he stocks up on shaving cream, razors, aspirin, and toothpaste on the pharmacy aisle. It begins easing his fury – all this plenty, filling his cart.

When he has a substantial pile, he heads toward the front of the store.

This is his favorite part. The gutsy part. The part he's sure most people could never pull off. Maybe he had his confidence shaken by Judith and his new dream shredded by Tom, but he still has *this*; he's undeniably good at this – and his pulse is as calm as if he were taking a leisurely walk.

He weaves back and forth behind the busy cash registers for a while, as if deciding which to pick. Then he parks his cart in a line and stays there for a few minutes as they inch forward.

'Oh,' he says out loud, and turns his cart around, pulling out of the line as if he's forgotten something. Then he takes a long tour around the back of the store, wraps around to the front, and finds the one closed register. It isn't chained off, luckily, so he powers right through it and heads for the door. No one notices him. No one cares about his full cart of groceries. He's done this many times before, and loves feeling both invisible and powerful at once. It's electric, and makes him push the cart harder – not because he's rushing to get to his car; no, he never rushes in these moments. Rushing would draw attention. He holds himself back, slows down, and is just leaving the last set of double doors when a voice behind him says, 'Hey.'

Paul keeps moving, pretending not to have heard.

'Hey.' Louder this time. So loud, in fact, that the two customers who left the store just ahead of him turn and look back. One of them, an elderly woman, raises her hand and points behind Paul to let him know he's being summoned.

Paul turns slowly around with a blank, confused look on his face.

'Did you pay for those?' The man is about Paul's age but heavyset, with a green vest pulled tight over his belly and a name tag that reads STORE MANAGER. Paul gives him an easy smile.

'Yeah, I did. I just grabbed these bags so I can pack up the groceries myself,' he says, waving his folded brown bags toward the man. 'I'm in a bit of a rush.'

The man squints at him, reminding him of Tom. Tom's doubt. Tom's fury. Tom's denial of what Paul wants. And now this fat little man, challenging other things he wants, things he *needs*. It's infuriating, but Paul tries his best to stay cool, seem calm.

'Can I see your receipt?' the manager asks. His face has begun to color, and Paul almost feels sorry for the guy; he isn't equipped for this, he doesn't know how to handle someone like Paul. Intelligent, educated, self-assured. He's way out of his depth and seems to know it.

'Sorry, I never wait for receipts, man,' Paul says, then waves at him as if saying goodbye and resumes pushing his groceries to his car. He thinks he's done it, but the man doesn't give up. Paul hears him huffing behind him, trying to catch up.

'Hey. I need you to come back to the store with me. Right now.'

Paul weighs his options for a moment. He could run to his car, push the cart away from him, and hope to peel out of the parking lot with the manager pounding on his windows, marking down his license plate. Nothing would probably come of it, but that isn't how he typically handles these close-call situations. He plays it cool. He talks reasonably. He seems unflappable and slightly amused. He decides that's the safer play – even though he's feeling a spike of anxiety – so he shrugs, turns his cart around, and follows the manager back to the store.

When he steps inside, Paul squints in the too-bright light and tries to smile as shoppers' heads turn. *Just a mistake*, he tries to convey – but the people keep staring. Paul watches the manager hail another green-vested employee and speak to him under his breath; he goes running to the back of the store. The urgency of the whole scene is comical, sure, but Paul can't help being rattled. When the manager directs him over to the line of cashiers, Paul complies.

'Can you point her out?'

'Who?' Paul asks, confused for a moment.

'The one who rang you up,' he says, looking at Paul with indignant, piggy eyes. Paul picks a cashier at random – an older, kind-looking woman who smiles as she moves items along the conveyer belt. She might not recall whether she rang Paul up – or she might look at him and say she did, just to be nice. Still, Paul feels a swell of nausea as they approach. He regrets following the manager into the store for this charade. He could – and should – be speeding back to the city now, puffing on a cigarette. This isn't fun anymore. The thrill is gone; he badly wants to leave.

'Maddie, can you verify if you checked this man out a little while ago? Maybe, what, five, ten minutes ago?' He looks to Paul for confirmation and Paul nods, then smiles at Maddie, hoping he's chosen well. He hopes she'll smile back and say yes, she thinks she did. But her lips stay pressed together as she looks him over.

'No, Harvey, I've never seen him before,' she says with weary certainty, and then turns away from them, returns to pulling goods off the conveyer belt.

Paul is starting to panic. He turns to Harvey.

'Look, if it's that important to you, I'll take the hit and leave everything here. Like I said, I'm in a hurry – my fiancée is in the hospital, I've got to go.' Harvey just stands there, looking over Paul's shoulder with a little smile. A piggy smile. When Paul turns, he sees a man walking toward them. In uniform. Local police.

4

Back in Harvey's office, across a desk from the two men, Paul tries to keep his rapidly vanishing cool. He's worried about going to jail for stealing groceries, sure, but he's more worried this officer will remember his name from the Judith Stanley case and will haul him in to be requestioned. This time with much keener interest. If he's one kind of criminal, after all, he might be another.

Paul Sorenson? the officer – Officer Prager – will say. *That name rings a bell…*

Thankfully, no such thing happens. Officer Prager covers grocery theft – not high-profile murders. He may have heard the suspects' names in passing – or not – but he doesn't seem to recognize Paul's. It helps that Paul's name was never batted around in the news coverage; he was mainly identified as a 'person of interest,' and once or twice as 'Judith's photography instructor.' It was Tom's name they liked the most – along with the classic husband-murders-wife storyline. Instead, Paul observes indifference in Prager's eyes, alongside a loosely veiled impatience with Harvey the store manager.

Harvey is oblivious, though. He sits straight-backed beside Prager, trying to borrow some of the man's swagger, scowling at Paul as if he's already been arrested, tried, and sentenced. *This little prick*, Paul thinks. But it doesn't matter. Prager looks at Paul and sees a well-dressed middle-class white man – a professor,

Paul made sure to tell him – and probably thinks Harvey has wasted his precious time.

Paul sniffs the opportunity, then seizes it.

'Officer Prager, I didn't steal anything. I paid for the groceries, and I just forgot to pick up my receipt. I was in a hurry, my fiancée is in the hospital. She's waiting for me right now. The old lady at the cash register –'

'She isn't that old,' Harvey interjects.

Paul gives the officer a meaningful look. 'Well, sir, she's old enough that she didn't remember me, even though I'd just been through her line and talked with her about her family. I'd say that's somewhat elderly behavior.' Paul sees the exasperated look on Prager's face and knows he's already won.

'Harvey, I don't think you've got a thief here. I think you've got a misunderstanding. Right, Professor?' Prager asks.

'Absolutely. And believe me, it's the last time I leave without a receipt, and the last time I spare the grocery bagger, too.'

'I think that's a good plan. Are you good with this, Harvey? Can the man leave with his groceries now?' He sounds deeply annoyed. Harvey's round face is red as a beet, but he eventually nods. He looks less like a prick and more like a chastised child, but he keeps his eyes trained furiously on Paul's face. Once Paul has shaken hands with Officer Prager, who strides away on more pressing business, Harvey follows him all the way out of the store.

'Don't come back here, *Professor*,' he spits. 'This is my family's store, and I'm adding your name to our blacklist.'

Paul barely stifles a laugh – but it's a nervous one.

'All right, Harvey. Sorry to have caused you such trouble. You have a nice day now.' He could torment the man a little, but he leaves it. As he pushes the full cart of stolen goods to the car, Paul knows without looking back that Harvey, stuffed into that pathetic green vest, is glaring after him.

5

Paul's evening class goes poorly. He's distracted and angry over the failed meeting with Tom – now two days behind him. And still nagged by the memory of the grocery store fiasco. *Near*-fiasco. He tries telling himself it doesn't matter, that it's over, but he was cocky and foolish and could have been dragged back to Judith's local precinct. He can't fully relax and let go of the experience – or the sight of Harvey's puffy red face. However comical, it was a bit harrowing, too.

But the real pill he can't swallow is Tom. Tom's resistance, his refusal to give him what he wants, what Judith herself wanted – or would have wanted, in time.

Paul has to fight the urge to yell, in the echoing classroom, that he *deserves* to have Judith's photographs. Doesn't everyone here think so? He'd look out at his students' stunned faces and feel foolish but cleansed, and possibly better able to move on. Instead, he holds it in and simply teaches without energy. The students reflect his unusual flatness by yawning, passing notes, and chatting quietly through his lecture. He isn't used to this, of course; he's used to commanding their attention, having their eyes trail every gesture, sensing them hang on every word only to frantically scribble it all down a minute later. But tonight, they give him all the attention and respect they'd give to a limp puppet mouthing his lines.

When class ends, he stands alone in the empty room, sliding papers, equipment, and sample photographs into his leather satchel, feeling the sting of yet another failure. A small one, but a sting nonetheless. He thinks of Judith fondly then, of how she would have stayed behind, waiting for his approval, his admiration. He looked forward to it after every session, even when he felt a hot pinch of envy looking at her photographs. Now he sighs heavily, pulls on his winter coat, and leaves the building.

Outside, a tall, heavyset man stands under the awning, letting the last students stream past. Paul's pulse leaps at the sight of Tom Stanley, but then he notices slight differences: this man is younger, his eyes are more widely set, and his nose is less prominent. It must be the way Paul looks at him that gives him the confidence to step forward with his hand extended, certain that he's found the right man. Paul sees Judith in his face when he speaks.

'Paul Sorenson? Professor? Tom Stanley Junior – or TJ. You can call me TJ.'

Paul fumbles with his briefcase so he can take the offered hand. He's flustered but manages to tell Judith's son that he's terribly sorry for his loss. That he was honored to have Judith in class, that she was a 'great, true talent.' The same thing he told Tom Senior, to little effect. TJ ducks his head and looks impossibly young and vulnerable for a moment: a slain mother's son.

'Thank you for saying that. I wanted to talk to you – about Mom's pictures.'

'Absolutely,' Paul says warmly, responding to TJ's tone. He opens the door to the building and waves him inside. They head back to the classroom, which is closer than Paul's office, and Paul wonders if the younger man is thinking, *This is where Mom studied*, or *This is the school where Mom died*. Or both. Or neither, maybe. He points out the seat where Judith always sat – feeling a bit silly, but he thinks TJ is pleased. Then they sit down across from one another in awkward silence. Paul decides to wait, to give TJ the space to say what he's come here to say. He's hopeful but determined to be cautious this time.

'Dad doesn't know I'm here,' TJ says at last. His cheeks color with the admission. 'He'd be upset if he knew. But I had to come talk to you myself. If it's true what you said – about Mom telling you she wanted her work to be... published? Displayed?'

'Published. But maybe displayed, too, ultimately. In a gallery.'

'I think you should do it. I think Dad should let you do it.' TJ shifts in the hard plastic chair as if he's suddenly uncomfortable. Paul doubts he's defied his father very often, if at all. 'I wanted to come and meet you first, though, to make sure...' He lets it trail off, not meeting Paul's eyes.

'Make sure I wasn't a con artist? A jerk?' Paul asks, grinning. TJ gives a single laugh and looks more at ease. Paul wonders what he'd think if he knew about Paul's run-in with Harvey the Store Manager at the Stanleys' local grocery store. They probably know Harvey, have probably shopped there for years. *Would Junior be so willing to entrust me with his mom's photographs then?*

'He told me you mentioned money,' TJ adds.

Paul rushes to clarify. 'Barely. I tried to mention money, just to get it on the table – because money will be part of it, eventually, if I can sell her pictures to a magazine like *Harper's* and possibly help mount a gallery show. That's... a ways off, but yeah. Your dad didn't like me bringing it up.'

'And you'd want a percentage, is that right?'

'It is,' Paul says, trying to sound professional. 'I'll be doing a lot of work up front, without pay, and I'll essentially be acting as Judith's manager, so thirty percent would be fair. That's the industry standard,' he adds, though he thinks the figure may be a bit high. TJ seems accepting.

'That sounds fair to me. I'll have to convince my dad, of course. Of everything. He and Mom have lived quietly, so the idea of public attention – of any kind – upsets him. Especially after all the coverage around… you know.' Paul nods to spare him saying it. 'But if she said she wanted to do this, then I think we should honor it.'

Paul stays stone-faced but lets excitement billow through him like a wave.

'I think so, too. I think it's the right thing to do. I think – Judith would be happy.' Paul wonders if it's a touch too much, adding this, but Judith's genial son smiles.

'Thank you. And thank you for braving my dad's wrath to get this done.' Paul gives a little laugh, shakes his head. 'I can't promise I'll be able to convince him, but I'll do my best. Can you give me your telephone number?'

Paul writes his number down, and the two men shake hands. After he's seen TJ off, Paul stands under the school's portico, deeply inhaling the cold air. This sudden lucky break makes him want to stand here, reveling, and light a cigarette. But ever since Judith's death, he's been wary of lingering in the parking lot. He thinks of how he strode to his car that night while Judith lay dying nearby. Her killer may have been watching from a distance, ready to attack Paul, too, if he'd found her, tried to help her.

Paul shivers. He squints into the darkness, staring at the spot where Judith died, imagining a different version of things. A version where he saw her, saved her life. It's just a fantasy, of course – but is it even one he would have wanted? If she'd lived, there'd be no getting her pictures *at all*. He's ashamed of even acknowledging this, so he flicks off the film scrolling through his mind and marches to his car.

6

DAYS PASS WITH NO WORD from TJ. Paul spends his evenings eating Chinese takeout in front of the television, glancing far too often at the telephone. It sits, doggedly silent, by the armchair in the living room. He grows tired of watching it but can't seem to tear his eyes away. One night, he drags himself from the apartment for a late-night drink. He figures it's after eleven o'clock, far too late for TJ to call. He sits at the bar at King's End Tavern alongside other regulars who are chatting while a football game replay runs on the bar's TV – Colts versus Vikings. It keeps any thoughts to do with the Stanley men at bay. He's just a guy out having an easy good time.

The next morning, Paul wakes late, hungover, and spends the afternoon grading quizzes by the kitchen window, staring at his neighbors' brick wall. He hands out As and Bs in place of rightful Cs and Ds, because he doesn't really care; he just wants to get through the work and be done. What does it matter if these kids learn 'key elements of composition'? What will they do with the knowledge? None of them are like Judith; none are even close. Most are taking the class for an easy A, and they'll go on to do other things – accounting, nursing, teaching – leaving photography behind, except when they need to snap shots of their children running in the park, starting kindergarten, posing in Halloween costumes one day. Maybe what they learned in class will flicker back to them then – but most likely not. So Paul goes on grading as lazily and quickly as he can.

On Tuesday night, whenever the door to the classroom opens, Paul snaps his head up, but it's never TJ. Of course not – he can't imagine shy, polite TJ just walking into his class. Still, Paul is jittery enough to look for him. He looks for him later, too, as he's leaving the building, but doesn't find him in the hall or under the portico. Paul casts his eyes around the parking lot in vain, and then he's struck by the thought that his telephone could be ringing – right now. He rushes home, then plops down in the armchair, determined to sit until the wee hours if he has to – though it makes little sense. He chain-smokes and stares fixedly at a spot across the room, his anxious mind thrumming as he listens for the telephone.

7

THE FOLLOWING MORNING, PAUL SEES a man with sallow skin and dark circles under his eyes staring back at him from the bathroom mirror. Though he shaves and tries to wash his face to brightness, he still looks a little sickly and pinched. He needs to get outside for a walk, at least, but when his eyes land on the obstinately silent, squat telephone, he knows he won't go.

The phone will ring today. It has to. It's been eight days, and he thinks TJ has probably called several times, always missing him. So he'll stay home and eat the last dregs of his grocery store spoils – one sleeve of buttery crackers, two mandarin oranges, and a small hunk of smoked cheddar cheese. Soon, he knows, he'll have to replenish his cupboards. He could just pop out to his closest bodega, grab a few things, run back… but no. The telephone. He has the urge to pull it from the wall and fling it out a window, to put an end to this ludicrous waiting. Maybe he should give up on the whole idea, even if it means relinquishing this fresh chance – his last chance? – to find footing in the art world…

And then the telephone rings. His mouth is full of crackers that he frantically chews and swallows, though he has no liquid nearby to wash them down. He clears his throat several times before lifting the receiver.

'Hello?'

'Hey, Paul. It's TJ,' he says as casually as if only a day or two has passed.

Paul drops into the armchair next to the phone and lights a cigarette to try to project a matching nonchalance. He inhales deeply, audibly, hoping to sound like a man who has the time and calm mindset to indulge in a favorite habit. But his whole body is tense, and even as he exhales he tenses more, waiting to hear what TJ will say.

'Look, my dad isn't too happy about it, but I convinced him to let you review all the photographs, select a few, and send them to a magazine – *one* magazine. What did you say the other day? *Life*?'

Paul pumps his free fist in the air.

'That's great news, TJ. I don't think we talked specifics, but *Harper's* would be my choice. It's the right place for Judith's work – it's edgier than *Life* – and I have a connection there.' He's talking too fast, partly to cover the tenuous nature of his 'connection': Marty Janowski, head of the art department, the man who published Paul's fight photograph years ago. Paul thinks Marty will flip for Judith's work, but first he has to get him to answer his call and agree to see him. That's a looming 'if,' one he won't share with TJ.

'All right. But you'll have to pass everything by my dad before you submit them. He wants to make sure there's nothing that could, you know, embarrass Mom. Her memory.'

'Of course,' Paul says, though his stomach tightens. What Tom thinks of as 'embarrassing' could encompass all of Judith's oeuvre. But he'll deal with that later. 'Did he say when I should stop by to pick up the photographs?'

TJ tells him he can visit Sunday afternoon, and that he'll be there, too. Paul is glad to have him as a buffer, especially if things get tense. He hopes they won't. He hopes he'll glide in and pick up the boxes, make promises he's not sure he'll keep, and be on his way. He tells TJ he'll need all of Judith's negatives and unprocessed film rolls, too, and TJ says he'll pass the word along. Paul thanks him and hangs up, then sits with the end of his cigarette clenched between his teeth, shaking his head in disbelief. And glee. He pours himself a very tall whiskey. It's only noon, but screw it. He's celebrating. He glances at his dining room table and pictures them there: piles of Judith's photographs like piles of gold.

8

With TJ's help, Paul packs the eleven boxes into his trunk as quickly as he can. He doesn't really think Tom Senior will change his mind, but the man hovers in the doorway, looking like someone who's ingested poison. Paul thinks he's gotten everything – except for whatever was in the filing cabinet down in Judith's darkroom. When he spotted the cabinet, he asked Tom about it, but he said it was full of Judith's 'personal things,' and the police had already been through it. No photographs in there – only bills, medical records, and memorabilia. Nothing of Paul's concern. Tom sounded defensive and ill at ease, and Paul didn't quite believe him. But he hesitated to push Tom at a crucial moment and decided to leave it alone, to stay focused on what he had: the photographs, the negatives, the film rolls. A treasure trove.

When the boxes are all loaded, the two Toms stand awkwardly by the car. Only TJ shakes Paul's hand.

'You'll let us know when you've made your selection and come by to show us, right?' Junior asks, glancing at his father.

'Yes. Absolutely. Wouldn't think of doing otherwise,' Paul lies. He's thought plenty of doing otherwise – of driving off into the sunset with the boxes and never having to deal with Tom Senior again. But in reality, he needs him. In reality, Tom is the one and only owner of Judith's photographs – however much it rankles Paul to acknowledge it. 'I'll treat everything carefully. And I'll be in touch. Soon.' Paul thanks both men again and begins to back the car down the drive. Just as he senses the onset of blissful freedom and fumbles across the seat for his cigarette pack, Tom Senior's face appears in the passenger-side window, his hand on the car. Paul tenses immediately. *Here it comes – either a retraction of permission or a whispered threat – or both.* Tom looks uncomfortable as he leans in, leans closer, and speaks low.

'Hey, if you happen to see anything out of the ordinary in those pictures she took of herself, will you let me know? Anything like... a man lurking in the background? The police have looked, but I thought maybe with your, you know, expertise...' He lets it trail off. It takes Paul a moment to realize what Tom is asking.

'Did Judith think she'd gotten a picture of him? Of the stalker?' Tom nods. He looks sick again, either from sharing this personal information or just from the mention of Judith's killer. Paul feels a bit ill himself, but it's an illness tinged with excitement. A picture of the stalker, possibly in one of the boxes in his trunk. *What a sensation that would cause.*

'She said he showed up in the background of those pictures. In *all* of them. She cropped him out every time, so the ones you saw were – fixed. After she died, the police reprinted some of her film, but they said they found nothing.'

'Really?' Paul says, stunned. 'Not a single one?'

'Nope. But I don't trust them. They've been nothing but sloppy. And if Judith said she saw it, it must be there.' There's defiance in his voice, though it shakes a little. *Here is a man who loved his wife*, Paul thinks with real feeling. A heartbroken man who's been cold to him, and dismissive, too, but if he could satisfy Tom Senior in this, it would be nothing but beneficial to them both.

Paul says he'll examine the self-portraits with exquisite care, reprinting the negatives if he needs to. Tom looks relieved – grateful, even. His face disappears from the window, leaving Paul to back the car out and drive off at last. Tom and Tom fade to blips behind him.

As he winds through residential streets toward the highway, Paul mulls over Tom's solemn request and wonders if he'll really find proof of the man in her pictures. He imagines how Marty would react… and the public, too. He gets carried away thinking about it until he merges with the highway. The flow of cars returns him to the present, to what he's just gotten: every last roll, negative, and print of Judith Stanley's. Pure elation takes hold of him, sends him speeding along.

He turns on the radio to hear the Doors. He doesn't love the Doors, but he pumps the volume anyway: *Come on, baby, light my fire, / Come on, baby, light my fire.* He feels ignited by the lyrics, for once. He feels like a fucking king.

9

He planned on waiting until the next day to start, but two hours after getting home, hauling boxes up the stairs and stacking them neatly by the dining room table, Paul stares down at the tidy piles he's made after inhaling dozens of Judith's prints. He's lingered with her in desolate small towns, felt the electric pulse of the city, and soaked in the eerie quiet of her suburban neighborhood. He's reunited with the sad girl at the parade, who seems just as vividly, painfully alive as he remembers, and he's examined Judith's face reflected in store windows, ponds, mirrors, toaster ovens, shards of glass... in every reflective surface imaginable. Her poses range from powerful to playfully arch; she stares a challenge at the viewer that is completely at odds with the Judith he knew.

But of course, he hardly knew her. Knowing what he knows now, and knowing how she died, he sees disturbing details he missed before: slumped shoulders, averted eyes, a haunted look. As if she'd seen the man over her shoulder and snapped the shot anyway. Paul finds himself squinting at every self-portrait for signs of him, even knowing these are the cropped prints, stalker-free. *Was he there?* Paul wonders, staring at Judith reflected in a window. Behind her, you can see the sidewalk across the street and a small part of a field beyond; that's all. But was he standing there, somewhere in that space, watching her?

He guesses he'll find out tomorrow, when he reproduces her

self-portraits, just as he promised Tom he'd do. He's as eager to look as he is uneasy. Even given the edge he'd have with Marty if he found Judith's killer lurking in her photographs, it freaks him out. To see the man who killed Judith – to actually *see* him, preserved on film.

Paul reaches for a glass of liquor that isn't there, the ghost of a drink like the ghost of the cropped-out man. He shivers. And steps away from the table – gratefully – to pour himself a few inches of whiskey and light a cigarette.

While he blows smoke into the cold night air, Paul remembers how he learned of Judith's death. He was sitting in this same room, in his armchair, watching local news about a 'shocking death' – a middle-aged housewife murdered in New Jersey. Paul didn't know it was Judith, of course – how could he? The housewives of New Jersey were legion. But when the announcer said the body was found in the parking lot at NJCC, Paul snapped to attention. He'd held class the night it happened.

Early the next morning, he called Betty in the main office and asked for the full story. When she said Judith's name, Paul felt a moment of vertigo. *Judith Stanley, really?* Betty had confirmed it softly and said she was sorry, though there was an edge to her voice. It wasn't long after that the police called, but in the quiet, shocked interim, Paul fixated on the way they'd described her on the news: as a stalked and murdered middle-aged housewife. When she was really, he wanted to say, a fucking *artist*, a brilliant photographer, an innovator. Should he call the TV station and tell them? He didn't. He couldn't. They wouldn't want to hear.

But here he is now, sitting close to the bounty of her work, the proof he needs to say what she was: *a fucking artist, a brilliant photographer, an innovator.* Soon he'll tell Marty, tell *Harper's*, then hopefully go on and tell the world. Yes, despite what Judith told him she wanted. She was wrong, though, wasn't she? And if she'd known how she would end – silenced and killed and deprived of her photographic voice forever – Paul is certain she would have changed her mind, she would have given her approval.

10

In the morning light, Paul studies the contact sheets he's developed from Judith's self-portrait negatives. Not *all* of them – it was too much work, and too slow, to do all of them, and he figures if Judith said the stalker was in *all* of them, he should see him in *any* of them, right? So he studies the selection under his loupe, moving slowly as he goes. He's afraid to see the figure – much as Judith must have been afraid every time she developed a self-portrait – but he longs to see it, too. Longs for proof.

He doesn't find it. Sets the loupe on the table and sighs. Maybe he's chosen the wrong ones? There shouldn't *be* wrong ones. Or he's missed it somehow, in these small versions? He could – and probably should – print them full-sized. He could – and probably should – print *more* of them, despite what Judith said. He should be thorough.

But it's eleven o'clock, his energy for the project has flagged, and he's anxious to call Marty now, while the day is fresh. He has his little speech about Judith memorized, and he wants to get things going. If it works out, he and Marty can discuss the elusive stalker another time. If it doesn't – well, he can't even think about that.

Thirty minutes later, he's on the phone with Tom sharing excellent news: Marty wants to see Judith's pictures – this Friday. Tom hardly reacts, which shouldn't surprise him, but it makes Paul rush awkwardly ahead without a careful transition.

'I'm sorry to say I struck out with the self-portraits. I, uh, redeveloped them and looked them over carefully, but... nothing. No sign of the man. I wish I had better news to report. It's possible I missed him, you know, though I did look thoroughly,' he adds, practically broadcasting to Tom with preemptive defensiveness that he *hasn't* looked thoroughly, that he's done a half-assed job.

'OK,' Tom says at last. Paul swallows his surprise. But he knows Tom simply distrusts him. He would have given the same response even if Paul had developed and scoured every last self-portrait for hours, for days, and found nothing. He only asked Paul because he had no other recourse, because Paul was the 'expert,' loathsome as he was.

'I don't know why I couldn't find anything,' Paul says, sounding desperate to his own ears but unable to stop talking. 'Just so you know, I believe Judith, too. If I have time later I can go through them again –'

'Don't worry about it,' Tom says stiffly. 'Let me know when you find the pictures you want to show the magazine. Tom Junior and I are anxious to see them.'

The words are delivered without malice, but Paul clenches all the same. When he phoned Marty and told him he had some 'incredible work' to share with him, work that wasn't his own and had a story around it as good – or better than – the photographs themselves, Marty said he was 'keen' to see it. When they hung up, Paul was shaking from head to toe – as if Marty had said he wanted to see Paul's own photographs, or as if Paul's personal artistic reputation were on the line. Regardless, Marty is eager to see the photographs *in Paul's possession* – and Paul is filled with urgency to bring Marty the very best set he can.

But what if he shows them to the Toms, and they veto them?

He tells himself to slow down. First he has to get Marty's approval; then he'll deal with the Toms.

11

PAUL RESENTS HAVING TO TEACH Tuesday night. He leaves his apartment reluctantly, but on the drive to New Jersey he reviews all the work he's done for his *Harper's* submission and realizes he's close, and getting closer, to finding the essential twenty prints that will blow Marty's mind. He calls up some of his favorites, analyzing their strengths and wondering in which order he should arrange them.

He's still caught up in this daydream when he steps through the classroom door. Hearing the low buzz of conversation and seeing his students' familiar, living faces wakes him from his art-induced stupor. Rich and meaningfully layered as they are, Judith's pictures are ultimately flat images, dead things. Or are they signs, images of death? Each one a testament to and proof of Judith's nullified existence? His students, though limited, are *living.* He needs the living tonight – though he didn't know it until now – and throws himself wholeheartedly into a largely improvised lecture on portrait photography.

His students respond in kind: tuning in, leaning forward, taking notes. The most visibly engaged among them are the three girls who sit in a row, dressed in tight turtlenecks or sweaters, miniskirts – god, those miniskirts! – and brightly colored tights. They smile at him with highly glossed lips, and sometimes he smiles back, runs a hand through his hair, tugs at his beard, struts a little. It adds vigor to an already vigorous talk, one he almost wishes would last forever. He wants to get back to Judith's photographs – and doesn't want to at the same time. He feels a chill now when he thinks of the pictures arranged on his table in all their gorgeous dead splendor. It's nothing like the dark, liquid gaze one of the three girls – the sexiest, Charlie – fixes on him now, sending sparks along his nerves. It makes him wonder if it might be worth ignoring the school's official policy on instructors commingling with students… again. It's been a while since he did, and it ended badly the last time. Got messy. He doesn't want or need messy right now, but the girl makes him ache for it all the same.

It's like she's read his mind. When class ends, she walks toward him, leaving her friends by the door. Watching her, images bloom in Paul's mind. Of her on her knees before him, looking up. Of her on his bed, spreadeagled and beckoning. He imagines pushing his lips into the pillow of her plush red mouth and his temperature rises. He tries to think again of Judith's dead pictures to gain control, but the nubile girl before him conquers all. He clears his throat.

'Hi, Charlie,' he says, as neutrally as possible.

She gives him a small, knowing smile. 'Professor, I – we – wanted to know if you knew how the investigation's been going.'

Paul blinks at her, stupid with surprise. 'What?'

'Into Judith Stanley's death? We know you were close with her.'

Close with her. He thought she might ask about some point from his lecture, something that gave her an excuse to talk to him. That's what she and her friends usually did, clumping around him, throwing their scented hair over their shoulders, blushing prettily. He certainly didn't expect her to ask about the murder investigation – or to insinuate that he and Judith were 'close.' He's shocked to know that Charlie and her friends are thinking of Judith at all. They must be drawn to the macabre drama of her death, the death of someone they 'knew.' Who knows. He can't have her thinking – and saying – that he and Judith were close, though. He doesn't need that floating around.

'We weren't close,' he says firmly. 'And I know nothing about the investigation, but I'm helping her family sort through her pictures now, for possible publication.' It gives him a thrill to say it out loud – especially when Charlie lights up.

'Oh,' she says. 'That's wonderful! I still think about that picture you showed us in class last semester. She and I were going to swap pictures sometime, before she – ' Her voice wobbles and she looks away. Paul nearly laughs at the thought of this girl and Judith swapping pictures.

'Anyway, I'd love to see more of them. Who's going to publish them?'

'Not sure yet,' Paul says, smiling tightly. He shouldn't have mentioned it. It isn't a sure thing, after all, and he resents her sudden eagerness. Leaning toward her, he says in a low voice: 'If we could keep that between us, that would be great, Charlie. Please don't share that with your friends.'

Paul expects her to reassure him, to say, *Yes, Professor, of course.* Instead, she gives him a long, measuring look.

'Are you still a suspect?' she asks. 'I guess not, if the family's asked you to help them.'

'No, I'm not,' he says, too loud. His voice echoes through the room. He doesn't appreciate her probing question or her sharp tone. 'I was never a serious suspect. That's all the time I've got, Charlie. Good night.' He has a sudden urge to grab and shake her, to startle the smugness right out of her. He turns away to stop himself from touching her – in one way or another – and makes a show of packing his bags.

'See you, Professor,' she calls, already clicking up the stairs.

He hears the girls' laughter echo down to him through the open door, and another wave of hot fury barrels through him. It takes several minutes of breathing in the quiet room to let it go, expel it from his body like a toxin. *She's just a silly young girl*, he tells himself, and longs for those dead pictures now.

12

THURSDAY AFTERNOON, PAUL STANDS ON Tom's doorstep with a pit in his stomach; will Tom ruin all his beautiful hard work? All the hours he's spent culling the best twenty prints – an impossible job – from the wealth of Judith's photographic archive? He could, Paul knows, but he tells himself *he won't let him* and grips the portfolio handle tightly, as if to keep Tom from snatching it. When the door swings open, Paul puts on a smile and simulates an air of relaxed confidence.

'How's it going, Tom?'

'Fine,' Tom says bluntly, leading him right to the dining room table. Paul hears the silent command: *Go on, lay them out.* He opens the case, glad to avoid any delay. He's brought ten backup photographs in addition to his top twenty, but he doesn't plan on using them. He's fiercely committed to the twenty he's chosen, to convincing Tom of their rightness. But he can't be *too* forceful with Tom Senior, he knows. He'll have to walk a careful line.

When Paul finishes arranging them in two neat rows, the men stand side by side, staring down with their arms crossed over their chests. Tom flicks his eyes over the photographs as if they were alien specimens.

'I don't understand,' he says quietly.

Though Tom's confusion doesn't surprise him, Paul blurts, 'What?,' then quickly shakes it off. There's a beat before Tom explains.

'I don't understand how these are good. I know I'm a rube, but can you explain them to me? These don't look like her other pictures – and they don't look like the pictures I've seen in *Life*.'

Paul feels a moment of impatience – *Pearls before swine*, he thinks – then reminds himself to tread gently, to be generous. Tom hasn't seen most – or any – of these before, and he must be shocked to see the *real* Judith – not the mother and wife, but the artist, the individual – in print after print. Paul switches into teacher mode and begins by pointing out the colorful self-portrait of Judith in front of the liquor store.

'OK, this one. First of all, she was right to use color film, instead of black-and-white. She's captured the light perfectly, the way it hits those bottles and makes them shine like gems. And Judith's face is beautifully lighted, too.' He pauses here, letting Tom soak up the image of his wife. Unless it's upsetting to see her so vividly alive. He can't tell from Tom's expression, so he pushes forward.

'If you look at the expression on her face, though, it's mournful. It makes a stark contrast, and we start to see those bottles in a new light – like brightly shining bottles of poison. Do you see what I mean?' Tom is nodding like one of Paul's rapt students. Has he won him over so easily?

'Her dad was a drinker,' Tom says. Paul tries not to show his surprise. 'He was unpredictable as hell. He wasn't around much, and her mother had died. Judith was mostly raised by her grandma. *Grandmother*, she called her. She was a real, uh, character. Not the warmest person, by Judith's account, but I never met her.' Paul makes a sympathetic sound. He wants Tom to keep speaking, keep sharing insight into Judith's life. He's envisioning a block of his own words printed boldly on a gallery wall: *Judith Stanley's work subtly highlights her personal struggle to overcome a troubled childhood haunted by a mother's early death, a father's alcoholism and neglect, and a grandmother's coldness...* Tom would be furious if that ever came to pass, but

Paul can imagine what he likes. When the silence drags on, he continues.

'You can see how her... background informs the picture. How the image is both a siren call to the drinker – a bright, colorful beacon – and a stark warning at the same time. It's poignant. Unnerving.'

Tom doesn't respond, only stares at the picture intently. Paul wonders if he's getting through to him, opening his eyes to the glories of Judith's artistry. He's patting himself on the back when Tom says, 'I don't know if Judith would want that one out in the world, then, if it's saying all that.'

Paul has to scramble now, kicking himself, to steer Tom in the right direction. 'I understand your hesitation, Tom, I really do. But I think we need this one. It really shows her prowess for composition.' Tom doesn't need to know that *every single one* of Judith's prints shows her prowess for composition. 'And remember, most people looking casually through a magazine wouldn't overanalyze it the way I have. They'd think it's pretty and move on. I can't help overthinking it – an occupational hazard, I guess.' He grins familiarly, but Tom isn't looking. He's staring down at the photograph.

'You can use this one. You can use all of them,' Tom says at last, waving his hand over the group of twenty. Paul gapes at him, speechless. He thought he'd be here all evening, haggling over every last print. He thought he'd have to swap out a few for his backups. But no, Tom is giving in – quickly and completely. After ten minutes!

What's the catch? he wants to ask – but wouldn't in a million years.

'I don't think the magazine is going to want them, though,' Tom says, breaking through the uproar in Paul's mind. 'I mean, I know you're an expert, but Judith was a housewife. A mother. She raised her kids and cooked dinner. She didn't have any art credentials or anything. She didn't have any fancy connections. I know you do, but… it's fine if you want to try. I'm fine with it.'

Paul understands now: Tom is giving in because he thinks Paul will fail. More important, he thinks *Judith* will fail. As much as Tom loved his wife, he can't see her clearly, even after her death – even with the evidence of her greatness staring him smack in the face. Paul was right; just as he thought, her exquisite photographs would have sat moldering in their boxes, unobserved and possibly discarded one day like trash. *A mother's hobby.* So he was right to lie, to force the Stanleys' hands. He wants to give a triumphant shout, but instead he presses his lips together until he can muster a semblance of constraint.

'Thank you, Tom. You're right, it may well come to nothing. But I'll try my best. And I promise to take good care of the photographs – all of them. I'll hold on to everything for now, if it's all right? In case *Harper's* wants to see more.' Tom agrees to this and the men shake hands – simple as that. Easier than Paul ever imagined it would be, which makes him nervous as he drives away. Now there's nothing between him and his meeting with Marty at *Harper's* tomorrow. A good thing, of course: the day he's been waiting for. But he doesn't feel jubilant or sure, the way he did when Tom acquiesced. He wonders if the man has infected him with doubt.

13

There's nothing for Paul to do in the bright, elegant *Harper's* lobby but watch the sharply dressed young man across from him flip nervously through an old issue – from start to finish and back again. Paul pities the guy, who's probably sweating it out in his dark blue suit and polished wingtips for an underpaid full-time position. Comfortable in his corduroy pants, wide-collared brown shirt, and fringed suede jacket, Paul's nerves have vanished, leaving nothing but an unwavering confidence in Judith's portfolio and certainty that Marty will love it. If he doesn't? So what. Paul will take it elsewhere.

When Marty appears, the well-dressed man stands up, touching his tie and clearing his throat, but Marty walks right to Paul and extends his hand.

'Paul, good to see you,' he says, directing him toward the back offices. He doesn't refer to their past history or ask after Paul's work – to Paul's momentary chagrin. He only says, 'I was intrigued by your phone call.'

As they walk along the busy and seemingly endless back corridor, Paul starts to lose his cool a little. Sweat beads at his hairline, prickles under his arms. Every last stylishly dressed person who passes by greets Marty while looking Paul over, sizing him up. Probably pegging him as yet another freelance photographer desperate for work. What he usually is – but not today, Paul reminds himself. Today he's the man bringing them a gold mine. If they only knew, they'd thank him. He stands straighter, meets people's eyes, and tries to calm the hell down.

'I really wanted to give you a first look at these, Marty,' Paul says once they're settled across from each other at Marty's desk. He can't imagine having the nerve to say those words about his own work – *I wanted to give you a first look* – but it feels good to say them regardless. Marty gestures toward the case like, *Hand them over*, but Paul keeps the portfolio close and waits a beat. He has to set this up right.

'Did you happen to hear about a woman killed by a stalker back in December? A mother, a housewife, lived in suburban New Jersey? Named Judith Stanley?' Marty shakes his head, reaches for his pack of cigarettes, and offers Paul one. Paul accepts but doesn't light it yet; he's too keyed up for a cigarette.

'That woman – the victim – was a student in my Introduction to Photography class. She was... extraordinary. Just an extraordinary photographer. But she was also very private and refused to publish her pictures whenever I suggested it. She changed her mind just before she died, told me she wanted my help. And then – she was murdered. Tragic, tragic loss, of course.' He waits for a beat. 'And that's what brings me here, with her photographs in hand.'

Marty has been listening intently. 'You have the family's permission?' he asks. Nothing about Judith's death or the serendipitous timing of her change of heart. Paul nods, relaxing when he realizes he won't be interrogated further: he won't need to clarify the limits of the family's permission.

'Well, let's see them, then,' Marty says, stubbing out his cigarette and stifling a yawn. Paul feels a sharp twinge of irritation, then fear, at the sight of that yawn, but he reminds himself that Marty can't possibly know what's coming, even with the story Paul's told. And why should he believe Paul anyway? He's just the one-hit wonder who can't sell his pictures to *Harper's* – or anywhere – anymore; can he even recognize great work? With a whiff of coming vengeance, Paul hands the portfolio over and watches Marty flip through the photographs. Nonchalantly at first, then with increasingly dense attention. He slows down, studies each image, and when he reaches the end of the stack, he simply goes back through them all, even more slowly this time. When he finally looks up, he appears vulnerable, moved, and electrified.

'This woman was your student?'

Paul nods.

'These are shockingly good.' Marty shakes his head and stares down at the prints again. Paul fights the urge to say, *I know*. Instead, he relishes being right in silence. And relishes being the one to *possess* such rightness. Such greatness. 'Tell me more,' Marty says then, folding his hands together and leaning back in his chair. 'She was murdered?'

'Yes, she was murdered. About two and a half months ago.' On a whim, he adds, 'I was the last person to see her alive.' Marty's eyes widen. 'Except for whoever killed her, of course. They haven't found the guy.'

'Jesus.' Marty picks up the prints and stares at the top one – of Judith reflected in the liquor store window. 'The self-portraits alone are masterful. And the street photographs – she's not treading the same ground as Diane, but she's in that general area, you know?' Paul agrees. His pulse quickens to hear Marty mention Judith alongside the great Diane Arbus, an art world darling.

'She's truly phenomenal, Paul. I can't thank you enough for bringing these to me.' Marty Janowski, *thanking* him. He gives the man his most generous smile.

'Of course. They belong here. I knew it the minute I saw them, and told Judith so. And this is just a slice of the archive,' Paul adds.

Marty stares at him over his glasses, his eyes huge. 'How many photographs are there?'

'Hundreds. I have them all at my place. I've made a deal with her widower to be her posthumous representative. Her manager.' A falsehood for now – but Marty nods his head distractedly.

'You found a real gem here, Paul. A real fucking gem. These are the twenty best? I believe you – they're exquisite. I want them all. We'll expedite this, do a portfolio in the issue after this next one, use one of her pictures for the cover. You'll write the introduction. And like you said, the story around these is almost as good as the photographs. *Almost.*' He reaches blindly for another cigarette, offers Paul one. Paul is still holding the one he hasn't lighted; he lets Marty light it now. *You'll write the introduction*, the man said, so nonchalantly. Paul will be published in *Harper's* again, after all this time. He takes a long, delicious drag and when he blows it out, he thinks of how he's building himself into a brand-new man: the man who speaks for the soon-to-be-famous Judith Stanley.

14

PAUL WANTS TO MARK THE occasion with steak and a whiskey or two, so he stops at Steiner's, his local grocery store, on the way home. When he's good and loose, he'll give Tom a call.

As he palms a sickly-looking banana, he realizes it hasn't even crossed his mind to steal. He hasn't wanted to for days, and he knows that has little to do with being caught by that buffoon last time and everything to do with Judith Stanley. He's too *full* to steal. Full of Judith's images, full of excitement about the opportunities opening up before him. Opportunities he *deserves*. Finally, finally, the world is cracking open, tossing him a well-earned, if overdue, pearl or two. And a nice juicy steak. He starts to whistle as he walks the narrow aisles.

Paul takes great pleasure – and a simple sort of pride – in watching his selected items travel down the conveyer belt to the clerk. He smiles at her, hoping for some reciprocal admiration, but this worn older woman with dark circles under her eyes ignores him as she picks up one item after another and tosses it carelessly into the paper bag. When Paul looks at her, he sees his old self, moving through life without purpose or delight. He's disgusted by the sight of her and pays without looking up. Then he hugs the two heavy bags to his chest as if they were small children, happy to leave the store with the fruits of his honest labor.

15

'It's happening,' Paul says into the telephone. Thankfully, both Toms are on the other end of the line – so the younger Tom can nudge the elder in the right direction, on hearing Paul's news. 'The art editor at *Harper's* wants all twenty of her pictures – all the ones I showed you, Tom.' There's a long silence on the other end before TJ speaks.

'That's – that's really something, Paul. Wow. When can I see them?'

Paul glances down to where the portfolio leans against the foot of his armchair. 'I'm sorry, Tom, but I've had to leave them at *Harper's*. I wasn't expecting to, but they need them. The issue will come out in about a month, so they're ramping up production.' He says this to make it true, to make it impossible for Tom Senior to say he won't let it happen. But he doesn't want TJ to see the pictures anyway, *just in case* he reacts the same way his father did. He won't risk losing TJ's support, not now. Better to leave him in the dark and let him see the photographs when they're beautifully and irrevocably printed in the pages of *Harper's*.

'I want TJ to see them before the issue comes out,' Senior says, gruffly.

'I know, Tom, and I'm sorry about this. I wish I could –'

'You need to call this Marty fellow and tell him to let TJ come by.'

'Dad,' TJ interjects. 'It's OK. Really. I trust Paul, and I trust you, too. You've seen them. You've approved them. I'm sure they're all right. I'm not exactly an art expert, anyway.' He chuckles, and Paul joins him. He's so grateful for this easy, pleasing man, he could cry. He's grateful, too, to have heard Tom Senior say a string of magic words: *before the issue comes out*. He isn't putting himself in the way, even though he's displeased. He's accepting it, allowing it all to happen.

Things seem solid enough for Paul to tell them next about Marty's generous offer: $1,000, which he'll split 30/70 with them, as agreed. He tells them he'll have 'his lawyer' – an old friend from college who'll do him the favor for a minimal fee – draw up a contract detailing the 30/70 split. Paul will make sure the contract covers *all* of Judith's work – not just these few photographs – and that Paul is listed as the caretaker of said work, though he doesn't mention this now. There are big things ahead, whether Tom Senior likes it or not.

Both men seem uncomfortable at the mention of money and the contract, but there's no outburst of anger, no denial or refusal. They're accepting it; they're going with the flow.

'I can't really believe it. Mom in *Harper's*. Holy cow,' TJ says.

'And not just "in" *Harper's*,' Paul adds enthusiastically. 'She'll be featured in the issue. The focus of it. And on the cover, too. Not sure which photograph they'll use – they'll let me know soon, I imagine.' TJ gives a low whistle and Paul risks saying that he sees this as an incredible way to preserve and honor Judith's memory.

'And her last wish,' TJ adds.

'Absolutely.'

'She really said that to you? She really said she wanted this?' Tom Senior speaks right into the phone, right into Paul's ear. Paul pulls the receiver slightly away for some distance. He clears his throat.

'Yes, Tom,' he says firmly. 'This is *exactly* what she wanted.' The lie has become so real to him, so true, that the scene unfolds easily in his mind: Judith approaching in her quiet way, requesting his help. She's wearing her long, camel-colored coat with a soft blue scarf, her brown hair done up in a tidy bun. She looks serious, a bit scared. Paul smiles and claps his hands together when she tells him what she wants – which is also what *he* wants. They're in total agreement.

'All right,' Tom Senior says, dispelling the joyful imaginary scene, and then Paul knows he's done it – he's won. He doesn't push it by adding the news that he's writing the introduction – it might complicate things; Tom Senior will surely have issues with anything and everything he writes. Instead, he thanks them both and tells them he'll stay in close contact, though he hopes to keep his distance from now on. When he hangs up, he blows smoke rings in the air for a long while, luxuriating in the solid double triumphs of the day: winning Marty over, and then locking down the Stanley men.

16

A BRIGHT SPLASH OF MORNING LIGHT illuminates the blank, lined page of the legal pad Paul bought with high hopes and determination. He sits staring at it, wondering where to begin his introduction. With Judith's first after-class approach? Or earlier, with what little he's learned of her childhood? He stares out his window at his neighbor's brick wall, feeling truly walled in, as his pulse hammers in his ear. He reaches for a cigarette. *Thousands of people will read what I write*, he tells himself, in an endless, aggravating loop. By noon, he's reaching for the whiskey bottle, too. Taking sips helps him quiet the voice in his head that says *failure is looming*, and by one thirty he's able to just let it flow: badly chosen words, lazy phrasing, and all. He doesn't stop until he has an awful first draft, and when he does, he celebrates by stretching out on the couch, yawning luxuriously, and rubbing his eyes.

Lying there, he thinks of Charlie, fleetingly at first, then intently, vengefully: what would she and her little cohort think of him now, writing for *Harper's*? Maybe she'd think twice before speaking to him the way she did in class the other night. Or would she? He stews over the question until he's furious and then his mind slips to her full tits in a white sweater, her round ass subtly swaying as she climbs the stairs. He unbuckles his pants, works himself to a full erection, and masturbates to the thought of her insulting him with that pouty mouth as he fucks her right to breathlessness, silence, and unwilling pleasure.

And then he's done. Alone on his couch with his spent dick in hand. He lets it flop to his belly and drifts off. When he wakes several hours later, confused and shivering in the dark, he gets up and stumbles to the bathroom for a hot shower.

Paul dresses quickly the next morning and leaves the building with his rough draft and red pencils in a shoulder bag. *Better to stay out today*, he thinks, as if last night's lurid fantasizing soiled his apartment for serious work. It isn't true, but he can't risk falling into another erotically charged haze; he doesn't have time. He heads for the nearby Hunger Pains Café to stay focused and fueled for as long as it takes.

After two raisin scones, five cups of coffee, and several more drafts, he thinks he's done it: polished the introduction until it shines bright enough for Marty, for *Harper's* and the *Harper's* reading public. He was right to come to the crowded café, to sit surrounded by the buzz of other conversations. Now he readies himself to head home and type it all up before sending it in. Stepping outside, blinking in the cold winter light, he feels haggard and stunned and in need of a long walk.

Two hours later, after dropping his introduction, sealed in a stamped envelope with a brisk and confident cover note, in the nearest mailbox, he strides through the neighborhood for over an hour. Soaking up the familiar sights and sounds, Paul says hello to a few shopkeepers and neighbors and begins to revive. He returns to his apartment, refreshed and also certain he'll hear good news from Marty soon. Glancing at the couch, he considers indulging in the somewhat tormented pleasure of jerking off to Charlie again, but it seems risky somehow. Dangerous and threatening to the work he's just done, and to Marty's reaction. *I'll wait to do it again until after Marty calls*, he promises himself, though he knows he's being oddly superstitious.

*

Marty doesn't call the next day, or the day after that. Paul finds himself sitting too often by the phone, anxious and a bit crazed. He stares at the telephone, the way he did when he was waiting to hear from TJ, startling whenever it rings. It's never Marty, though. He knows Marty must have received his introduction by now. Does he hate it? Is he rethinking Paul's connection to the feature? Will he find someone else instead, a famous photographer perhaps, to write the introduction? He could call the *Harper's* office, of course, confront Marty head-on, but he doesn't want to seem desperate. Instead, he drinks himself to sleep but sleeps poorly, plagued by bad dreams that feature Charlie somehow holding his introduction and laughing over it, wide-mouthed, her head thrown back. He wakes thinking of the soft white expanse of her throat, with his stomach crimped in anger and fear.

When the telephone rings at 10:00 am on the fourth morning, it's finally Marty. He's effusive in his praise, says the piece is 'almost perfect,' and gives Paul a list of minor tweaks he wants him to make. When they hang up, Paul sits in the silence of his living room, his stomach and mind fully eased. He smiles stupidly around at his familiar belongings: wooden chairs, crammed bookshelves, shoes lined up in the small apartment vestibule. *Of course* Marty loved the introduction. Paul has known all along that he did a great job. Marty said something to him about 'beautifully shaping Judith Stanley for the public,' and Paul puffed up at that. He likes to think of it that way – of his having *created her.* His mind flashes, then, to his dream of Charlie's exposed throat. The image sends him quickly to the couch, where he pulls and grunts until he's satisfied.

17

THOUGH PAUL IS ALMOST DIZZYINGLY busy in the days leading up to the *Harper's* publication date, time passes slowly. He sends the finished contract to the Stanleys – which Tom signs and sends back, surprisingly without complaint, and seemingly without noticing how much power it gives Paul, or how much leeway there is for future endeavors like gallery shows. He visits the *Harper's* office, too – this time, thrillingly, as part of 'the team' – to review the portfolio layout. Even in its unfinished state, the feature looks stunning. They've chosen the butcher shop self-portrait for the cover, and soon Judith's face will be staring back at him, slyly, from the cover of every *Harper's* on every city newsstand, alongside the phrase *Introduction by Paul Sorenson*. It will link them forever in the public mind.

In this time of impatience, Paul smokes and drinks more to try to quiet his anxiety-infused glee – or his glee-infused anxiety. He masturbates to Charlie, too, but when his fantasies grow darker, tinged with violence, and he emerges from them shaking and ashamed, he resolves to try something more purifying: taking hours-long walks up and down the length of Manhattan in the bitter cold. He returns home exhausted and peacefully emptied out, but the feeling doesn't last; he'd have to walk forever to retain this placidity. But it does pass the time, and one day he finds himself on the eve of the issue's publication, just like that – after seconds, and long centuries.

Paul drags himself to class in a jittery, scattered state without his lecture notes, unsure of what he'll do: give an impromptu talk about photography as a profession? One he's abandoned, he thinks with a twinge of pain. Fainter now, though, very faint. He stares around, speechless, feeling the students' eyes – and Charlie's in particular – boring into him, and starts to speak about the only thing filling his mind these days. He was going to save it for the end of class, but why not start now, tell them about the forthcoming *Harper's* issue, the process of building the portfolio, writing the introduction, and so on? The students will like that. He'll enjoy it, too.

'Everyone, I wanted to let you know that your former classmate, Judith Stanley, who, uh, died so tragically a few months ago, as you probably know, will have twenty of her photographs featured in this month's *Harper's*. It comes out tomorrow.'

He waits for the murmurs to subside, and inadvertently locks eyes with Charlie when he adds, 'It features an introduction written by yours truly. I selected the photographs with – on behalf of Judith's family, too.' Paul senses a slight and sudden shift in how his students perceive him: he's no longer their insignificant community college instructor – however charming – but a big shot, a cool guy, a man of real substance and importance in the world.

A few hands shoot up and he happily answers their predictable questions.

'How did you choose which twenty to use?'

'Will they mention NJCC?' This one gets titters.

'Did you include that one of the couple you showed us last semester?'

'How can I submit my photographs to *Harper's*?'

When he looks around for the next question, Paul spots Charlie's raised hand, her darkly intent gaze. He could pass over her, pretend not to see her, but that would be weak – and he isn't weak, is he? Still, he dislikes the serious set of her face, the way she looks at him like she's prying him open. He's pried her open many times, in his head, but the thought doesn't protect him. It feels instead like he's done something wrong, something gross, and that everyone here has seen him do it, too. He hasn't and they haven't, but still he cowers a little and calls on Charlie without using her name, pretending he doesn't know it.

'How much was her family involved in the process?' she asks. A seemingly innocent question, but Paul is unnerved.

'Oh, uh, they trusted me to do the hard work,' he says, stretching his lips into a semblance of a smile. 'But I ran my choices by them, of course, and won their approval.'

Charlie receives this blankly and carries on. 'Amazing, too, that *Harper's* let you do the introduction. Congratulations.' He nods but bristles. *Amazing* because it's wonderful? Or *amazing* because it's a job for someone better? They didn't *let* him do the introduction; they begged him to. An exaggeration, sure, but Marty offered it to him without question, without hesitation, at the same moment he proposed publishing Judith's portfolio. Paul takes a breath and tries to remind himself that she's just a young know-it-all. She probably doesn't intend her tone. He needs to calm down, be mature, be *the professor.* Or be the man with a feature coming out in *Harper's* tomorrow.

'Yes, thank you. Not really surprising when you consider I worked with her on the photographs quite a bit and knew her work better than anyone else. And since I'm a professional myself –'

'And you were the last person to see her that night, too, right, Paul?' Charlie adds, interrupting. She sounds almost helpful, just listing another reason he might have been chosen, but Paul isn't fooled. He hears the dark implication; so does everyone else. The room stills. All eyes are fixed on him, all ears tuned to hear how he'll respond. *Careful, Paul. Careful.* Paul lets out a breath and shakes his head.

'I was. I hate thinking about it. I wish I – could have done something to stop it. But I was in here, and she was out there, and by the time I came outside, well…' He lets it trail off. Folds his arms across his chest and stares into the distance, to the back of the classroom, safely above and beyond his students' unwavering attention.

'I only wish Judith were here to see that *Harper's* issue tomorrow.' He says it softly, conveying real regret and sorrow with his voice. He thinks that should get them on his side – even if it doesn't win over Charlie.

'Me too,' Charlie says, her snide little voice echoing through the room. That's it: *Me too.* As if she knew Judith at all. As if she has any right to talk to him this way, like a fellow collaborator on the Judith project. He fights the urge to march over and pull her up by the ear, in front of everyone. He wants to drag her –

'I can't wait to see the feature tomorrow, Professor,' a young man whose name escapes him says in the awkward silence. Saving him. Paul's simmering rage retreats; he looks over and smiles at the male student. A real smile.

'Thank you for saying that. I can't wait to see it, either. I think you'll all appreciate the photographs in the feature. Now go out tomorrow and buy one! Or two!' he says, laughing as they laugh, even though he's still seething in Charlie's direction. He turns around to hide it as students leave, half expecting to hear her cough quietly to announce her presence behind him, but there's nothing, and when he turns around, she's gone. Everyone's gone. He's blissfully alone, though he doesn't feel blissful. Not blissful at all.

18

PAUL WALKS BRISKLY TO THE newsstand the next morning, his heart pounding in his chest. The *Harper's* issue is there, front and center. He stops walking, stops breathing. His eyes land first on Judith's face: wry, reserved, unknowable. *I exist*, it says. *I'm here.* And even though Paul knows better, it's suddenly as if she *were* here, staring him down, challenging his bogus story of her 'last wish.' *This isn't what I wanted*, she's saying with that closed expression of hers, and Paul checks over his shoulder to see if anyone else has witnessed his exposure as a sham. But there are only strangers passing by, utterly indifferent, and Amir gives his usual kind smile when Paul pays, asking him why he's buying several copies. When Paul points a finger at his own name, under Judith's on the cover, Amir claps his hands with real glee. He rummages behind him then and pulls out a cigar – a good one, Paul notes – and Paul takes it gladly, gratefully, his mood shifting like the ground beneath him. He's happy again, proud of what he's done. Who he's become. *A true success.*

Amir lights the cigar for him, leaving Paul to stand on the sidewalk, puffing, staring at the cover, which reads: *JUDITH STANLEY, Suburban Housewife, Murder Victim, Visionary Photographer: A Portfolio. Edited and Introduced by Paul Sorenson.* He loves seeing his own name but hates the descriptors they've used for Judith. He tried to get them to change them – or their order, at least – but the editors (not Marty, who agreed with him) won out. They said it would sell, and Paul concedes the point; those descriptors alone could compel people who aren't usually interested in art to buy the issue in droves. And Paul wants it to sell. If it doesn't, then what will he have to show for his hard work, for the risks he's taken?

Paul buys a croissant and coffee, then heads to the tiny park not far from his apartment. He sits on a bench, takes a deep breath, and flips through to the portfolio. It's right in the middle: a centerfold. He smiles at the sight of his byline but doesn't read the introduction yet; he skips ahead to Judith's pictures. It's like seeing them for the first time, in all their vibrant, playful, breathtaking beauty. He stares at each one, knowing that *he himself* selected these, put them in order, had them published – and here they are. He feels as though he's floating in air, observing himself from above. He seems to watch himself flip back through the pages to his introduction. And then his own words bring him back to earth; he shuts out everything but the lines before him, the lines he's written:

To the everyday observer, Judith Stanley would have seemed like an average woman: a housewife, a mother, and the unassuming resident of a suburban New Jersey town. Like so many women of her age and middle-class status, she had a hobby, too: taking photographs. When she enrolled in my Introduction to Photography class at New Jersey Community College, I, too, was fooled by her appearance. I saw her as a quiet, self-contained woman, probably trying to fill her empty evenings now that her children were gone. I didn't give her much thought at all; though older than my average student, she blended in, became just another face among many in the lecture hall.

When she handed me her photographs one night after class, everything changed. It was like I'd been sleepwalking, and Judith's pictures smacked me awake. That's how good, how original, how startling they were. Especially the self-portraits. I'd never seen anything like them, and I was well-versed in the current trends of portrait and self-portrait photography. Judith was doing something thrillingly new, yet she had no idea. She may have known that she was 'good' at photography, that she had a knack for seeking out idiosyncratic subjects and views, but she didn't know how uncommonly gifted she was – and neither did anyone around her. I'm honored, and so grateful, to have been the one to first recognize Judith Stanley for the major talent she is – or rather, sadly, was.

I didn't know, when we met, that Judith was being stalked. Sometimes by telephone: it would ring and no one would answer, or the caller would say terrible, intimate things to her over the line. He followed her, too, as she traveled around taking photographs, keeping his distance but always there, and appearing, she said, as a shadow in the background of many self-portraits – though she religiously cropped him out, and you'll see no sign of him in this selection. He approached her a handful of times and then finally, tragically, he stabbed her after class one late fall evening. He left her for dead in the parking lot, then vanished into the night. I'm haunted knowing that if I'd left the building sooner and spotted her lying in a pool of her own blood, I might have saved her. Her killer has yet to be found.

It was – and is – a terrible loss. To her family and friends, of course, but also to the rest of us, as you'll soon discover yourself. I never knew Judith the mother, Judith the wife, or even Judith the friend, but I did know Judith the photographer. And she was mighty. She is mighty. She was struck down far too soon, but her work will endure. Over the past weeks, I've worked diligently to select twenty of her most striking photographs for the portfolio that follows – a true feat, given that nearly every photograph in her substantial oeuvre is striking.

Judith had been wary of sharing her photographs publicly; she was a private person. But on her last day in class, which was also, sadly, the last day of her life, she asked me to help her publish her work. I was eager to do so. She was eager, too; I only wish she could have lived to see this exquisite portfolio come to fruition. Welcome to the world of Judith Stanley: small-town parades, suburban parties, self-portraits, lovers' spats, outcasts, and city sights as you've never before seen them. Enjoy these glimpses of our mundane lives made wholly new through the lens of Judith's incredibly uncanny eye.

Paul Sorenson, Photographer and Photography Instructor

Paul looks up and around, almost expecting the oblivious passersby to tell him, *Well done.* He thinks his introduction is really quite good, and aside from that, no one who reads it will miss the glaring proof of his interwovenness with Judith Stanley. Tom Senior won't like it; he won't like how Paul has rendered the details of his wife's ordeal in print, either, though he's hardly said more than the newspapers and television news did in their lurid accounts. He's done it more tastefully, more respectfully. Tom would have to acknowledge that. And how could he tell the story of these pictures, and of Judith, without that essential background? He takes an overlarge bite of his croissant and washes it down with a fast, hot swallow of coffee as if swallowing down Tom's disdain, cleansing it away. He chews and sips more slowly after that, determined to enjoy this moment that may be a turning point in his life. And when he wipes the last crumbs from his mouth, takes the last drink of coffee, he heads home. After all, his telephone might be ringing.

19

THE FOLLOWING DAYS UNFOLD LIKE a dream. Journalists and gallerists begin to write and call, circling like kind, subservient vultures. *Mr Sorenson* this, *Mr Sorenson* that... Paul responds to all of them with confident ease, as *Mr Sorenson*, naturally, would. By the end of the first week, this new identity has blotted out the old one so thoroughly that he forgets all about his real job: teaching photography. He calls Betty in the main office to cancel class at the last minute with only a twinge of disappointment that he won't face Charlie while wearing this new, unassailable skin.

But there's so much more to think about than Charlie. Though no one ever says it aloud, Judith's gruesome death has amplified the public response to her work, and Paul feels himself at the center of a maelstrom almost immediately. He's booked for radio, television, newspaper, and magazine interviews, during which he speaks somberly, respectfully, about Judith's last day in class, how she broached her desire to publish, and what exactly he saw and heard when he left the school building that evening. *Nothing*, he tells one mournful-looking host after another, shaking his head. *Absolutely nothing.* On one occasion, he hears the live audience's collective moan and thinks it sounds slightly ecstatic. They're feasting on Judith's tragic story – and on the story of 'Judith and Paul.' Not quite a love story, no – though some are already speculating about this in the press – but still something for his listeners to tear into.

Not one of his interviewers has come out and said, *If Judith were alive, you wouldn't be sitting here, would you, pal?* And thank god for that! But Paul still hears it as a subtext to certain questions: *How long ago was it that your own work was published in* Harper's, *Paul? Are you still an active photographer, or do you simply devote yourself to your teaching now?* As time passes, though, he grows inured to it all, sets aside any focus on possible subtext. What does subtext matter, anyway, in the mind of the public, which has no mind? The public wants surface, only surface, and he's good at giving it, so good. He knows he's the best possible champion of Judith's work – much better than Judith would have been herself. Marty reports that sales of the issue are 'through the roof,' and he treats Paul now like the son he never had – though the *Harper's* check still hasn't arrived.

Before long, Paul's tireless efforts secure a glowing prize: a one-woman show at Doven Gallery, the crown jewel of the New York art world. When Paul brings fifty of Judith's photographs to share with Jahan Davani, Doven's famed owner and head curator, the man is so moved by them that tears spill down his cheeks. He blots these elegantly with a monogrammed handkerchief while Paul stares; what surer proof of his own elevated status, his sparkling new life, than the sight of this ethereally handsome, successful, stylish man weeping over his pictures?

Once Jahan recovers, clears his throat, and declares the work 'dazzling,' he lights two cigarettes from a slim gold case and hands one to Paul. Then he recites a litany of promises and intentions: Doven will mount a one-woman show; it will draw thousands of viewers; Paul will be 'consulting curator,' essential to the mounting of said show; a contract will be drawn up and work will begin post-haste, as Jahan wants the show to open in April – or at the latest, May. Jahan shakes his hand and claps him on the shoulder, then kisses him on both cheeks while bidding him goodbye. Paul, ecstatic and dazed, stands on the sidewalk outside the gallery, wondering if what happened was a dream. *Consulting curator*, the man said. Paul has no idea what the job will entail, and he has no credentials for it either, but it's his and he wants it badly. He'll be the best goddamn consulting curator the world has ever seen, and Judith's show will be the hit of the season – or of the whole year.

And after that, who knows? The world will be his fucking oyster.

20

The dampening reality, of course, is that he'll have to tell Tom about the Doven show. He's waited several days, letting himself bask in the glory of Jahan's offer, but now he has to fulfill his contractual obligations to Tom. Though Tom signed over managerial control of Judith's photographs to Paul – when he believed it to be unlikely they'd even be published – he retained the right to be 'informed of all consequential decisions related to the public display of [her] work.' So telling Tom about the show is largely a formality, Paul knows, but it could be an unpleasant one. Or not – he was surprised by Tom's silence when the *Harper's* issue came out; the man didn't call him ranting about the introduction – or anything else. They spoke once, in the aftermath, and Tom sounded almost elderly, bewildered and aged a dozen years by his late wife's sudden transfiguration into an overnight public sensation.

Paul hopes for the same reduced man when he calls today and delivers the latest news as gently and as coolly as he can.

'A show?' Tom asks, as if Paul were suggesting they mount a Broadway burlesque, a cabaret, or even a topless dance at a gentlemen's club inspired by Judith's work.

'Yes, Tom. This is, you know, the best possible outcome. The pinnacle for any artist or photographer. It's the best thing for Judith – and for you and TJ,' he adds quickly.

Tom snorts. 'Not for us.'

'Well, for Judith, then. Think of –'

'Don't tell me "Judith would have wanted this." She asked for your help with submitting a few photographs to magazines, and now you've gone and whipped up a circus. *You* want this. That's why you're doing it. You love the spotlight. You've been giving interviews left and right, don't think I haven't noticed. Putting up a gallery show? That's something you're doing for yourself. You'll get more money that way, won't you?'

'There could be sales, yes. But you'll get the bulk of those profits. Seventy percent, remember?'

'I don't want it.'

Paul leans his head in his hand, as if Tom were there to witness his weariness. 'Look, if Judith were alive, she would have understood this as the natural next step. This isn't –'

'This is about *you*, Paul. It's all about *Paul Sorenson*,' Tom says with disdain.

'I'm building her legacy!' Paul practically screams.

'Her *legacy*? Thanks to you, everyone on earth knows she was brutally murdered, and took weird photographs. It wasn't enough for you to write about it, either – you had to go shouting it on every TV show, in every newspaper. To hell with you and your show, Paul. I'll have to read through that contract again and see if it holds up. If it doesn't, *our lawyer* will be in touch.' And with that, Tom Senior hangs up.

Paul holds the receiver in his hand and stares blearily around the room, listening to the dial tone. He hasn't slept well since the issue came out but he's been riding adrenaline for days; now exhaustion lands like an anvil. He looks at the boxes of Judith's photographs, his small desk piled high with correspondence related to her work, and the hall table smothered in unopened fan mail. He sees it all as real, substantial evidence of everything he's done to bring a great artist's oeuvre into the world. If Tom sees him as some kind of narcissistic opportunist, he's a fool. And he *is* a fool, isn't he? He knows nothing about art or the art world; he couldn't even appreciate his own wife's photographs.

Still, Paul feels sullied by Tom's words, and afraid of what he said about a lawyer. He didn't know the Stanleys *had* a lawyer – it's the first time he's hearing it, and it could be a bluff. Contracts can be broken, though; they can be torn into bits and flushed down toilets, or burned to ash. He wouldn't have the resources to fight, should Tom take action. But all he can do now is wait and hope that Tom's words were just bluster, or that TJ will talk sense into the man. Again.

In the meantime, he has to focus on other things – there are so many things in need of his attention, and he has so little energy for them all. He reaches for a cigarette, lights it, gets a burst of uplift with the first inhale. His eyes land on the stack of unopened fan mail: one of his less urgent tasks. He's told himself he doesn't have time to read those letters right now. He's told himself it isn't important – what Middle America thinks of Judith's work.

But he's curious. And it doesn't take much to open and read a few letters.

21

Paul slits open the first envelope with his dagger-shaped letter opener and settles into the armchair to read. Margo in Illinois calls Judith's work 'disturbing, unladylike, and harmful to the general public.' Not exactly a fan letter but it makes him laugh, and laughing feels good. When did he last laugh? Everything has been so serious and intense for days – though it's all going well. Except for Tom. He turns to another letter, quickly: this one from a fellow photographer in Idaho who says Judith's work has been a great inspiration. There are more like this, one after the other, thanking Paul for what he's done. He pours himself a generous glass of whiskey and toasts himself, then takes a burning sip. He's having fun, and he deserves to have fun, doesn't he?

The next letter is written in a childish hand and signed by someone named Eddie. There's no return address. Eddie asks if Paul knows 'who knifed the lady photographer,' and if he watched it happen. What did it look like, how did it sound, what did Paul feel? Eddie asks. Suddenly, the whiskey sits like acid in his empty stomach. Paul should have eaten, though he had no appetite – and now he has less. He knows 'Eddie' is just some wacko, but he feels guilty somehow – as if he encouraged men like Eddie to write things like this. He didn't, of course; he blames the interviewers, forever asking him about Judith's morbid end. He has no choice but to answer them, does he? To the twisted delight of the Eddies of the world.

Paul tears up the letter and tosses it into the trash.

After a brief pause and a deep inhale and exhale of clarifying smoke, Paul keeps moving through the diminishing pile, gaining a sense of small accomplishment. It's suspenseful, too. He keeps wondering what's next. In one letter, a woman from Arkansas thanks him for helping women artists everywhere. 'We've been neglected and dismissed out of hand, but in helping Judith rise to the top, you've helped the rest of us,' she writes. Paul rereads it several times, smiling as the acid in his stomach fades to mellow warmth. He thinks about sending this one to Tom, along with some others that sing his praises. But it might just enrage him, all these strangers weighing in on his precious 'private' wife.

Forget Tom, he tells himself, and picks up another. This one comes in a plain white envelope with no return address; Paul's name and address are written in block letters. Hopefully not another odd one – the handwriting reminds him of 'Eddie's,' though it's bolder, cleaner, and more assured. He opens the envelope, unfolds the single piece of unlined white paper inside, and reads the message written there, also in tidy block lettering:

YOU'RE A FUCKING PARASITE

LIVING OFF JUDITH'S WORK

I BET YOU'RE GLAD SHE'S DEAD

DID YOU KILL HER, PAUL?

FUCKING LOWLIFE

MONSTER

He rereads it several times, just as he reread the last one, though he isn't smiling, isn't pleased, and the paper trembles in his hand. He tells himself this is just another crackpot like Eddie, but it feels different. Worse. He reaches for his whiskey bottle, unscrews the top shakily, and takes a long, hot swallow. As it pools heavily in his stomach, he burps. He lets the letter and envelope drop to the floor instead of tearing them up – he isn't sure why – but then he stares down, compulsively rereading.

The truth is, he *is* a parasite. What else could he be? Though technically he isn't 'living off Judith's work' – the *Harper's* check still hasn't arrived, and even when it does, it won't give him any great financial boost. But he *is* profiting from her work in other, less material ways, and he may profit greatly after this gallery show, so… the label will be irrefutable then. He fixates on the word and takes it in, lets it settle inside him. It almost feels good – cathartic, anyway – to let the word *parasite* attach to him – like a parasite itself. *A parasite living off a parasite*, he thinks with a dry chuckle. The word pierces the skin of the dream he's been living since the *Harper's* feature appeared, and for the moment he welcomes it, savors its blunt truth.

A blunt truth he would never publicly own, of course.

A blunt truth he'll soon shove to a shadowed corner of his brain.

After a long while, he reaches down to pick up the letter with thumb and forefinger, scanning the words, wondering for the first time who wrote them. Certainly a woman; he can almost taste her woman's rage.

But what woman? A deranged stranger, or someone he knows? Someone like his student Charlie, maybe. He doesn't believe it *is* Charlie – not really – but someone like her: drawn to Judith's work and the drama of her death, eager to blame Paul in the absence of anyone more deserving of blame. The writer is frustratingly unaware, too, of her own hypocrisy – because she would never have known about Judith *without Paul's involvement*. And she'd never have had the opportunity to hate him, then.

He wonders if she's written more.

He returns to the pile, recoiling from the thought of finding another but still sifting through the letters quickly, almost eagerly. Finally, he dumps them all on the floor and gets on his knees to survey them.

After a few minutes, he's certain: there are no other envelopes addressed to him in block letters with a missing return address.

He should be relieved – and he is, to some degree. But he also wants more. *More information*, he tells himself, so he can figure out who this epistolary enemy might be. But he also craves more nastiness and hurt: the delicious pinch of real feeling at a time when his life often feels unreal. Wonderful, but sometimes unbelievable. *Fucking parasite*, though, he can easily believe.

He picks up the letter and rereads it, letting it prick him all over again.

22

THE NEXT MORNING, WITH A hot cup of black coffee in hand and rays of sun warming his kitchen, Paul rereads the scolding letter and laughs out loud. It's childish. Pathetic. A missive from someone's deranged mind. Why did he let it bother him so much? Paul isn't a parasite; he's a hero for bringing attention to Judith's work. Other letter writers have said as much – like the woman artist from Arkansas, and many more. Why listen to some hateful outlier when most voices praise and thank him? *It's a choice*, he tells himself. *And I choose not to listen anymore.*

He folds the letter up and slides it into its envelope. Sets it carefully on his desk. He won't destroy it the way he did 'Eddie's'; destroying it would mean it has power over him. He'd rather treat it like just another letter in the pile. And the letters – good or bad, admiring or outraged – don't mean much anyway. Far more important and worthy of his notice is the day ahead: his first as consulting curator at Doven Gallery. The most important job he's ever had.

He takes more care than usual getting ready. With his brown pants he wears a white button-down shirt he forgot he had. A little tight across the chest, but he likes how he looks when he checks the mirror: serious, quietly stylish, and mature. Professional. He's trimmed his beard and carefully combed his hair. His worn winter coat won't make much of an impression, but he doesn't need to make an impression – he's already *in*. He heads for the train in high spirits, relishing the clear blue sky and hardly noticing the frigid air. The world feels electric, rich with possibility, and the usual sights and sounds of the city – even the frosted bags of garbage piled on the sidewalks – delight him.

When Paul enters the gallery, Jahan welcomes him with a firm handshake and a beaming smile.

'Mr Sorenson, so wonderful to see you.' Paul thrills to the sound of *Mr Sorenson* coming from Jahan Davani's lips but tells him to call him Paul – just as he did when they first met days ago. The two men take their seats on the aggressively modern, uncomfortable chairs Jahan seems to favor, and Jahan leans forward, his brown eyes warm and keenly focused.

'I want this to be an iconic show. Legendary. And, Paul, you will play a huge part, involved in everything – but not the tiresome things. My staff will handle those.' He gives a big laugh, and Paul tries to match it. The thought of staff handling 'the tiresome things' is extraordinary, thrilling – but he tries to act as though he's long been a stranger to grunt work.

'The show is about Judith, yes, but it's also about you,' Jahan goes on, pointing his forefinger at Paul. *About me?* Paul wants to ask, letting himself imagine, for a moment, that Jahan saw his old photograph in *Harper's* and wants to feature his work alongside Judith's. 'You and Judith are fused in the public mind. Judith is the star, of course,' Jahan says, evaporating Paul's little dream. 'Her work will be the centerpiece. So will her death – whether we like it or not. But the story of "Judith and Paul" is compelling, too, the one about this singular talent discovered by her brilliant photography instructor. People adore stories like this, so you must know how crucial you are – both behind the scenes and out on the main stage.' Here, Jahan makes a sweeping gesture with his arms. Paul has the sudden impulse to stand and take a bow – and he's almost giddy enough at Jahan's words to do it.

'Now. Let me give you the grand tour, introduce you to the

staff. They're absolutely dying to meet you.' Paul floats up out of his chair and drifts after Jahan, allowing himself to revel in the moment as he shakes hands with one eager staff member after another. With each handshake, he discards more and more of his old self – the shabby college instructor and has-been photographer – and leans into the bright new person who belongs in this golden world.

23

OUTSIDE, PAUL LEANS AGAINST THE window of a closed florist and lights a cigarette. The smoke fills him up, tastes delicious. He lets his mind drift over the past several hours: meeting Tasha, Jahan's gorgeous assistant, who seemed to instantly like him; seeing the rooms to be filled with Judith's framed photographs, and his own printed words; signing the contract that said *CONSULTING CURATOR* in all caps.

In all caps like: *FUCKING PARASITE. I BET YOU'RE GLAD SHE'S DEAD.*

The words jolt him out of his reverie. He forgets the glory of the day and fixates on the letter again – especially the accusation that he's 'glad she's dead.' He isn't *glad* she's dead, but he can't deny that things are working out for him *because she died.* If she hadn't, and if she'd ever published her photographs – which was doubtful – he'd have been a brief mention in her interviews at most. *I had a photography instructor who pushed me to send out my work. I resisted but finally did it, thanks to him...* She wouldn't have named him, because who would need to know his name? Only hers would have mattered.

But now his matters, too. Maybe he won't be the great photographer himself, but he'll be the next best thing: the one who recognized genius and ferried it deftly into the world. A few might share the letter writer's view – like Charlie, maybe – but most will see him as a generous mentor and promising young curator.

He exhales a great cloud of smoke at this vision and the vision slowly disintegrates; the city returns. A hobo walks by, dragging behind him a cart stuffed with paper bags and old electronics. Paul thinks of Judith: how she could have captured this man's image, made him into something magnificent. He lets the fleeting joy of this thought swell inside of him, generous and unenvious. Judith had her talent; he has his own – and yes, she's gone, but he's still alive.

Instead of heading home, he ducks into a bar in Chelsea and stays until midnight. He thinks he might go home with one particular pretty girl, but she says she has plans and slides him her number for a 'rain check.' Once he finally leaves the dim, cozy glow of the bar and finds himself back on the street, alone and wobbling drunkenly, the unwanted phrase pops into his head and repeats, repeats:

FUCKING PARASITE

FUCKING PARASITE

The words trail him down the subway stairs. Standing and swaying in the train car, he sees nothing but strange characters, some of whom catch and hold his eye: a man with a deeply scarred cheek; a woman with a swollen-shut eye, compulsively knitting; two shockingly thin young women, possibly twins, leaning together as if conjoined at the temple. Paul thinks he may have entered some kind of hell, after having lived in paradise briefly. But it isn't hell, of course, it's just the *city*, flaunting its mundane horrors. They're nothing new, they just seem especially horrible after his time at Doven Gallery.

He's relieved when he's climbing the steps to the door of his building. He thinks about going straight up but instead heads to the row of metal mailboxes with a quickening pulse. He pulls out a small stack of letters and bills and shuffles through them, spotting another envelope with the address written in block letters. Are they the *same* block letters, though? He can't tell. He tears it open and unfolds a sheet of yellow legal pad paper bearing a message from someone who signs off, 'An ex-con.'

Did that bitch really take those pictures or did you take them? Is there really even a Judith Stanley or did you make her up to make money? That's what I think. I watch a lot of television and I never saw a news story about a Jersey housewife getting killed so I think you made it up. I don't really care except I hate bitches like her. Glad she's dead.

The last line sends a chill through him. Despite the half-witted, delusional content, Paul can't ignore how this letter echoes the other one at the end. *Glad she's dead.* Could this 'ex-con' be the same writer putting on an act, trying a new way of goading Paul? His instincts tell him no, they're different people, but even so, he compares the two envelopes when he gets upstairs. His eyes flit back and forth between them but he can't be certain they're the same – or different. They look similar, but one slants slightly to the left; the other is nearly perfectly vertical.

But who cares? He sets both letters aside. He's just had one of the best days of his life; it doesn't matter what an ex-con and an angry woman (or just one angry woman) wrote in their unhinged letters. No one will see these letters but him – and he isn't required to open them! But he does have to eat something, change, and drive to New Jersey to teach his class tonight. It's been two weeks, and he'll have to dip himself back into his old life for a while – though he can hardly imagine it.

24

AMIDST THE SMALL CROWD OF students stopping to congratulate him on the *Harper's* feature, Paul spots Charlie leaving and calls her down. When he first saw her tonight, surveying him with those dark eyes, he felt skittish and guilty. He thought of all the time he'd spent with her in his mind, lonely on his couch, and the sad shabbiness of it made the glamorous day he'd spent at Doven wither and recede; he wanted badly to grasp it back. He thought maybe if he could grasp *her* – or jostle her, unsettle the girl who *might* be his letter writer and *was* the girl who liked challenging him in front of the class – he could regain his confidence and recapture the loftiness of his newly minted existence.

But as she nears him, coming into soft focus like a classic movie queen, he catches himself staring at her breasts beneath the thin fabric of her sweater, the dramatic curve of her hips in her bell-bottomed jeans. He struggles to meet her keen and questioning – and laughing? – dark brown eyes.

'Hey, Charlie,' he says, feigning nonchalance. 'What did you make of the *Harper's* portfolio? I assume you saw it.'

'It was out of this world. Fantastic,' she says, her face lighting up. It stirs something in Paul; she's become warm again, readable. *Fuckable.* She's impressed with what he's done and she can't help showing it. Glowing with it, even.

'I just love her work so much,' she goes on, cheeks flushing. 'I can't believe I was in class with her. Her pictures are so –

powerful. Like magic, almost. They speak to me – and to so many people I know. She was a genius,' she says reverently. Paul could be anyone – one of her peers, or a table, for all his presence matters to her. His lust shrivels to nothing.

'I agree. I, uh, enjoyed writing the introduction,' he says, giving her an unsubtle nudge.

She doesn't notice, or pretends not to. She stares at him and simply nods, holding his gaze. Says nothing about his introduction. He knows she read it; curiosity alone would have driven her to read it. Her silence resounds in the empty classroom like a booming judgment. Paul scrabbles at his jacket pockets for his cigarettes. He'd be all right, he'd handle this just fine, with a cigarette.

'Professor – Paul – did you want something else? I'm about to miss my ride,' Charlie says, and a swift, bright fury rears up in him. He drops his hands, forgetting the cigarettes – he wants something else. He wants to grab her arm, press her up against a wall, grind into her with a hot hand smothering her mouth. He wants to hear her trying to scream.

'No, no,' he croaks out. 'I just wanted to get your take on the *Harper's* thing. Glad you enjoyed it.' He spits the last words, but she misses – or ignores, again – the bitterness.

'I loved it. I've looked at the pictures like a million times.' No mention, again, of his introduction, of anything to do with him, even though *he* made the portfolio happen – as she damn well knows. He can't help thinking she's withholding that praise intentionally. Because she hates him. Enjoys pricking his ego in person, and maybe also in neatly printed block letters.

Charlie turns and walks briskly up the stairs, giving him nothing but her beautiful behind.

When he's certain she's gone, he smashes his fist into the table beside him and stands there, breathing heavily, holding his throbbing hand, until the anger fades. Depleted, he gathers his belongings.

He finally lights a cigarette when he steps outside, and stands smoking it under the awning. His is the only car left in the lot. The nicotine doesn't calm him like he thought it would; he starts staring around at still and moving shadows, at the swaying tops of trees. He feels nervous and observed. He's been so focused on Charlie tonight, but what if there's someone far more dangerous out there now, watching him? Judith's killer must be aware of the *Harper's* feature; he may have even read or watched Paul's interviews. If he has, he knows Paul was here that night and could have heard something, seen something. And Paul is easy to find. Especially easy to find in this dark parking lot. He takes one final inhale before crushing the cigarette beneath his heel and walking quickly to his car. As he fumbles for his keys, he senses a presence just behind him. He whirls around as he opens the car door, seeing nothing, no one there. Only the darkened school entrance and the bushes around it, slightly stirring like the trees.

He gets in the car, tosses his bags beside him, and forces himself to sit there with the doors unlocked and his window down while he lights another cigarette. Why in god's name would Judith's killer come after him? If he'd been useful to the police, they would have caught the guy already. Paul isn't thinking clearly. He blames Charlie for rattling his confidence the way she did. If she'd just given him *one word* of praise or thanks or congratulation, he wouldn't have walked out feeling twitchy. But she couldn't spare it, could she? She had to make it all about Judith. If Charlie *is* the one writing to him, it's because she's eager to puncture the bubble of his success. She thinks he deserves to have it punctured. Well, he won't let her. He's been handing her the power to harass him, when he's the powerful one. The *someone*. He starts his engine, revs it, and goes peeling out of the parking lot.

25

He tosses the latest batch of letters onto his dining table, tells himself not to mess with them, then starts picking through them anyway. He needs a hit of something nice, something to lift him up after dealing with Charlie's ugly silence and the paranoia that overtook him back in the parking lot.

He zeroes in on a promising-looking one. The handwriting on the envelope, all elegant loops and curves, tells him it's from a woman, one as sane and orderly as his own mother, whose handwriting resembled this. The letter starts promisingly enough; Farrah from Minnesota calls Judith 'a visionary who made [her] feel seen.' Fine, good. But then she goes on to lament Judith's death in a long, winding paragraph, and closes without mentioning Paul at all. His absence is central, slighting – a replay of what happened in the classroom. He crumples the letter and envelope viciously in one hand and drops them in the trash.

So long, Farrah from Minnesota.

One more, he tells himself. Catherine of Chicago is just as impassioned as Farrah was – or more – and while she does thank Paul briefly for his work, she spends several paragraphs detailing her responses to each of the twenty photographs from the feature. She's an amateur photographer herself, she notes, and discusses the originality of the angles, the perspectives, and the use of light – as if Paul needed a lesson in the merits of Judith's work. At the very end, she asks Paul if he would look at her photographs, which she will 'happily send.' He laughs out loud. It's not the first of these solicitations he's received, though it's phrased more eloquently than most. He's flattered and pleased by this sign of his new prominence, but not enough to do more than send Catherine's letter floating to the floor. He sighs and eyes the significant pile. One more? Then he can give it a rest. He shuffles through and finds a neatly typewritten envelope addressed to 'Mr Paul Sorenson.' He likes the touch of respect. Appreciates it. There's no return address, which strikes him as a bit at odds with the rest of the envelope's formality, but he tells himself it doesn't matter. This one will be good, it will give him what he wants. What he deserves.

Dear Mr Sorenson,

I find it absolutely unbearable that a draft dodger like yourself would be the man to profit by Judith Stanley's work. I feel sorry for the woman herself and for her family, who may or may not know the truth about you. If I had the power to expose you for what you are, I would. Alas, I only have the power of sending these private words. I admire Ms. Stanley's photographs greatly and only wish they were in the hands of someone with a real sense of duty, honor, and integrity. I'm certain you'll go on profiting from her work in many ways, and I want you to know that if I could do anything to stop it, I would.

Sincerely,
David

A man who didn't even have the 'honor and integrity' to sign off with his last name, or include his return address, accusing Paul of being a draft dodger – when Paul was too old for the damn draft! Paul snorts and rips the letter right in half. Then he grabs up the whole pile and nearly strides into the kitchen to light it on fire in the sink but stops himself before getting there –

it will make a mess, he'll set off the fire alarm, it's too cold to go out on his fire escape and do it in a metal trash can out there… He throws the letters back on the hall table. Some of them slide to the floor, and since Paul can't stand disarray, he scoops them up and stacks them neatly, his stomach churning violently the whole time.

He wanted something, needed it, and didn't get it. But why was he looking for what he needed in the damn letters anyway? Or from someone like Charlie? Or *anyone*? It was just a craving he'd given in to – a craving for affirmation, a sense that he was good and what he'd done was right. But no outside voice will give him that; he resolves not to read any more unless he wants pure entertainment and has absolutely nothing better to do. He finds an empty cardboard box and dumps all the letters – even the opened, threatening ones – into it. Neither threats nor compliments matter; he won't let them distract him anymore. He has a catalog introduction to write, and a job at Doven Gallery. He will no longer let the insignificant insults of angry girls, women, or men have any impact on his upwardly mobile life. In the end, he's still winning.

26

PAUL IS SO IN THE flow of writing the next morning that when the telephone rings he lets it go for a while, hearing the sound but not responding until he thinks, *Jahan. It could be Jahan.* It's 11 am and the gallery is open; Jahan might have a question, or he might be checking in. Paul strides over to the armchair and grabs the receiver.

'Hello?' he says. Silence on the other end.

'Hello? Jahan?' he says, as if Jahan would call and say nothing. Paul listens deeply, pressing the telephone against his ear, and begins to hear the sound of light breathing. It reminds him of standing alone in the parking lot last night, straining his eyes for some solid threat he could sense but not see. He felt foolish and scared; he refuses to feel the same way in his own living room, and from something as trifling as a late morning phone call. But he does think of Judith – of what she endured. Calls like this – but worse – as her stalker pressed closer, boding bad things to come. Paul swallows.

'Hello? Anyone there? I'm hanging up,' he says firmly, but he doesn't, and the hand pressing the receiver to his ear shakes slightly. He listens hard, trying to discern if the breathing he hears is male or female. He thinks… female, but how can he possibly tell? He's thinking of Charlie, that's why, however incongruous it is to imagine a girl like her sitting at home alone, playing around with prank calls. He can see her penning a cruel letter or two more easily than he can imagine her doing this.

'Hey. You need to cut this shit out,' he says at last, hearing a little gasp, or intake of breath – or was it a swallowed laugh? Paul slams the receiver down and stares at the phone, waiting for it to ring again. It doesn't.

As the minutes pass, Paul stands smoking at the window, turning to stare at the telephone more often than he'd like. He wants another chance with the caller – maybe it *was* Charlie? Maybe she and her friends were grouped around the phone, listening to Paul panic and curse, when one of them let a single syllable of laughter escape. He can see it: those gorgeous girls from class sitting cross-legged on a shaggy bedroom carpet, pressing their heads together to hear, pressing their hands to their mouths, eyes bulging with merriment. Charlie wouldn't do it alone, but she might do it with friends. And she would be the leader, the one passionate enough about Judith's work to fuck with him. The others were just –

The telephone rings.

'Hello,' Paul says brusquely. There's a pause; Paul can hear muffled background noise, but no laughter. The noise of a busy workplace carrying on beyond a closed door. He's instantly relieved.

'Professor Paul Sorenson?'

'Yes, speaking.'

'This is Detective Grant Schuyler of the Harrington Police Department. We questioned you not long ago in relation to the Judith Stanley murder?'

Paul's relief vanishes; his stomach twists. 'Y-yes,' Paul stammers. As if he could forget the small gray interrogation room where they held him after Judith's death. Not *held* him, really, but it felt as if he were being held. He was so nervous he thought he might crap his pants at any moment, and everything he said sounded suspicious even to his own ears. But this isn't the officer who questioned him. He can't remember that officer's name, but he remembers the voice: higher pitched than this

Detective Schuyler's. He's somewhat relieved that it's a different person. But why should he be?

'As you probably know, the case remains unsolved.' Paul tries to say yes, but it comes out a flippant-sounding *Yeah*. 'Well, I've taken over, and I'm starting from scratch. Reviewing suspects, paperwork, photographs, everything. Looking at some new angles here, too, and I'd appreciate you coming by the station this week to answer some questions.'

Paul swallows. *New angles*. What 'new angles' might those be? Did Schuyler learn of Paul's near-arrest for grocery store theft and think it worthwhile to reconsider 'the professor' as a suspect again? But there was no record of the near-arrest, because it wasn't a *full* arrest; he doubts the officer would remember his name. He doesn't remember the officer's – and it certainly wasn't Schuyler. All he remembers is *Harvey* – the ridiculous, red-faced manager who chased him out of the store.

'Of course, Detective. I'd be happy to come by,' Paul says, trying to sound relaxed, though he's grateful the detective can't see how hard he's gripping the receiver. 'How's tomorrow morning?'

'Excellent. Nine thirty all right with you?'

'Yes, that's fine,' Paul says, because what else can he say? When they hang up, Paul reaches for a nearby glass. It hasn't been washed, but it will have to do. He pours whiskey in it almost to the rim and swallows it in two gulps. It doesn't even begin to help, at least not immediately.

What the hell? Schuyler didn't sound like he was winding up for an interrogation, but you never could tell. He might have played it like that on the phone, sounding polite and mild, but then Paul could arrive at the station tomorrow and find himself in handcuffs.

You didn't kill her, though, Paul reminds himself with surprised relief; the call briefly made him forget his own innocence – not that innocence always matters. He wonders if

Tom Stanley has anything to do with this – but Tom distrusts the Harrington PD more than he does Paul. It's possible the detective saw the *Harper's* issue or one of Paul's interviews and thought, *Here's a man who's profiting nicely from Judith Stanley's death*, and thought to bring him in. Or what if his harasser sent one of her pithy anonymous notes? *You should take another look at Paul Sorenson, that vile worm.* He directs a surge of helpless rage at Charlie and latches on to her image as he sits, mind and stomach roiling, staring toward the table where he sat not long ago, peacefully working on his catalog introduction.

27

At the station, Paul is led straight to Schuyler's office – not to an interrogation room. He takes this as a good sign until he meets the detective's penetrating gaze and suffers his brief but crushing handshake. If he'd faced Schuyler right after Judith's death, he might have confessed despite his innocence. He only hopes the man can't hear his rabbity heartbeat in the small, closed room.

But not an interrogation room, Paul reminds himself. *An office. It's just an office.*

His first impulse on sitting down is to reach for a cigarette. But there's no ashtray, and no sign of the comforting cloud of smoke that hangs over the rest of the station. It adds to his unease, but he holds off from pulling out his pack. Tries to focus all his attention on looking the detective squarely in his gray-green eyes.

Schuyler opens a file, takes out a yellowed paper, and slides it across the desk.

Not what Paul expected – an old newspaper article?

'Have you seen this?' he asks. Paul shakes his head as he studies it: an article from the *Somerset Daily Register*, from June 1934. 'Local Girl Attacked by Afternoon Intruder.' Ancient history. Below the title, there's a picture of a young, unsmiling girl. Her head slightly tilted, her shoulder-length hair neatly curled.

A high school portrait, Paul notices first.

Judith, he notices next. Judith is the 'local girl.'

He looks up at Schuyler, who doesn't speak. Paul reads the article, learning how Judith, sixteen, was attacked in her home. She was making herself an after-school snack when the screen door opened and shut behind her. A large, middle-aged man strode in, grabbed her, and pushed her to the floor. He pinned her down with his heavy body and told her he'd kill her if she struggled, so she lay still. Then he *touched her inappropriately*, the article says, and afterward *harmed and disfigured her*. Harmed and disfigured her… chilling in its vagueness. Paul feels disgusted but curious, too – where and how did he disfigure her? He saw no sign of disfigurement, though he only ever saw Judith's face, neck, and hands. Does the detective know? He looks up again to find the man watching him, gauging his reaction.

'This is shocking. Terrible,' Paul says, hoping to sound sincere because he *is* sincere, but it's hard with the detective's gaze boring into him, judging him. 'Where did you – how did you find this?'

'In a locked file cabinet of hers, down in the darkroom. Mixed in with bills, medical records, that kind of thing.' Paul remembers seeing the file cabinet and asking Tom about it; he remembers, too, Tom's halting response.

'Did Tom know about this?' he asks, gesturing toward the paper.

The detective shakes his head. 'Not until I showed him. He seemed genuinely shocked.' Paul nods, taking this in. He is and isn't surprised that Judith hid this from Tom. He is, because they were married for so long; he isn't, because he could see Judith stuffing this away, trying to keep it from tainting her wholesome family life. But how could she have hidden her 'disfigurement' – wherever it was? She must have lied about it to Tom.

'Does that track?' Schuyler asks. Paul looks at him, confused. 'Does it make sense to you she would have kept this from her husband?'

'It does,' Paul says. 'She was extremely private, you know.'

'But this was her husband. You think they had a good marriage?' Schuyler asks, lightly enough, but Paul knows he's being asked a serious question – one whose answer could have serious consequences for Tom, the former prime suspect. Is he back at the top of their list? Paul thinks it's highly unlikely that Tom is the killer, but his answer could nudge Schuyler away from suspecting Paul himself. And if Tom were the focus of the murder investigation again, he wouldn't have time to deliver on any of his various threats to Paul's – Judith's show.

'I don't really know,' Paul says, not wanting to overplay it. 'I think so? They seemed – well, it was a long marriage, wasn't it? I never saw them together, and I've only met Tom a few times, but I can't imagine he'd be the type of man who'd appreciate knowing… *that* about his wife. I can see why she might hide it from him, or even be afraid he'd find out someday,' he said, shrugging as he delivers this suggestive last line.

'It's sad, and strange, isn't it?' Schuyler asks, and Paul thinks, at first, he means the state of their marriage. He's about to agree when Schuyler goes on. 'To go through something like this as a kid, and then to go through a similar experience *again*, some thirty years later.'

'And die,' Paul adds, then clears his throat. Why did he mention her dying? But Schuyler doesn't seem to hear; his eyes are fixed on a spot to the right of Paul, who sits wondering over the sudden change of topic. What happened to Schuyler's interest in Tom?

'Yes,' Schuyler says finally. 'And die at the hands of yet another unidentifiable attacker who vanishes into thin air. They never caught the first assailant, either.' Schuyler folds his arms over his chest and keeps gazing into the distance.

'Could it be the same man?'

'He'd be old.'

'It *is* possible, though.'

Schuyler shrugs. 'I suppose.' Paul, relieved not to be Schuyler's focal point, warms to the idea of the two of them sitting here, batting ideas back and forth. But he does wonder where the man is heading. Schuyler leans forward then, steepling his fingers, and stares at Paul as if scouring him, measuring him up, making a decision.

'The thing is, there was only one set of fingerprints on the knife found at the scene in the parking lot: Judith's.' Paul nods solemnly; he read that in the newspaper. He didn't find it strange. He figured the killer must have been careful and worn gloves. He waits for Schuyler to say something to that effect, but the man sighs and squints through the glass wall of his office, still weighing his words.

'Look, there are details I can't divulge, but I will say it's a – it's a strange case. Made even stranger by this background information,' he adds, nodding toward the old article still in front of Paul. 'So, as you know, I wanted to ask you a few questions. We got a bit sidetracked here, but I needed you to know the context, if you weren't already aware.'

'I was not,' Paul says, wanting to reiterate his ignorance. Paul swallows dryly, longs again for a cigarette. Finally asks if he can smoke.

'Sorry.' The detective offers a wan smile, the first sign of vulnerable humanity Paul has seen. 'My wife made me quit last year and I've stuck to it. I can't have anyone smoking in here or I'll pick it up again. Dying to, by the way. But she says it's bad for my health.' He chuckles at this funny notion of his wife's, and Paul tries his best to chuckle along.

'What was your relationship like with Judith?' Schuyler asks, his gray-green eyes fixed again on Paul. Paul tries not to show his sudden alarm at this shift in topic – to his *relationship* with Judith. Did Schuyler emphasize the word, or was it his imagination? He wonders, too, if it was all a ruse, that story of Schuyler's wife. Maybe he uses nicotine deprivation to make his suspects squirm. Paul struggles to master himself. To be still. To remember how the two of them were bantering just now, and how interested Schuyler has been in *Tom*, not in him.

'Um, it was good. I was sort of her mentor. You know, encouraged the photographs she was taking. They were incredibly good.'

'Yeah, I saw them in the magazine. *Harper's*, right? You were responsible for that, weren't you?' He makes it sound like a crime.

'Yes,' Paul says, swallowing. 'And next up is the Doven Gallery show. Should be a pretty big deal. Judith told me – she asked for my help publishing her work just before she died – so I did what I could.' He regrets speaking, but Schuyler's silent stare pushes him on. 'I just want as many people as possible to see her work. She had real talent...' he says, letting his words trail off. He waits anxiously for Schuyler's follow-up questions, sounding in his mind just like his harasser's: *Are you a fucking parasite? Did you kill her, Paul?*

But Schuyler only nods distractedly, as if Paul has said nothing of consequence.

'Was she – happy when you knew her? How did she seem in class?'

'She seemed... perfectly fine, but looking back, she couldn't have been, could she? While being stalked, harassed. She was like that, though – reserved, very private, as I said.'

Schuyler nods in his distracted way. Paul lets himself relax again. The man doesn't seem interested in *him*, but he still can't tell where his interest lies. He doesn't understand these odd questions or why he's chosen to share the news article about her early attacker. Is there new evidence of some kind? Schuyler's next question is another surprise.

'Professor, do you think a person's photographs can reveal their state of mind?'

'Absolutely.' Paul nods energetically, slipping right into professor mode. He's glad to find himself on solid ground. 'They can reveal the photographer's background, his perspective on life, his hopes and fears – and yes, his state of mind, too. Or hers,' he adds, giving Schuyler a significant look.

'So you see all of that in Judith's work?'

'I do. All that and more. In fact, now that you've told me about what happened to her… early on, I can see evidence of it in the work. Of her psychological scars, I mean. You must have seen her self-portraits, Detective?' Schuyler nods. 'They're quite something, aren't they?' Paul asks, like a proud father.

'They are. They're – disturbing.'

'I agree. And even more so now. I can see how those shots of her own face in shop windows, water, and mirrors must have helped her… plumb her own depths. But in a safe way. A way that kept her from looking too directly at them. What she didn't want to see, the mirror saw for her, the pond saw for her, and so on. I can understand now why she was so private about her photographs, why she didn't want to publish them – until she finally did,' he says, catching himself. He twists his empty hands in his lap and longs for a damn cigarette. He wouldn't have slipped like that if he'd had a cigarette.

'Why do you think she changed her mind?'

'I don't really know. Maybe because I'd asked her so many times that she finally gave in just to shut me up,' he says, grasping for levity. Schuyler doesn't laugh.

'I was struck by the picture in the butcher shop window.'

Paul nods, preparing himself to lecture on the striking photograph *Harper's* chose as the cover for their issue, but Schuyler continues.

'It's odd, isn't it? To take a picture of yourself with all those hanging sides of beef, and then a few days later, you end up dead? It seems…' He searches for the word, looking at Paul.

'Tragic?' Paul offers.

'No. Purposeful,' he says bluntly. 'Meaningful. You know, we studied those photographs – and the negatives, too – for any sign of her stalker. The first team did it, and now I've done it, too. She told her husband the man was in there, in *every* picture she took of herself. And we didn't see a thing. Don't you find that strange?' Schuyler's favorite word. This time, though, it rings in Paul's ears. *Strange.* It's *very* strange. Just as Paul catches Schuyler's meaning, the revelation ringing like a bell in his head, the man abruptly stands and extends his hand. As if he wants to stop him from saying it aloud.

'Thank you for coming by, Professor. It's been very helpful.' Paul can do nothing but extend his own hand and let the man crush it.

A few minutes later, he's outside the station gulping cold, fresh air. He's able to light a cigarette – at last, and just barely – with his trembling hand. *They think she did it herself,* he thinks, over and over, without any sense behind the words. *My god, she did it herself.*

28

Schuyler didn't come out and say it, of course, but it's what he was insinuating: that Judith was mentally ill, that she invented the stalking story, that she… *killed herself.*

Stunned by the phrase, Paul forgets to exhale a chest full of smoke and bends over, coughing. A woman wearing an unfashionably long skirt walks a wide circle around him; he focuses on the black leather of her low heels, the reassuring sound of an ordinary woman walking. When he recovers, he straightens and looks around at the small, orderly houses lining the streets. They all resemble Judith's house: small brick ranches with tidy lawns. He thinks of Judith in this destabilizing new light with a deep, physical pang, and begins putting one foot in front of another.

Loosened a little by the forward movement, Paul asks himself if what he's thinking – what he thinks Schuyler is thinking – could really be true.

Having known her – calm, steady, and quiet as she was – he can't see the detective's idea as anything but outlandish, even offensive. But he felt it, didn't he? Felt the truth of it in that stifling small office? And beyond that, there was evidence – or a *lack* of it, rather: no stalker in Judith's portraits, no fingerprints on the murder weapon, no sign of her attacker anywhere. And now he knows how psychologically scarred she must have been – and he himself has offered photographic proof of her troubled mind. Schuyler let the various strands of this theory hang separately, but Paul gathers them together quickly and hangs on, despite his own revulsion and resistance: *Judith did this to herself.*

It only makes sense, he thinks, walking now at a furious pace, if Judith's mind were warped enough to make her *believe* she was being stalked, to see the man over and over again, to hear his words, even feel his touch. Was that possible? And most of all, could her mind have really brought her to the point of stabbing herself? Killing herself? He thinks instantly of Malcolm, his psychologist friend. They haven't met up for a while, but he could buy him a drink and run it by him – in strictest confidence.

My god, if it were true… it would be a stunning draw for the show. He flinches from the thought at first, but as the seconds go by, he begins to understand why it might be not only beneficial but also *necessary*. This is part of Judith's story, after all: Judith the artist, the photographer, the public figure. Posthumously, sure, but that's all the more reason for Paul to broadcast what he's learned. The story of her life doesn't belong to him, or even to Judith anymore. And certainly not to Tom Stanley. All of it, all of *her*, belongs to the viewing public: art critics, gallerists, and Judith's growing cadre of fans. Even fans like Charlie, yes, he thinks with an internal flinch. They need to approach her work and view it with the full story in mind; it will change how they perceive and critique it, how they place it in the scope of art history. This has nothing to do with Paul, really! He's merely the vessel, the mediator, bringing it all to light for the public good. He has a duty to do it, as her mentor and manager.

Paul loops back to his car with a determined stride. Tomorrow, he'll visit the library to search for the *Somerset Daily Register* article; he wants to be able to refer to its specifics while he's writing. Because even if he ends up discarding the suicide theory, he *has* to use her childhood attack. That alone would alter the narrative around Judith: the woman who survived one attack only to die, years later, in another. He'll also read any follow-up articles he can find, about the search for her attacker.

Schuyler said the man had 'vanished,' just like Judith's murderer; Paul wants to make sure that's the case, and he wants to glean anything else he can from Judith's hometown rag. Then he'll run it all by Malcolm. He veers toward the nearest pay phone booth to make his call. He reaches Malcolm's secretary and leaves a message that reads: *Please call Paul Sorenson. It's urgent.*

29

MALCOLM IS ALREADY SEATED AT the bar, foamy mug of beer before him, when Paul arrives a half hour late to the King's End. He's spent all day in the basement of the main library, scrolling through rolls of microfiche until his head was pounding. It paid off, though; he found the original article and several follow-ups about the fruitless search for Judith's assailant. Seeing them made Schuyler's story come alive: it really did happen, and though the articles were written with standard neutrality, Judith's suffering vibrated through the words. What she must have endured in the aftermath, with minimal comfort from her withholding grandmother, who's quoted tersely in one of the articles as saying, 'It's a shame.' What an odd phrase to use about your granddaughter's molestation: *It's a shame*. As if it were a slight accident, or as if Judith were somehow to blame. Paul starts to think it *must* be true – that this formative incident, probably long smothered, simmered in Judith until it spilled over, flooding her vulnerable psyche. He doesn't have the right words or means to express it – that's why he's come to Malcolm – but he senses he's right.

Paul claps Malcolm on the back and sits beside him, simply relishing the pleasure of reuniting with an old friend for a moment. So much has changed in his own life since he last saw Malcolm that it's almost like seeing a ghost – or perhaps *Paul* is the ghost, a new iteration of himself living a surreal new life. Even watching Kent, the bartender, pour two fingers of whiskey over rocks and slide the glass toward him with a nod is slightly disorienting. But the first burning sip sets him right, brings him back to his body and the present and his purpose.

'How you been, Malc? How's things?' he asks.

'Can't complain, I guess,' Malcolm says, baring his straight white teeth when he smiles. Paul knows it's an understatement: Malcolm's fit, handsome, and married to a gorgeous girl. He has a thriving psychology practice in Midtown, too, and Paul has always envied him as much as he's liked him. But things are different now. Paul has been released from his former envy, all thanks to Judith Stanley. *Thanks to Judith Stanley's death*, he corrects, before batting the thought away.

'How's your fancy art show going? Saw the piece in *Harper's*. You're moving on up, buddy,' Malcolm says, grinning. Paul grins back.

'Hardly. But yeah, it's exciting. I mean – Judith, my student, should be here to see it. The glory is all hers – but yeah, it's still gratifying.'

'Think you'll make some big bucks?' Paul laughs uncomfortably and doesn't respond. He shrugs it off, the way he's tried to shrug off those nagging words: *fucking parasite*. Does Malcolm think the same of him? No. He can see from Malcolm's face that he's happy for him – maybe too happy, in fact. *Thank god Paul has gone and done something, at last*. It irks him so he plays it up, tells Malcolm that yes, 'big bucks' might be in order, even though his 30 percent is purely imaginary right now, except for the *Harper's* check that has yet to arrive. The show will have to succeed, and people will have to buy a lot of Judith's prints for any whiff of 'big bucks.' But he keeps that to himself for now.

The two men catch up for a while longer, but when they signal the bartender for their second round and light fresh cigarettes, Paul's impatience gets the best of him. He clears his throat.

'Listen, Malc, I have something to ask you. As a – you know, a shrink, not a friend. In strictest confidence.' Malcolm raises two fingers in the air in a mock Boy Scout pledge. 'It's about Judith Stanley.'

'What about her?'

'Well, it turns out she experienced something traumatic as a teenager, then stuffed it under the rug –'

'Was she raped?' Malcolm asks bluntly.

'Uh, maybe.' Paul is taken aback. But he reminds himself that hearing of rape must be commonplace in Malcolm's line of work. 'Something like that. Look, it's easier if I just show you the article.' He unfolds the copy he got from the library and hands it to Malcolm, eyes darting around the bar as if someone might be spying. He knows it's comical to suspect his fellow bar patrons, some of whom he's known for years, of being the least bit interested in this conversation, but that doesn't stop him from feeling ill at ease.

'This is in strictest confidence right now, of course,' Paul repeats nervously, unnecessarily. His friend nods, still immersed in his reading, then shakes his head when he's done and looks up, handing the article back.

'Could you see the scars?' he asks.

'No. No clue… how he disfigured her. Or where.'

'It's all very sad,' Malcolm says after a long drink of beer. 'And I'm guessing she didn't visit a psychiatrist after this happened, back in 1934?' Paul shrugs but says he assumes she didn't. He clears his throat.

'Is it possible this experience could have made her… see things, imagine things, later in life?' His face reddens just the way it did with Detective Schuyler, as if he were guilty of something. Malcolm stays in pure professional mode, though, looking thoughtful.

'Are you asking if it's possible she made up the stalker story?'

'I am,' Paul says, giving a quick nod. Malcolm gives a long, low whistle under his breath.

'Who killed her, then? The husband?' Paul doesn't answer. He stares at Malcolm until he gets it, which doesn't take long.

'Jesus. You think she did it herself. Stabbed herself.'

It isn't a question. Paul shivers to hear Malcolm say it – to hear it spoken aloud, made a part of the world. Even if it's only the cloistered, muggy world of King's End Tavern.

'I went to the station yesterday and talked to the new lead detective. He said he had questions for me, and I thought I might be a suspect again,' Paul says, trying to chuckle lightly, as if it didn't rattle him. 'But then he showed me this article and started asking me questions – about Judith's mental state, about how I perceived the psychological content of her photographs. He emphasized the lack of evidence they had, too. He never said it aloud, and I didn't put it all together until I'd left, really – then it shocked the hell out of me. I thought it was bullshit at first – I *knew* Judith, you know? – but then I kept turning it over in my mind, seeing how it made sense in a fucked-up way. If it were even possible, probable. That's where you come in.' Malcolm nods, looking deadly serious.

The two men stub their cigarettes out in the ashtray at the same time. Paul immediately lights another to steady himself as Malcolm asks questions.

'Did you ever see any sign of it in the way she acted? What was she like in class?'

'Normal. Perfectly friendly, but reserved. She was a deeply private person.'

'Not anymore,' Malcolm says, lifting his eyebrows and giving Paul a brisk stab of guilt.

'Hey, I'm carrying out a last wish. She wanted me to publish those pictures,' he says convincingly, through the bitter taste in his mouth. Malcolm says he understands.

'Look, repressed trauma can really come back to haunt you – even years later. If the police – and you – are right, it sounds like she could have had something called dissociative identity disorder,' Malcolm explains.

'If she did, would she have known what she was doing? The Judith I knew wouldn't have done this intentionally. I didn't know her *that* well, but I do know that much.'

'Technically no, she wouldn't have. But there's a lot of controversy about this. About dissociative episodes. About dissociative identity disorder in general. Some practitioners in my field dismiss it entirely. I don't. I think it's possible that her past trauma could have triggered out-of-body experiences or hallucinations. Strong ones. But why *then*, why that particular moment in her life?' he wonders out loud, turning his nearly empty glass on its coaster. 'Did anything happen in her life that might have triggered them?'

'No clue,' Paul says. He regrets not having more access to Tom now, probably the only person who could answer Malcolm's question. But it's moot; Tom has closed and locked the door against him. Paul might even have exhausted Junior's patience by now.

'I'm guessing something did – a recent incident, a shock, a loss. Look, I don't really know, but what I've learned most after years of study and practice is that… anything is possible, and mental illness is highly subjective. An experience like the one she had as a teenager could have affected someone else entirely differently. Especially if they had treatment for it, had a supportive family, and so on.' Paul takes this in, finishes his cigarette with a deep drag, and stubs it out.

'Does the family know?' Malcolm asks.

'About this – theory? No. I don't think so. And the husband just learned about this past incident when the detective showed him the same article. She hadn't told him, it seems.'

'Wow, she really was… private.' Paul nods, recalling Malcolm's sharp-edged *Not anymore*. There's an uneasy silence between them. Then Malcolm asks, 'So, what's the plan? Is this just for your own curiosity?' He sounds hopeful.

'Well, I have to write this catalog introduction for the show, and I'm sure I'll be doing interviews. I feel like – I think I have a duty to share this with the public,' Paul says. 'To give them background to the work, you know? They'll understand the pictures better if they know what she was going through.' When he thought this all out the day before, on his walk, it felt lofty and righteous. Now it sounds craven. Malcolm stares at him for a long moment.

'I think you mean it will pack the room and sell pictures, right? I mean, I get it, I know you want the show to succeed, but you don't have the right to share someone's *possible* psychological condition. What would her husband think?'

'Well, he'd hate it. He's going to despise me even more than he already does,' Paul says, giving a bitter chuckle. He tells Malcolm about Tom's hostility toward him and how he knows Tom would never, ever accept this theory as the truth. And how enraged he'll be if it comes out.

'So it's simple, then: leave it out, leave it alone,' Malcolm says, waving his hand as if giving an order.

'I don't really want to,' Paul says, heating up. 'I don't think I can. And when I tell Jahan – the gallery owner – I know he'll want me to use it. It's –'

'Don't tell him, then,' Malcolm says gruffly. He's looking at Paul with real disgust now.

'I *will* tell him,' Paul says, defiant. 'Besides, like I said, I feel I have a responsibility to tell the truth.'

Malcolm scoffs. 'You don't *know* the truth, Paul. I don't either. It's all just speculation. It's not like you have solid evidence. What I've said doesn't amount to a diagnosis.'

'I don't need solid evidence – I don't need your diagnosis, either. I'm not a cop or a judge. I'm the curator of an *art show.* My only concern is taking care of my show. Judith's show. Like you said yourself.'

Malcolm swallows the last of his beer and stands. 'Well, count me out. Forget what I said about dissociative disorder and trauma-induced hallucinations. And for god's sake don't quote me. I don't want anything to do with this.'

With that, Malcolm leaves him, dropping a few bills on the bar. He doesn't shake Paul's hand or wish him well or even say goodbye. Paul leans heavily into the bar, feeling soiled and gravely alone. He catches sight of himself in the mirror behind the rows of liquor bottles and winces at his asymmetrical features, the slight droop to his right eyelid, his beaky nose. His own ugliness startles him, confuses him. Hasn't he always been handsome? He tries to smile, to make it right, and fails. He looks queasy and his features stay unbalanced, malformed.

'I'll have another,' he tells Kent. 'A double this time.'

30

PAUL WAKES EARLY TO GRAY morning light, an upset stomach, and a pounding head. He stayed at the bar until 1 am, pouring liquor over the sting of Malcolm's self-righteousness. But Paul had gotten what he needed from Malcolm, hadn't he? Blinking awake in pain, he remembers that, clings to it. He can go to Jahan now with a newly compelling story about Judith's death, one that should, yes, *pack the room and sell pictures*. But it will also enhance the experience for Judith's viewers. He wasn't wrong when he said that – Malcolm was just too stubborn to hear. He stares carefully in the bathroom mirror after rinsing his face and trimming his beard. Better now, isn't it? Better than the man he saw reflected back at him in the bar mirror last night. More human, more civilized. This version of himself could debate Malcolm winningly – but the moment for that has passed, and Paul tells himself it doesn't matter, he doesn't care.

At Doven, Jahan welcomes him warmly. Paul never tires of this happy welcome, of Jahan treating him like *someone important*. But today it unsettles him. Will Jahan view him the way Malcolm did, as a craven opportunist? He could always invent some other reason for coming in, but he finds it's impossible; the story he came to tell fills his brain, fizzes his nerves, demands to spill out. And it's important. Paul takes a seat across from Jahan and gives a wobbly smile.

'Is everything all right? Introduction coming along?' Jahan asks with a touch of anxiety.

'Oh, I've made great progress,' Paul says, relieved to tell an easy lie. It loosens him up like loosening a necktie. He begins to see a path forward, a way to play this conversation more wisely. He leans on his side of the desk and clasps his hands, warming to his task now.

'I came because I have to share something with you. Something – sensitive.' At this, Jahan hops up to close the door. When he sits again, Paul looks him in the eye.

'Judith may have killed herself.'

Jahan's face falls in shock. He listens intently as Paul tells him everything, beginning with his trip to the Harrington PD. He details Detective Schuyler's leading questions, his own realization of what Schuyler was intimating, and the talk he had with a 'respected psychiatrist friend' who confirmed the detective's theory as valid and even offered a diagnosis.

'My friend thinks she had dissociative identity disorder, or something like it,' Paul says, and Jahan nods as if he's heard of it. Malcolm would be horrified, of course, but it's not as if he's made the diagnosis public – yet. 'I couldn't sit with this by myself any longer. I had to run it by you, had to get it out.' *Like a confessional*, Paul thinks. Like a man who's come to his priest for spiritual relief and has no intention of spreading the word outside of this closed circuit.

Jahan nods again, then sits staring at a spot on the wall to the left of a towering stack of art books, papers, and manila folders. *How has the man accomplished so much in such an overwhelmed office?* Paul wonders idly. It's relaxing to think of something entirely unrelated to himself or Judith or to how Jahan might react to his 'confession.'

Finally, Jahan shakes his head sadly and looks again at Paul, but with a gleam in his eye.

'Poor woman. She did this to herself? Invented it somehow? And believed it, too.'

'It certainly seems that way. I had a hard time accepting it –

but the more I learned, the likelier it seemed. And the likelier it seemed, the more disturbed I was.'

'Well, it's terrible. Truly terrible. Almost worse than having a stalker in the flesh. She must have been very ill. And you say her husband didn't know?'

'He did not. And I don't think he would accept this diagnosis or the idea of Judith committing suicide… if it ever came out,' Paul adds, carefully watching Jahan's face.

'Hmm. Well, as sad and horrifying as this is, and as much as I hate to say it… this could mark an opportunity for us, and for the show. For Judith herself. For the legacy of her work.'

Paul tilts his head as if he doesn't entirely understand what Jahan means.

'Paul, I know it's a bit… delicate, but I think we should share this revelation – carefully and with qualifications, of course. Our press release has already generated excitement, but this? Something like this could absolutely *ignite* the show.'

There. Jahan has done it, given him a directive, couched in that comforting use of the collective pronoun. Maybe Paul will be the spokesman – his head on the proverbial chopping block for the Stanleys, the Malcolms, and the avid fans, but he'll have the weight of the gallery and Jahan's impeccable status behind him. *We* decided to release this story. *We* felt it was a necessary addition to provide context for Judith's work.

When Paul feigns hesitation, Jahan leans forward over his desk, looks Paul in the eye.

'I never knew Judith in real life, but, looking at her pictures, I believe she would have wanted this. She would have wanted her viewers to know the truth, don't you think so?' Paul gives a slight nod and shrugs. 'She's an artist who fearlessly plumbed the depths and revealed stark truths. Isn't that how you'd describe her?'

'Absolutely. But she was a private person, Jahan, I don't know…'

'She isn't a private person anymore. She asked for your help with publication and you gave it. She has since become a public figure, and is about to become an even *larger* public figure. And she is – gone. There's no help for it.' It's a comfort to hear Jahan voice the rationalizations that Paul has told himself many times, even if one is a half-truth at best.

'I want to do right by her,' Paul says softly. 'And if you think this is the best way – the best way to be fully honest with the public, to give them the full picture, then… I'm on board, whatever it will cost me.'

Jahan claps him on the back, grinning from ear to ear.

'It won't cost you anything, my friend. If you're worried about Mr Stanley, he signed a contract, didn't he? Handed over her work to you. He can make a fuss – it will only add to the attention, honestly – but I have a *very* good team of lawyers. Very, very good. You'll be protected, Paul.'

Paul thinks of Jahan's beautifully groomed, suited lawyers encircling him. Protecting him. Shielding him from the worst possible outcomes of the world. He's become one of those people at last: The safe, exalted ones. The ones with teams who whisk danger away. The notion fills his stomach with warmth and his eyes with tears. He has to look away quickly to hide it – though he supposes this show of emotion only enhances his performance of hesitation and gratitude. Jahan leans toward him.

'Paul, you'll be doing a great service. You'll bring a more sensitive, multidimensional portrait of Judith Stanley to light. The truth about her life – and death – will make her photographs even more resonant with viewers. They'll see her complex, flawed humanity, something every single person on the planet can relate to.'

Paul nods along, feigning a growing enthusiasm. He remembers making this same argument with Malcolm, who swiped it away. Spat on it, essentially. Malcolm could have profited by this, too, Paul thinks, appearing with him on television and radio as the 'psychological expert' in Judith Stanley's case. But he lost his chance, and Paul doesn't need him now. He doesn't need anything but Jahan's unwavering support – and he has it.

31

SEVERAL WEEKS BEFORE THE GALLERY show opens, Paul sits in *The New News Hour*'s small but sleekly furnished green room, staring around at the black-and-white photographs of New York landmarks that line the walls. His hands are trembling, his stomach unsettled. He admires the tray of fresh pastries and the plate piled high with fruits he can never afford, but he can't force himself to eat. He desperately wants more coffee, too – and a cigarette, of course – but he's afraid of getting too wired. He tells himself he'll be *fine*; he's done interviews before. But he's never done an interview like this one: on national television, telling viewers that Judith Stanley, the tragically murdered, now-famous photographer, was a lunatic who essentially ended her own life. Even with Jahan's blessing and that influential *we* lifting him up, he can't nullify the sense that he's doing something drastic and outlandish – something *dangerous*, even.

A surge of pain in his chest confirms it; Paul wonders if he's having a heart attack. At least he'll die wearing a beautifully tailored suit (courtesy of Jahan's staff). The makeup artist knocks on his door, comes in to apply foundation and pat down his shine. Chatting with her helps calm him, and then, once she's packed up her supplies and left, he stares at what's to come: the walk to the sound stage, the mindless introductory banter with the host, and the weight of those bright, hot lights as he makes his unsavory announcement.

He thinks of Tom sitting lonely in his living room over a TV dinner of Salisbury steak and potatoes au gratin, hearing the host announce his name. *Paul Sorenson to discuss the new retrospective of Judith Stanley's work at Doven Gallery...* He thinks of Charlie, too, scoffing at the sight of him onscreen. Again Paul's chest throbs with pain. He presses his fingers deep into the spot, hoping he can at least delay the heart attack for twenty or so minutes.

There's another knock at the door, then a slim, smiling young woman in a perfectly fitted maroon suit steps inside. 'You ready, Paul?' she asks. He drops his hand from his chest and smiles back. Trembling Heart Attack Paul is unfit for national television, so he does his best to banish him.

'You bet,' he says, rising to his feet. He follows her down a narrow, turning hall that leads to a bustling studio. Don Gregor, beloved former football star and *The New News Hour*'s host, is suddenly before him, shaking his hand, ushering him onto the stage to take a seat in the show's faux living room. Before Paul has a moment to take a sip of water or adjust to the glare in which he sits, exposed, he hears the cameraman counting down to one.

Paul sits, tense and unmoving, as Don introduces the segment. He recounts the official Judith Stanley story, ending with the known details of her 'tragic death.' Then he turns to Paul and asks about his 'discovery' of Judith and the journey to publishing her photographs. Paul finds, despite his nerves, that the more he speaks, the more relaxed he becomes, and the easier it is to be the man the audience wants to see. They aren't here in the studio with him, but he can sense their gratifying attention, their warm approval – of his looks, his flair for storytelling, his bright conversational manner.

'Paul, how does it feel knowing this gifted artist can't produce any more work because a still-unknown assailant killed her?' Don asks.

'Well, it's – it's terribly sad and disturbing,' Paul begins. The words catch and start to carry him; he only has to follow their flow. 'It's an incalculable loss to those of us who knew her. Especially to her family, of course. It's also a loss to the art world, and to the many, many people out there who've become fans of her pictures.'

Don nods solemnly. 'And what about this man, her attacker. Is there any new information on him? About who he could be? I understand you were questioned, too, as the last person to see her alive.'

Paul doesn't appreciate the jab, but it's given him the perfect segue. 'I was questioned, yes. But never treated seriously as a suspect, Don. And what I've learned since – through research and conversations with… extremely knowledgeable people, is that there may not *be* any assailant. At least, not in the way you might expect. Judith may not have been murdered.'

'What the heck?' Don asks, looking genuinely stunned. 'What exactly do you mean, Paul?'

'Well, this is hard for me to say. Very hard,' Paul says, the story rolling out of him now. 'But as you said yourself, there's been no sign of her assailant, and it was her own knife, with only *her* fingerprints on it, that was found beside her. She also claimed that her stalker appeared in the background of all of those marvelous self-portraits of hers. Well, I – and others – have gone back through every last one and scoured them for any sign of this man. We found nothing, Don. Absolutely nothing.'

As the drama of his own words crescendos inside him, Paul sees this effect mirrored in Don's face. The host's next questions come stuttering out.

'So you're saying – but who killed her, then? And why?'

'She may have taken her own life,' Paul says bluntly, and one of the studio crew members, out of sight, lets out a gasp. For Paul it echoes what must be a chorus of gasps in all the tuned-in living rooms and kitchens of the country. Paul feels it run through him like an electric current – crackling, unstoppable.

'I think she may have been… very ill. I've spoken to a trusted psychologist about this, as well as the police. Judith was assaulted and… injured in her home as a teenager. This may have festered in her until now and made her mind turn against her.'

'All these years later?' Don asks. Paul nods. He knows Malcolm and Detective Schuyler will be furious to hear him expounding on this on national TV, even if he's withheld their names. But he goes on, carried on the current and the knowledge that the people out there, watching him, are *riveted*.

'So her death was… a suicide?' Don asks, so genuine now that the two men might be lounging in a café, having a private conversation. But Paul flinches at the word. He knows he's all but said it himself, but he's purposely avoided saying it. America doesn't like that word, *suicide*; doesn't Don know better? Paul backpedals.

'This is a *theory*, Don. I want to be clear on that. But it's a strong one, backed by expert advice, and I felt obligated to share it with the public. It's changed and deepened the way I look at her photographs, and I hope the same will be true for other people, for her fans. She has a lot of them, I know,' Paul says, smiling out at the viewers, reassuring them. Don nods but looks lost as he veers toward the wrap-up.

'Well, that's certainly some shocking news we've had from Paul Sorenson, consulting curator of the upcoming Judith Stanley show at Doven Gallery here in New York City. That's all the time we have for now. Paul, thank you for joining us.'

When the cameras stop rolling, Don leans toward Paul.

'Well, that should boost your attendance, shouldn't it? Not to mention picture sales.' Paul can't read his tone. Half impressed, half annoyed by the surprise? Not angry, though. He's smiling, so Paul smiles back.

'Sorry you weren't prepared for that. We had to keep it under wraps.'

Don waves this away.

'All the better. The higher-ups loved it, I'm sure. Great for ratings.' He shakes Paul's hand briskly and then strides off the stage. Paul envies him, leaving this interview with his life unchanged. Paul rises shakily to his feet, feeling the pain in his chest return as he follows the maroon-suited girl, now grimly silent and unsmiling, to an exit. Outside in the cold, he tries to recapture the warmth he felt while connecting with his countless invisible and captivated viewers. He shivers; it's vanished now – and he may have invented it anyway.

32

MORNING SUNLIGHT SNAKES THROUGH THE blinds. When Paul blinks awake, he hears the telephone, ringing and ringing. He was dreaming of wandering through a ragged old house – a nightmare version of the Stanley home with the same furniture, the same blue carpeting – searching for Judith. There were signs of her everywhere: her Nikon sat on a side table, her winter coat hung limp in a closet above a pair of worn leather boots. *She must have just left*, he kept telling himself, turning in circles. But he couldn't concentrate with that shrill ringing sound somewhere in the background – where was it coming from?

When he rises up on his elbows, the headache descends.

He went to a bar after leaving the studio and got smashed in its gloomy, welcoming darkness. The place was called… the Pig & Whistle? The Pot & Kettle? Something like that. The jolly bartender kept filling his cup, so by the time he stumbled out to the sidewalk at 2:00 am, he'd forgotten where he was, and all thoughts of what he'd said about Judith on television had long since gone sodden in his brain.

Once home, he fell into bed without remembering to unplug his telephone. He's paying for it now as he reckons with the wrenching noise, his wrecked head, and the swift return of unwanted – if foggy – awareness. He wants silence and peace – only silence and peace! – but knows there can be none, not after yesterday. The phone's endless screaming is the sound of his longed-for success. And, speaking of that, damn it all, the caller could be someone important. He groans and swings his legs out of bed, stumbles in his underwear to the phone.

'Hello,' he croaks, then clears his throat. He can't sound like some hungover slouch.

'Fuck you, Paul Sorenson,' a woman's voice hisses. 'Fuck you and your lies about Judith Stanley.'

'Fuck you, too, you loony bitch!' Paul shouts, banging the receiver down. He almost said, *Fuck you, too, Charlie*, even though it didn't sound like her. Even though he's probably incited a whole mob against him after his TV appearance, and any of them – not just Charlie – could ring him up. He sighs and shuffles into the kitchen. He needs coffee and a cigarette. Coffee first. As he's waiting for it to brew, he spots the day's printed schedule Tasha gave him; it's chock-full of interviews. Today's task will be to rehash his suicide theory all over again, for one outlet after another. Though the first sips of coffee bring a jolt of energy, he still longs to hide in bed in the semi-dark until the whole day has passed.

The first thing he'll do, after coffee, is call the telephone company and change his number.

33

After a week of interviews and appearances – each more focused on the possible truth about Judith's death than the last – Paul returns early one Friday evening, exhausted and profoundly relieved to be home. He's so glad to have changed his telephone number. He'll have silence tonight, after a day filled with noise – most of it coming from his own mouth. He drinks a cool glass of water from the tap, folds his suit over a bedroom chair, takes a hot shower, and slides into worn pajama pants and an old white T-shirt. He sits in his chair with his whiskey glass and a cigarette and feels like himself for the first time in days. Like the old Paul, the guy he was so eager to shuck off. Now he revisits the comforts of this former self – tartan plaid slippers, his view of the neighboring brick wall – and tries to sink back into them. Hide in them.

But it doesn't quite work. He can't fully relax, hard as he tries. Part of him remains rigidly observant, on alert to answer a question like, *Why do you think Judith's earlier trauma affected her the way it did?* That was one he got today from a *New York Times* reporter, and he desperately wanted to answer with, *I don't fucking know, man.* Maybe he should have. It would have been more honest. Instead, he theorized – bullshitted – for several minutes with the journalist staring at him as if he could see right through Paul's skull to his squirming, scrambled brain. Paul sighs, takes a long swallow of whiskey, and stares at a brown grocery bag bulging with letters by his dining room table.

Maybe this is another reason why he can't relax: the letters. They've poured in since that first fateful television interview – in such great number that his landlord, Cyrus, collected the mail and left a note in his otherwise empty mailbox that said, *See me.* Paul expected to get a lecture from the old grump, but instead he greeted Paul with a painfully wide grin that bared his yellowed teeth and said, *You've hit the big time now, ain't ya?* while licking his lips and handing over the bag. Paul didn't answer; he wondered how much Cyrus knew. Had he seen the interview? Had he seen multiple interviews? And what did someone like Cyrus think about all of it – all the art world drama, the psychological intrigue? Maybe he didn't think about it at all, Paul mused. Maybe he just saw his tenant, newly notorious, and the bright light of that revelation blotted out everything else.

Paul grabs the bag and reaches in for a handful of envelopes. He riffles through, his eyes half closed. He's doing it aimlessly, with no intention of opening and reading any of them now, before a well-earned early bedtime, when he spots it: the slanting block letters screaming his name. He tears the envelope right open, all the while knowing he shouldn't. He shouldn't, but he has to. The letter inside reads:

PAUL SORENSON

YOU'VE SHOWN YOURSELF TO BE

A LEECH

A NOTHING

A THIEF

AND NOW A LIAR, TOO

HOW DARE YOU SPEW LIES ABOUT JUDITH???

ALL FOR MONEY & FAME

BEWARE

YOU'LL GET A PAYCHECK SOON

WE'LL DELIVER IT WHEN YOU'RE LEAST EXPECTING

Paul crumples the letter up and throws it in the trash. After a long minute of staring at the trash can, he grabs the letter out, smooths it over his knee. The final *we* rattles him; the *I* was less concerning. What if Charlie is gathering a tribe around her? A tribe that loathes him. A tribe of angry women bent on delivering justice. This isn't an idle threat; it's one promising action. If it were still just an *I*, just a Charlie, it wouldn't bother him so much – but what if there's really a *we*? A *we* with a plan. Maybe he *should* call the police? Then he remembers he's aired Schuyler's semi-unspoken theory on television and needs to avoid him. He's surprised the detective hasn't come knocking already.

Paul lights a cigarette, takes a quick, harsh drag, and sets the letter aside. Gently, as if it were made of a volatile substance. He tells himself to calm the hell down, to move on and read something normal and nice to take the sting out of Charlie's – or whoever's – poison. The next letter he opens is from a retired schoolteacher in New Jersey who raves about the *Harper's* portfolio. After that, a man in Ohio who describes himself as 'an avid collector' thanks him and asks about acquiring Judith's work. Paul sets this one aside for Jahan's team; the man seems like a legitimate potential buyer. He's glad to be doing this, to be moving on through his correspondence with calm and poise. He's a professional, isn't he? He's such a professional, in fact, that he can glance at the wrinkled letter now and then and feel nothing at all.

A letter from 'Barbara' in New York starts by praising Judith's work but ends badly: 'I saw your first interview, and some of your subsequent interviews. You should be ashamed of yourself, dragging Judith's personal history into the light. It isn't your business. And it's overshadowing her work, which was your intention, I suppose? It will sell more photographs, I know.' Paul grunts in disgust; he hates the way she calls Judith by her first name, as if she'd known her. *I knew her, you stupid cow*, he thinks, but Barbara can't hear. She wouldn't hear him, anyway, even if she were here, spouting her nonsense to his face.

He opens more letters, each time thinking he'll find something that will give him a hint of satisfaction. But more and more of the letters mirror Barbara's now: expressions of admiration for Judith's photographs interspersed with disgust or even outrage. It's as though a knitting circle were railing against him with a set of stock phrases: *You have no right*, *You should be ashamed*, *Your greed is astonishing.* It would almost be laughable if there weren't so damned many of them – at least forty so far, and he's only halfway through the bag.

Female soldiers for Judith, Paul thinks with a laugh that sounds strange and lonely in the air of his apartment. *Possibly led by the dark-haired girl who used to sit near the great photographer in class. What would Judith think of that?*

Paul lets the letters drop back into the bag and kicks it away from him. The action helps return him to himself – to his armchair, his glass of booze, his burning cigarette, his warm slippers. He's had enough. Whatever the rest of the mail says, it can wait until after the show – or forever.

34

PAUL FINDS HIMSELF BACK IN class – unprepared and unmotivated to teach – exactly two weeks before the gallery show is set to open. He stands where he's always stood in the ugly, institutional lecture hall, staring at bright-faced (if not always bright) young men and women in the seats around him, but he feels like an actor in a play about someone else's life. He used to relish playing the part of expert photographer, sharing his wisdom and his love of photography with students, but now that role is dead to him, like a husk he's long since discarded. He has nothing he really wants to say and no energy for discussing 'setting up your darkroom,' as it reads on the syllabus. He used to enjoy giving this lecture, didn't he? He can hardly remember, and he can hardly bring himself to begin class. But he must, so he does.

Looking around as he speaks, his eyes land on Charlie. He's thought of her so often lately that it's jarring to see her in person – and to see that she's just an ordinary pretty girl, one of several in the class, not the powerful figure he's imagined sometimes, the leader of an enraged, self-righteous women's gang. She *is* giving him a sour look, though – and he can sense animosity rolling off her in waves. Probably because of the interview. Interviews. He remembers the old Charlie, from back in September, who used to cross her beautiful bare legs and look up at him as if he were a demigod. That girl has been extinguished by her passion for Judith's photographs; it's twisted and deformed her in some way.

He can't even see her now as the object of those masturbatory fantasies he had – only days ago.

He looks away from her stony face and carries on.

'Many of you may already know this, but I'm co-curating an exhibition of Judith Stanley's photographs that's opening in two weeks at Doven Gallery, in the city. If I've seemed a little distracted lately, that's why,' he says, smiling. 'I've been doing some, uh, appearances lately that have taken up a great deal of time.' Speaking frees him, and locking into his new identity gives him an added boost – as do the knowing looks on his students' faces. They've watched the interviews; of course they have! Their lowly community college professor has suddenly been elevated to the highest of cultural heights. He puffs up with their regard – until he looks Charlie's way. While his other students tune in admiringly, Charlie's hard stare cuts him and sends his mind back to those hateful phrases in the letters he's received. Reminding him of the sound of cruel laughter on the other end of the phone line. It doesn't matter right now if she's responsible or not; she's simply guilty of the look she's giving him. It's enough.

'It's going to be an extraordinary show. You may have seen a taste of her work in *Harper's*, but this will be really comprehensive. I encourage you all to see it,' he says, more emphatically than necessary. As if he were trying to convince Charlie of his unimpeachable status and worth. A hand goes up in the back: not Charlie, he sees with relief.

'How did you get involved in all this, Professor?' The young man sounds mild, friendly even, but Paul still bristles. Is there a provocative undertone? He doesn't think so, but he can't help answering with a touch of defensiveness.

'Well, I was Judith's mentor, and the only person she ever shared her work with.' A possible exaggeration, but who would ever know? He made the claim in his catalog introduction, the final draft of which he's just handed in to Jahan, so it was on its way to becoming historical truth; it would lead the catalog and be stamped on the gallery walls for the exhibit's myriad visitors. 'Just before she died, she told me she was ready to publish her pictures and asked for my help. I worked with her husband to choose them and contacted *Harper's*. The rest just… fell into place,' he says, skimming over the stress and numerous difficulties he's endured. The student looks satisfied, impressed.

'You're all invited to the opening, by the way – it's Friday, April 10, at 7:00 pm. You should dress up, or at least not look the way you usually do in class – get cleaned up for god's sake!' This earns him a big laugh, and more than a few students exchange excited glances, jotting down the date and time in their notebooks.

Through all of this, Charlie sits silent and brooding. She really must be the one spewing venom from a safe, anonymous distance instead of confronting him head-on. He decides to face her, question her, once the others have left. He wants to force her into the open, make her admit that she's been hounding him.

He plods through the rest of class somehow. He knows Charlie enjoys seeing him struggle; after his smooth delivery of the Judith Stanley news, he has trouble recalling the smallest details of setting up a darkroom – like what chemicals to use in the developing bath – even though he's given this lecture a hundred times and has a home darkroom himself. Every time he stumbles, he senses Charlie's pleasure and a tide of fury builds in him.

Once he's dragged through the final minutes of class and reminded everyone about the opening, he calls Charlie down to see him. She doesn't react, not even when her friends lean their sleek, pretty heads close, presumably to question or strategize. Once they've left – probably to linger in the hall outside – Charlie walks slowly down to him in the emptied room. For a moment, Paul is overwhelmed by déjà vu. If this were some months ago, it would be Judith approaching – though Judith's gait was lighter and her demeanor, unlike Charlie's, was deferential, reserved. He yearns to look up and see Judith standing before him once more – then he pulls himself together to face Charlie's piercing gaze.

'Hey, Charlie. You must be jazzed for Judith's opening. I know you're a big fan,' he says as lightly as possible. She cocks her head at him and nods; that's all. Then, after a beat:

'Did she really say that, before she died?'

'Excuse me?'

'Did she really tell you she wanted to publish her photographs? She didn't seem the type, honestly. I'm the type, but I don't have the talent.' She lays this out before him with plain-spoken confidence. Doesn't even look ashamed of herself, or daunted by saying this to her professor's face. It's so galling Paul has to grip the edges of the table he's leaning on to keep his hands from reaching out for her, grabbing her the way he imagined in class the other night.

'I don't make things up, Charlie. I know I seem like an easy-going guy, a friendly, approachable professor and all that, but suggesting that I lied about something like that is – is –'

'Unconscionable?' Charlie offers.

'No, I was going to say… incredibly rude. You shouldn't talk to your superiors that way.' Charlie bursts out laughing while staring straight into his eyes. Paul wants to smack her. So hard that her head would snap to the side with the force of it. So hard it would leave a dark red handprint on her cheek. And maybe give her a black eye, too, if that were possible. He can see her, standing before him with her dark eyes spilling over with tears, blubbering her apologies in the aftermath. *Sorry, Professor. Sorry, sorry.* Apologizing for speaking that way but for the rest of it, too: The letters, the threats. All the hatred she and her friends and the others like them have been aiming his way.

When he returns to himself, to the real present, where he hasn't slapped her, he finds her still staring at him with that amused, challenging look. She hasn't excused her rude outburst and she never will, he knows.

'If I don't see you before then, I'll see you at the opening, Professor.'

Did he imagine the mocking emphasis on *Professor*? And what did she mean, 'before then'? Why and how would he see her *before* the show? Next week is spring break, and he's canceled the following week's class for the opening. He thinks of the line *We'll deliver it when you're least expecting* and shudders a little. He could confront her right now, call her on it – but why bother? She'd only laugh again. She wouldn't tell him the truth. She's brazen as hell and he suddenly wants to kill her. Not really, of course, but his hands curl into fists at his sides, and he stands there, enraged and impotent, as she turns to leave.

35

PAUL SLUMPS SIDEWAYS, LETTING HIS head rest against the subway car window warmed by afternoon sunlight. *Spring* sunlight. The season has changed without his noticing; he hasn't had a chance to notice. He thinks about getting off at the next stop and walking the rest of the way to Doven to appreciate the weather, but he doesn't have time. Jahan asked him to be there by four, and he's running late. His third interview of the day ran long, and he realized he hadn't eaten since breakfast; he made a hasty sandwich and rushed to the train. Now he wants nothing more than a nap. He lets his eyes close, but Charlie, laughing in his face as she did last night, pops into his mind. He remembers his immediate urge to hit her, to harm her. He wouldn't, though, he tells himself; he isn't that kind of guy.

She's the one who's pushed him – with her prying questions and rudeness and evil letters and calls – to the *edge* of wanting to hurt her. He hates spending time stewing over Charlie, especially now, with so much forward, upward movement in his life, but he has the sense that he can't fully enter his future without dealing with her somehow. When he opens his eyes again, he searches the darkness of the tunnels that blur by for an answer. *What to do about Charlie? What to do about Charlie?* No ideas come. He racks his brain for an answer as he climbs the subway stairs to the street, and all the way to Doven's front door.

But everything shifts and brightens when he walks inside; all thought of Charlie drops away as if the rarefied air has instantly cleansed his mind. He looks around reverently at the white walls hung with Judith's pictures now, at the workers mounting caption cards beside each one, and he catches the eyes of assistants and junior curators who nod or wave and say his name. When Jahan comes striding toward him from a back room, welcoming him with open arms, Paul smiles in anticipation.

'There he is!' Jahan crows, clapping him on the back like he's a war hero returned home. 'What a star you are, Paul, what a star! They'll come pouring in here on opening night. This is wonderful – for all of us,' he says, and gestures toward his staff, who've arranged themselves quickly in a semicircle and, to Paul's pleased embarrassment, have started to applaud. A few of them say *Woo-hoo*, and Paul feels it all like a much-needed warm embrace – until his eyes land on two female employees, standing together, who stare at him with mild disgust. They're clapping, but limply, reluctantly. They remind him of Charlie, of course, but in this case, Paul knows he could tell Jahan later, get them disciplined or even fired. But why give them the satisfaction? He decides to ignore the women instead, these nameless assistants who blame him for his faultless act of airing the truth about Judith – on their boss's orders, though he doubts they know that.

Following Jahan to the room where they've mounted the best of Judith's self-portraits helps to clear his mind. They're all beautifully framed and arranged in the order he himself suggested, and together they make an astonishing sight. He loves this work as if it were his own. He loves it more than his own – much more. He knows Judith's work isn't *his*, but who else alive can feel even a sliver of this sense of pride and ownership? Only him. Jahan may be a close second, but it can't be very close – Paul was the one who discovered her, mentored her, after all.

'Stunning, isn't it?' Jahan asks, sighing.

'I can't quite believe it's real – that her work is *here*, at Doven. It's – it's a dream come true.' His face heats with the childish admission and because it's *his* dream come true, not Judith's, even though the work is hers. Jahan laughs and claps him on the back for the second time.

'It's real, Paul. It's all very real. I can't thank you enough for bringing her work to us. And for everything you've done since. I think audiences will be wowed.' The two men pace around the room, staring in silence at Judith's eloquent and innovative self-studies. Paul thinks her face might be more familiar to him than his own, after studying it for so long: days and weeks of his life. His own face gets minimal attention when he stares in the mirror – and only a practical sort of attention, not the searching, philosophical contemplation he gives to Judith's.

'It's a terrible shame, what happened. What she did to herself,' Jahan says, pausing at the image of Judith centered in a car's side mirror, the tall buildings looming behind. Paul doesn't want to think about Judith's death right now – or the noise around it, most of which he's made himself. He wishes Jahan hadn't brought it up. He makes a vague sound in the back of his throat, and the two men move on.

'Have you heard from the Stanleys? Since the broadcast?' Jahan asks. Another thing Paul would rather not discuss.

'No. They've been ominously silent,' he says simply, and gives Jahan a tight smile. He doesn't tell him what he's afraid of: that they'll show up at the opening to make a great big embarrassing fuss. His only comfort is knowing how out of character something like that would be for the Stanley men. 'But other people haven't been so quiet. I've had some – odd calls. Threatening ones. Letters, too. It started when the *Harper's* piece came out and it's gotten worse since the recent interviews.' He feels slightly relieved, if foolish, too, to have blurted this out. At least speaking it makes the harassment real: a thing in the world, not just in his head.

Jahan looks at him with a furrowed brow. 'Paul, ignore those fools. When someone succeeds, people want to drag them down. I've had my share of this kind of ugliness thrown my way. More than my share, really, given my ethnicity. It isn't right, but it's something to be endured. And ignored, as much as possible.' Paul nods along, wishing now that he'd told Jahan sooner.

'Thank you, you're right. It's made me feel kind of… sleazy,' he says with an awkward chuckle. The word brings to mind his old friend Malcolm's scorn.

Jahan shakes his head. 'No. Don't believe it for a second. You did what you did for Judith, ultimately. You granted her last wish, and then you worked to make the show a success. And now all of us prosper, together. Of course, Judith won't prosper, but her family will – whether they like it or not. These other people are insignificant. Ignorant. Unhappy souls,' he says, waving his hand in the air as if dismissing flies. 'What have they done in their lives? Aside from write a nasty letter, make a nasty phone call? These are stunted, sad people, Paul, and are only to be pitied and ignored.' Paul nods and feels absolved, as if Jahan were a priest who banished his demons with a handful of words. He wishes he could write the words down and reread them – the way he's reread the threatening letters, absorbed the phrases – *fucking parasite, monster, thief, liar, leech*. If he could replace those hateful words with Jahan's, he might hang on to this exuberant well-being forever. Or at least until the show opens.

After they've walked the length of the room, Paul suggests moving Judith's self-portrait with mannequins to a new spot that will connect it with the other store window portraits – to highlight it more. Jahan tells him he has a great eye, and Paul swells with pride. He scans the room for other suggestions he can make to earn more of Jahan's praise.

'You not only have a great eye but an excellent business sense, too, Paul. I can't wait to introduce you at the opening. There will be so many collectors, curators, museum directors, artists… the crème de la crème of the art world. So many doors are about to open for you. And you've earned it.' Jahan winks – actually winks at him – and then excuses himself from the room. Paul sits on the nearest bench – situated in front of an enlarged version of Judith's liquor store portrait, a centerpiece of the show – to absorb Jahan's words. To try to feel what it means to have *so many doors about to open* for him.

Because you used Judith's pictures and exploited her life, Charlie and her friends and those two angry assistants and countless unknown others would add. He tries to shake the thought by shifting his gaze to the gorgeously framed picture – the one he caused to be hanging here, resplendent in its frame. The image, sorrowful yet transcendent, is enhanced by the knowledge of Judith's death: you can see through her body as if she were already a shade. But her face looks wholly alive; she stares at him like she can see it all: his pride, his ambition, his fraudulence, his awareness that he's wronged her – first by lying about her desire to publish, now by publicly sharing the possible truth about her death.

He starts to look away in shame, but something catches his eye: a dark spot in the top right-hand corner of the photograph. He rises from the bench, getting so close to the glass frame that the tip of his nose nearly brushes it. Could he have missed a sign of the man in a picture he's studied repeatedly? And could the man be real after all? Sweat prickles at his hairline. But when he's close enough, he sees that what he glimpsed is just the shadow of a bush. *Thank god*, he thinks, and jumps when someone speaks behind him.

'Everything OK?' He recognizes the bright, anxious voice as Tasha's, Jahan's assistant. He turns to her with a big smile to hide how shaken he is.

'Thought I saw something. But it was nothing. Just a shadow.'

'Oh, I'm glad. If there's a smudge or anything at this point, there'll be hell to pay,' she says, laughing, but meaning it, too. Paul hasn't witnessed Jahan as anything but jolly, but he's heard stories of his ruthless perfectionism.

It's when she turns to go and he watches her walk away – that lovely round ass like Charlie's moving in a tight, short skirt – that the idea comes to him: he'll follow her. Not Tasha, of course; Tasha has been nothing but gracious, appreciative, polite. But Charlie. He'll follow Charlie once or twice, to give her a scare and a nudge. A warning. Something to shake her up and shake her off, to let him move forward, as he damn well deserves to, without her constant nagging intrusion in his life.

36

PAUL HAS BEEN SITTING IN his parked car across from Charlie's brick apartment building at 135 Van Houten Street for several hours, doing everything but having fun. He's been restless and bored, nervous as hell, excited when he thought he spotted Charlie's car two times, and regretful, too. More than once, he's turned on the engine, tossed his cigarette out the window, and prepared to pull away from the curb. But he hasn't. He's stayed. He left once, on foot, to pick up food at a nearby burger stand, but aside from that, he's stayed in the car, his eyes glued to Charlie's building, to the street in front of it, to every passerby. He knows it's the right address because he got it from the NJCC secretary, telling her he had to mail a graded paper back to a student who'd been absent for weeks. He's fairly certain Charlie will be driving, and he knows her car: a dark brown Chevrolet. He's seen her drive off in it after class – which makes him realize that she lied that time, weeks ago now, when she told him she was 'about to miss her ride.' She said it just to get away from him. More disrespectful behavior from Charlie, who has yet to arrive.

He's gearing up to leave again – it's almost eight o'clock, and he's cold and tired, and feels foolish, too – when Charlie drives right past him and pulls into the parking garage. He doesn't turn his head to look but hears her singing along to the radio. The sound of her voice gives him a jolt of pure fear.

He grasps the ski mask beside him with trembling fingers. He looks down at his outfit, too, to make sure, again, that he's dressed in nondescript clothes he's never worn to class. He wants to look like an everyday thug, and he thinks he's managed it. Or close enough. He pulls the ski mask on over his face, checks himself in the mirror – looking like a disturbed and disturbing stranger – and feels a spike of shame. Disgust, even. What the hell is he doing? *It's just a lark*, he tells himself. *Giving her a much-needed, much-deserved nudge, remember?* Still, he pulls off the mask but holds it as he gets out of the car. He doesn't pass anyone on the dark street but waits to put on the mask until he's in the dimly lit garage, watching Charlie from a distance as she opens her car door and collects her coat and purse. He creeps closer, ducking behind each car as he goes. But when he gets near enough, almost, to reach out and grab the long rope of her dark, shiny hair, his nerve fails him. He finds he can't move from his crouch behind the long back end of an Oldsmobile, so Charlie gets away, walking languidly to the door. Humming the song that was playing on the radio, something he doesn't recognize. She's confident, unafraid – and why shouldn't she be? She's the same as she always is in class, and Paul is the same, too: he folds, he fails.

When another car pulls into the garage, Paul stays put. He yanks off his ski mask and stays there, fuming, crouched on his aching legs for several minutes after the other residents have slammed their car doors and gone inside.

At home, he drinks and stands smoking at his window, glaring at the neighboring building's brick wall. He isn't mad at Charlie – he's mad at himself. For being weak and afraid, for letting his chance slip away. But as the minutes pass and the smoke and booze start to lull him, quiet him a little, he begins to forgive himself, bit by bit. This wasn't a failure but a successful practice run, he decides. Now he knows what time she comes home from work, and he knows her parking spot, too: number 35. He'll go back again tomorrow night, and tomorrow night he'll rise from his crouch and come up behind her and… scare her. Scare the living hell out of her.

37

EVERYTHING IS EASIER THE SECOND night; he's steadier and his mind is calm. He knows where to park for the best view of the garage, and he's even packed a sandwich this time. He's fairly certain she'll be home after eight, but he arrives at six to begin his watch, and at seven forty he leaves the car, ski mask in hand, to crouch quietly in a shadowed spot close to her parking space. If anyone happens to see him, he'll pretend to be looking for a lost key. He'll give a sheepish grin: *I know it's here somewhere, I heard it drop.* But no one spots him, and soon enough, after his legs have tired and his heart has jumped multiple times at the sound of cars arriving, Charlie drives past. He watches her red taillights drift by and pulls the ski mask down over his face; he doesn't feel silly now or obscene, but focused, purposeful. Like an expert, too, as if he's been doing this for months, or even years.

He crawls to the edge of the Chrysler he's been hiding behind and waits for the sound of her car door creaking open, Charlie stepping out. When she does, he coughs once, loudly. He watches through the car window beside him as she pauses, peers around, looks for the man who's made the sound. When she doesn't see anyone – a friendly neighbor's face, or at least someone she knows – she slams the car door and starts walking quickly toward the building.

He didn't plan to do things this way but decides it's fun – to frighten her by doing so little, while staying out of sight.

He coughs again, louder this time, and now she's running for the door. He wants to yell *Bitch* so badly, but he won't risk her recognizing his voice. He doesn't need to yell anything, though – the simple sounds he made have done their job. When Charlie reaches the entrance, she turns, looking wildly behind her, before walking through and slamming the door shut.

The sight of her terrified, beautiful face does something to him. It sings to him. He's wanted her to look that way in class so many times: after she's insulted him, or asked him a probing, inappropriate question about Judith, or *laughed in his face.* He drinks in the sight like nectar and lets the image imprint in his mind. Long after she's gone, after she's taken the elevator or stairs to her snug apartment and locked the door and leaned against it, breathing hard, after she's called a friend and cried a little over a glass of wine that she holds in a trembling hand, he savors the image he's made – of Charlie, terrorized.

38

At home, after a celebratory jerk-off in the shower – still relishing the sight of Charlie's twisted face – Paul towels off and stands, drained but exhilarated, drinking in the middle of his living room, swaying naked to Charles Mingus on the radio. That was much more fun, he decides, than even his ballsiest theft, which was probably the time he stole fifteen rare books at once, cramming them into his backpack and walking right past the snobbish, oblivious clerk. He has no physical reminders of the past night – like the books he has on his shelves to this day – but the high is more intense, and probably longer lasting.

To affect someone deeply, to snatch away their sense of wholeness and security. Especially someone like Charlie, so deserving of the fear. Much more gratifying than pilfering groceries or books.

Before long, Paul is staring drunkenly at the neighboring building's brick wall, toasting each and every individual brick – the dark red brick; the light, chipped-away brick; the yellowish brick loose in its slot. 'To Charlie!' he yells. 'To my-goddamn-self!' And the last one: 'To Judith!'

When he finally sits and begins smoking one cigarette after another, he quiets. The nicotine is clearing his head, dissolving his buzz. He begins to see the night differently, to doubt what he's done – or hasn't done. He really didn't do *much*, did he? All he did was *cough*, without even emerging from his hiding place. She didn't scream, she didn't run – she *jogged*, but she didn't run. Was she really that scared? Her face conveyed fright, but was it enough, provoking her from such a distance? Has he taught her what it's like to be hunted, to be harassed, to be made to feel miserable and insane, the way he has in recent days? He doesn't think so. He thinks she'll recover quickly, and return to her usual haughty, provocative self, with the memory of one night's fear fading fast.

So: he has to go back, to leave a lasting impression. Just one more time, then he'll be finished with Charlie.

After spending the next morning and part of the afternoon on the phone with Jahan and a journalist from *The Washington Post*, and with only two days before the gallery opening, Paul dresses carefully despite his speeding pulse and drives out to Charlie's place at sunset. While he follows the now-familiar route, he dwells on how utterly estranged the two halves of his day are from one another. He doesn't judge himself for any of it, but isn't it weird? How he's Paul Sorenson, rising curatorial star, and also Paul Sorenson, mask-wearing avenger. He chuckles a bit at this and pulls thoughtfully on his cigarette before tossing it out the window.

This time, when Charlie pulls in, she parks in a different spot, one closer to the building entrance. It throws Paul a little, but not enough to dampen his plan. He likes seeing her, through the eyeholes of his mask, hastily lock the car and look around. Like a scared little bug ready to scuttle to safety. As soon as she turns, he's on her. He catches her by the shoulders and pulls her back, screaming, clamping a hand over her mouth and an arm around her neck. She tries but fails to bite his gloved hand.

He drags her into a shadowed corner by the door, letting nothing escape but the sound of his breath, hot and urgent in her ear. He doesn't whisper *bitch*, like he's tempted to do, or say her name to scare her – he'd be stupid to let her hear his voice. Instead, he pins her against him so she can feel his erection and wallow in a moment of paralyzing fear. After that, he'll loosen his hold enough to let her go. But before he can, her hands flail up at him somehow, and something sharp comes slashing at his arms. A knife. He sees the blood darken his shirtsleeves before he feels any pain. But when the pain comes, it's searing. He groans and loosens his hold. Charlie twists out of his arms, stumbles forward, and grabs for the door.

Another man might follow her, might chase her inside, up the stairs, might pull her back and put an end to things. But he isn't that man – though he has to remind himself of that. The urge is strong to do it and the pain eggs him on but *he isn't that man*.

He drives off in his ski mask without giving his arms more than a glance. But before he gets on the highway, he pulls over and peels off his mask and shirt to examine the stinging wounds. There are quite a few slash marks, all bleeding profusely, but he doesn't think they're that bad. That knife of hers didn't do so much.

It was he who'd done much. He'd terrified her. Touched her. Physically attacked her where she lives. And even though she struck back, like a little mouse with its claws, he knows she'll be the one to suffer, to carry that night for a long, long time. It will scar and subdue her. And Paul? He's on his way home, where he'll shower and tend to his injuries, knowing he's finally secured Charlie's silence, that he'll never be bothered by her hateful letters or calls or insolent harassment again.

He's run an obstacle course, really, from the moment he stood on Tom Stanley's front porch all those months ago to lobby him for Judith's pictures. He is bone-tired and weary – but energized, too. He's done it, he's cleared his path of every obstacle at last. He's free now to shine all night at the opening, to step through the doorway to his bright new world.

39

BY 7:00 PM THE NEXT night, the opening is in full swing, the din in the rooms nearly deafening. Enthusiastic viewers move slowly in a line along the walls, and in the middle of each room, groups stand chatting loudly with champagne glasses and cigarettes in hand. Paul has been caught and circulated like the miniature crab cakes from one lively, elite group to the next – and he's been happy to be so praised, politely questioned, and consumed. He's seen the eyes of every single person light up when he's recognized or introduced: *Paul Sorenson, the man who made Judith Stanley.* His name alone is powerful in this milieu, and it's thrilling to see its effect on the myriad art leaders in attendance – like Brian Ellis, owner of the world-renowned B. Ellis Gallery, or Artie McElvoy, art critic for *The New York Times.* Now and then he might glimpse a hint of disdain on someone's face, but it's a passing, trivial thing, overwhelmed and demolished by the praise he's won from the likes of Dorian Murphy, legendary street photographer, who tells him he has 'quite the eye' for recognizing Judith's genius.

Everything is going beautifully, Jahan says – not with words but with a glance he and Paul share across the overheated, boisterous room full of images of Judith's face.

Paul, inhabiting his role seamlessly, tells everyone he meets 'how it happened,' how he recognized Judith's genius the first time she showed him her pictures. As the evening wears on, his voice grows hoarse. His jaws ache from smiling.

'I thought she was just a bored housewife, trying to pass the time by taking a photography class,' he begins, laughing along with his listeners for the hundredth time. 'I wasn't that interested when she asked if I'd look at her work, but it's my job, so I said I would. When I slid them out of the envelope, they took my head right off.' Here he makes an exploding gesture with his hand at the top of his head, and his listeners respond with murmurs and exclamations of wonder – and once, even a round of applause. He tells them *Parade Girl* was the first one he really fell for, he couldn't look away from the stark pain and beauty of it.

'Of course, knowing what we know now about Judith's... troubles, it's easy to see how *Parade Girl* reflects her own damage, her... mental distress,' a teacherly Paul says to one small group of solemn, sympathetic faces. They pepper him with questions: *When did you first suspect Judith had killed herself? Do you really believe it's true? Do you think she knowingly staged it to look like murder?* He's certain they've heard him answer these questions in interviews, but they still clamor for the live version.

With a grimly set face that's something of an act by the end of the first hour, Paul tells them he hates to say it, but yes, he truly believes she killed herself. He walks them through his evidence and reasoning, reminds them he confirmed his suspicions with a psychologist, and thinks gleefully of Malcolm, who would hate to hear him airing his professional opinion to everyone in sight. He thought Malcolm might pop back up to berate him when the first television show aired, or when subsequent interviews aired, but he never did. His silence and absence are damning, Paul supposes, and their long friendship is over, but so what? Here he is, after all, making new connections, new friends, left and right and all around. His pockets bulge with business cards.

When he's finished telling his version of Judith's story, the women make tutting noises; the men sigh – and then eventually they shake his hand and move on to other groups, where they share what he's said, and Paul is left, drained yet elated, to face a new threesome or foursome of eager listeners.

In rare free moments, Paul scans the growing crowd. Though he hasn't thought of them lately, the Stanley men come to mind. How could they not, on this night? Paul looks idly around for their faces, unsurprised when he doesn't find them. He doubts they'd brave an event like this, even if they wanted to confront him in person. They'd be afraid to see Judith's photographs boldly displayed on gallery walls – getting the much-deserved attention Paul has ensured – and they wouldn't love the crowd, either. He's relieved by their absence, but he hasn't been that worried about the possible threat of Tom and Tom. It would be unpleasant, of course, if they berated him or tried to sue him, but he's protected now, just as Jahan promised he would be. Cushioned by the eminent Doven Gallery and his own growing fame. And soon enough, the Stanleys will start getting checks in the mail – the room is full to bursting with eager buyers, after all – something sure to make their gripes evaporate for good.

Paul greets several groups of his students as he moves through the room, all of them awed by the glamour of the night. But there's no sign of Charlie. Unlike with the Stanleys, he almost *wants* to see her. It's a twisted desire – he wants to see her *as she is now*, after what happened between them. But he can't really imagine she'd be up for a night on the town. *She might never again be up for a night on the town*, he thinks, like a friend sympathetic to her pain instead of the man who traumatized her. It's hard to think of himself as *the man who traumatized her*, especially when he looks around at the bright walls, the rich crowd, the glorious photographs; it doesn't jibe with where and who he is now. He tells himself to imagine it never happened, and it isn't hard to do.

'Paul, Paul, it's so wonderful to meet you. Tell us how you found Judith…' A stout, elegantly dressed couple approach, standing before him and smiling deferentially. Collectors, he thinks, from the look of them; he's getting good at recognizing every type of art lover in the room.

In the midst of retelling his tale, Paul hears the faint sound of a spoon tapping the side of a glass. He clenches for just a moment, thinking of the little speech Jahan asked him to give. Just a few brief lines about himself and Judith, but the thought of speaking in front of this enormous group – now spilling out the propped-open front door – is daunting. The room quiets more quickly than he imagined it could, and he finds himself on the front row of a loose circle of all the attendees, who've cleared a small space around Jahan. Jahan looks him in the eye as he lifts his glass.

'We welcome you all to the Judith Stanley show!' Jahan says, and there's a roar of mingled shouts and applause. 'So many people have been involved in putting together this fantastic show…' With mounting anxiety, Paul listens to Jahan praise his hardworking staff. He hopes the gallerist will forget about his speech – but Jahan is not a forgetful man. Soon, he winds inevitably toward his conclusion, which includes Paul's name… 'and would never have been possible without the extraordinary Paul Sorenson.' Another rowdy round of applause, and Paul steps forward, feeling abashed, but also like a rock star. He's fine to speak now, more than fine. When the crowd quiets he begins, making sure to scan the circle and hold people's eyes as he speaks.

'Judith Stanley was a remarkable talent, as you can see here tonight. I'm so grateful to Jahan and his team for making this possible, and so thankful, really, for the moment when Judith walked into my classroom, all those many nights ago, out in the wilds of suburban New Jersey,' he says to laughs. 'She was taking the class as a hobbyist, I assumed, as a woman whose children had grown and left the house and needed –'

His eyes catch on a particular pair of eyes. Dark and liquid, shimmering.

Charlie stands across the circle from him, somehow. Has she just arrived? He notes her satiny, sleeveless blue dress and the two black circles around her eyes. The long, deep-looking scratch along her right cheek. Dark bruising around her bare neck like a choker and bruises evident along both her bare arms, too. Did he do all that? He didn't, no. He knows he didn't. She's wearing makeup, he thinks, she's putting on an act, but it doesn't matter – people are casting their eyes in her direction as she stares at Paul. She reminds him of *Parade Girl*, which hangs just behind her, over the heads of the crowd. But Parade Girl's look is full of hurt; Charlie's is full of rage.

She knows, he thinks, and swallows. Was it the groan that escaped him when she cut him? Or had she already recognized him by then? It doesn't matter now.

He has to go on – the crowd is shifting, exchanging glances. Jahan is staring at him, slightly open-mouthed. Worried Paul's nerve has failed him.

'And I – I had never seen such beautiful photographs, really. She was just – Judith was just – just a unique –'

Charlie steps forward to the center of the circle, holding Paul's gaze as she bares her pale, damaged flesh to the crowd. Paul sees men and women in the back row standing on tiptoes, craning their necks to see her. He can't let this happen. He has to take control somehow, be the first to speak, try to contain her, whatever her intentions.

'Folks, this is one of my NJCC students, Charlie Levin. Incredibly bright girl and a huge fan of Judith's. I've invited her here tonight to talk about Judith's work, to give you the student's perspective. Charlie?'

He gives her a hard look, a look to match the man in the ski mask. He can almost feel the mask's fabric against the skin of his face, feel the power it gave him. Feel her fear along the length of him, thrilling him.

'Paul Sorenson did this to me,' Charlie says, her clear voice ringing out. 'He followed me home last night and attacked me in the parking garage. He's been stalking me for a while now, mostly through letters and stuff, but he didn't touch me until last night.' She lifts her arms as if to display them and immediately, a flashbulb or two pops. Paul jerks his head to the right, sees journalists, photographers, pushing through the crowd. They don't have to push hard; the crowd parts for them. Several photographers kneel in front of Charlie to get the best angle. She changes her pose then and clasps her hands before her, looking demure and sad and traumatized.

'She's lying,' Paul says, his voice croaking. 'Look at her closely, it's makeup!'

There's a collective horrified gasp. Jahan, across the way, his face drained of color, looks at Paul like he's an appalling lump of flesh – not the man he's thanked and praised profusely in recent days. Paul notices people edging away from him, drawing back from him as if he were diseased.

'I did nothing wrong! This girl has been harassing me. She's the one who wrote letters, called me, made threats. Terrible – terrible threats. She's a sick fan, that's all. Obsessed with Judith. This is revenge for – for telling everyone how Judith died. For telling the truth. Trust me, everyone. This is all a show!' His voice echoes in the silence. The people stare at him as if he were mad, and he feels mad, he feels like Judith must have felt in her final moments, pressing a knife to her own flesh.

'Look, look what she did to me! You can't make this up!' He pushes up his shirtsleeves as quickly as he can with his trembling hands and tears off the bandages covering his wounds. They look like nothing, simple cuts next to the severe – if fake – damage to Charlie's flesh, but he flashes his arms around to the audience, who watch in riveted silence.

'Those are defensive wounds I made when he attacked me. I had a little knife. Just like Judith had,' she adds, tears clotting her voice. 'I wonder if there are other scars on Paul's body somewhere, where Judith swiped at him before he killed her.'

Another collective gasp.

'I didn't kill her! You and everyone know I didn't kill her! The police cleared me! She did it herself! You all *know* this!' Paul screams, and scans the faces for a single sympathetic soul, but everyone frowns his way – even the ones who smiled and simpered just minutes ago.

Precious minutes ago. When he was the shining star.

'I did *not* kill Judith Stanley! I did *not* attack Charlie Levin!' he screams, and then he turns, pushes through the bodies packed tightly around him with their mouths agape, and runs for the door, their voices shouting after him:

'Stop him!'

'Someone, grab him!'

But no one does. He pushes out into the night and runs as fast as he can, certain there are footsteps pounding, voices shouting after him. He runs faster, dodging traffic and heading south toward home as he imagines the scene back at Doven. The crowd will be clustering around Charlie now as she accepts a man's large mackintosh, buttoning it up so her bruised-looking body is covered, protected, no longer visibly shivering. People will ask if they should call the police, if she needs medical attention, and Charlie will nod with a soulful, damaged look in her eyes – or she might say no, that she's already contacted the police, already sought medical help. She's all right now. Now that he's gone. Now that people know what he did to her, and what he probably did to Judith, too. Everyone will want to hear her theory of how Judith died. She'll tell them she doesn't know for sure, but since Paul attacked her, why wouldn't he have been the one to attack Judith, too? Out of jealousy, or the sense of an opportunity – or both. Her listeners will nod thoughtfully or shake their heads as if they've never heard anything worse, as if they can't believe they were just fawning over such a depraved man.

Meanwhile, in the background, Jahan will be quietly assuring his collectors and comrades that Paul Sorenson is gone, out of the picture completely. His introduction on the wall will be painted over, the catalogs will be edited and reissued, his name will be erased from any connection with the show. *And in the meantime, here are Judith's pictures. Aren't they marvelous?* he'll ask. *These are the real focus of the night. Don't let that terrible mess with Paul convince you otherwise.* They won't – Paul knows they won't. They'll buy every last print, and Jahan's staff will collect orders from those demanding more. The gallery will profit, Jahan will profit, the Stanleys (grudgingly) will profit – even Judith will profit, in posthumous fame. Not Paul, though, who'll be left without a shred of all the bright things he's gathered to him in the exhausting, exhilarating weeks since Judith died.

When Paul finally stops running for a moment and stands, wheezing, by a house on a quiet residential street, he hears no sounds of pursuit, only the normal city noise: cars honking on the adjacent big avenue, a cat yowling in a nearby backyard, someone pulling his trash can to the sidewalk. When Paul turns to stare wild-eyed behind him, there's no one. Nothing. Only the circle of yellow light cast by a nearby streetlamp. He stands outside of it, tense and waiting, watching from the shadows.

Acknowledgments

Thank you to Chris Clemans for his brilliant insights and edits, his tenacity, and his endless support.

To my editor, Tarini Sipahimalani, for her dynamic and diligent caretaking of this novel, and to my outstanding publicist, Kristen Bianco. To the rest of the top-notch Putnam team, for the second time around: Ivan Held, Lindsay Sagnette, Ash McClay, Alexis Welby, Jess Lopez, Erin Byrne, Erica Rose, Maija Baldauf, Almudena Rincon, Eric Fuentecilla, Lorie Pagnozzi, and Aja Pollock.

Many thanks to Jenna Gordon and the always outstanding VERVE Books team in the United Kingdom. To the incomparable Jason Richman at UTA, too.

To Margaret Lewis, always my first reader and tireless cheerleader.

To my family and friends, with special thanks to my early readers: Kimberly Arin, Mona Awad, Courtney Brkic, Camille Guthrie, Amelia Kahaney, and Corey Mead. Special thanks also to Lee Seidenberg, whose photography knowledge greatly informed the novel (mistakes/moments of artistic license are mine alone) and who took an author photo that my dad called 'the best photograph I have ever seen.'

To Marcia LeBeau and The Write Space for giving me the quiet place I needed to engage in the hard work of making this book. And to my current and former coworkers, who make library work even more joyful and meaningful than it already is.

Finally, my heartfelt thanks to the booksellers, librarians, bookstagrammers, BookTokers, book clubs, fellow authors, and readers who've championed my past novels in one way or another. This one is for you (they're all for you).

Book Club Questions

1. Why do you think Judith, with her exceptional photography talent, has remained a hobbyist? How have both personal and societal factors affected her life as an artist?
2. What makes her self-portraits so unique and revolutionary for their time, and why do you think she only sees 'the man' (at first) in the background of these self-portraits?
3. What experiences in Judith's life – past and present – contribute to her being stalked by the man?
4. Why does she respond so powerfully to Professor Paul's praise, even while resisting his urges to publish her work?
5. Were you surprised by the end of Part One? How did your response to it change, if at all, by the end of the novel?
6. How does your perception of Paul change from Part One to Part Two, and how would you describe his complicated relationship to Judith and her work?
7. Why does Paul respond the way he does to the various criticisms he receives (via letter and telephone, primarily) after he goes public with Judith's work? Although this story takes place in the late 1960s, can you think of correlations to the present day?
8. Why do you think Paul fixates on Charlie in particular? Why does she get under his skin, and what leads him, finally, to act out against her?

9. What's your interpretation of the final scene? How would you describe Paul's journey from start to finish? Does it mirror Judith's in any way?
10. Which of the men in this novel do you think of as 'the man', and why? How does your answer reflect our societal conceptions of manhood and masculinity?

About the Author

(Author Photo © Lee Seidenberg)

Laura Sims's previous novels *How Can I Help You* and *Looker* have been featured on Best Books lists in *The New York Times Book Review*, *Vogue*, *People* magazine, *Entertainment Weekly*, *Real Simple*, *Publishers Weekly*, and more. An award-winning poet, Sims has published four poetry collections; her essays and poems have appeared in *The New Republic*, *Boston Review*, *Lit Hub*, and *Electric Lit*. She lives in New Jersey, where she works part-time as a children's librarian.

laurasims.net

@LJSims50

@LauraSims2121

Also Available

A razor-sharp psychological suspense about two librarians whose lives become dangerously intertwined, *How Can I Help You* explores the dark side of human nature and the dangerous pull of artistic obsession.

No one knows Margo's real name.

Her colleagues and patrons at a small-town public library only know her middle-aged normalcy, congeniality and charm. They have no reason to suspect that she is, in fact, a former nurse with a trail of countless premature deaths in her wake. She has turned a new page, so to speak, and the library is her sanctuary, a place to quell old urges.

That is, at least, until Patricia, a recent graduate and failed novelist, joins the library staff. Patricia quickly notices Margo's subtly sinister edge and watches her carefully. When a patron's death in the library bathroom offers a hint of Margo's mysterious past, Patricia can't resist digging deeper – even as this new fixation becomes all-consuming.

VERVEBOOKS.CO.UK/HOW-CAN-I-HELP-YOU